Highland

HARMONY

AVELINA & DREW

KEIRA MONTCLAIR

DEDICATION

To Sharron Gunn:
Thanks for being so willing to share all your knowledge about the
Scottish and their history. You are a charm, for sure.

THE CLAN

Grants
1. Laird Alexander Grant, and wife, Maddie (#1)
   a. Twin lads-James (Jamie) and John (Jake)
   b. Kyla
   c. Connor
   d. Elizabeth
2. Brenna Grant and husband, Quade Ramsay (#2)
   a. Torrian (Quade's son from first marriage)
   b. Lily (Quade's daughter from first marriage)
   c. Bethia
   d. Gregor
3. Robbie Grant and wife, Caralyn (#4)
   a. Ashlyn (Caralyn's daughter from a previous relationship)
   b. Gracie (Caralyn's daughter from a previous relationship)
   c. Rodric (Roddy)
   d. Padraig
4. Brodie Grant and wife, Celestina (#3)
   a. Loki (adopted)
   b. Braden
   c. Catriona
5. Jennie Grant and husband, Aedan Cameron(#7)

Ramsays
1. Quade Ramsay and wife, Brenna Grant (see above)
2. Logan Ramsay and wife, Gwyneth (#5)
   a. Molly (adopted)
   b. Maggie (adopted)
   c. Sorcha
   d. Gavin
3. Micheil Ramsay and wife, Diana (#6)
   a. David
   b. Daniel
4. Avelina Ramsay and Drew Menzie(Book #8)

CHAPTER ONE

Summer, 1260s, Lothian, Scotland

I love you.

Those were the three words Avelina longed to hear. She so hoped to fall in love and share her life with the most perfect lad. Being the youngest of four and the only lass of the Ramsay brood relegated her to the task of taking care of the family bairns. She was the only one yet unmarried, and she longed for a relationship of her own. But therein lay the problem—how could Avelina Ramsay ever possibly fall in love if she froze whenever a lad came near her? She would have to change, though she knew not how.

She was pondering this problem one eve as she made her way back to the keep at dusk, her arms full of flowers from the garden. The smithy's son, Keith, passed her, a sly grin on his face. He always looked at her in a hungry way she did not like, so she increased her pace, but panic stole over and she closed her eyes for a moment, intent on calming her soul and starting fresh.

That was her mistake. The lad she had just passed apparently spun around, shoved her from behind, and propelled her into the end of the stables. Her entire body responded with terror, yet she couldn't scream.

"Daft lass. That's what you are." Keith's heated breath drifted to her ear from behind as his grip on her waist tightened. "Still cannot speak, can you?"

Rough hands shoved her atop the mound of hay. She lurched forward and caught her fall, the straw scratching the tender skin of her arm as she attempted to spin around to shove her attacker away. Panic coursed through her body, giving her tunnel vision where naught else existed but herself and the crude lout whose hands were everywhere. She had to get away; she just had to fight with everything she had. The shock of seeing him fumble with his pants forced her into action. Shoving at him and kicking any part of him she could reach, she scrambled to get away.

Her heart threatened to explode out of her chest while a rushing sound echoed in her brain, threatening to dim her vision. What was his intent? The lad had never treated her thus before. He had oft followed and teased her, but this was the first time he had dared touch her. Her breathing came out too rapid, and she did her best to calm it as she tried to shove away from him. Then something hot and hard hit her hand. A piece of flesh.

She knew what it was and tried to scream, but naught came out. With all her strength, she pummeled his arms, but he slapped her and she fell backwards.

"Cannot even scream, can you? How perfect is this? You flaunt that body around and do not allow anyone to touch you. You have tits better than any lass I have ever seen, and I plan to feel them for myself. I'll be the first to take you, and I do not care if you are the laird's sister. And if you say aught to anyone, I'll hurt you worse. Though 'tis foolish to think of you talking, is it not? You may be a beauty, but you're daft. 'Tis time to take what I want after your stupid brother made me dig out those trenches."

Keith forced her back onto the hay and held his arm across her throat as he tore the ribbons on her dress. Pinning her down with all his weight, he groped for her breast and smiled. "Just as I thought." Gasping for air, she managed to free one foot to kick him, but he struck her again. Her hand came free and she raked his arm with her fingernails, but he continued to hold her down and tug at her skirts. Tears blurred her vision as she realized just how powerless she was against the brute.

In an instant, an unknown force lifted him away from her and flung him across the barn, sending him against the wall with a thud. Logan. She could tell by the fierce growl that came from him. Her brother had saved her.

"You filthy piece of slime! How dare you touch my sister! I'll kill you now with my bare hands." Avelina managed to stand up and grope her way toward the door while Logan punched the lad's face and belly. Before she reached it, the door flew open and her eldest brother, Quade, the laird of their clan, flew in with Logan's wife, Gwyneth, directly behind him. As soon as Quade saw her disheveled appearance, his eyes widened, and a fury set into his gaze the likes of which she had never seen. Quade definitely possessed more self-control than Logan. She pushed past Gwyneth and Quade and ran out the door. Holding her skirts in her hand, tears blurring her vision, she raced toward the keep. She could hear Gwyneth shouting her name, but she couldn't stop. She just couldn't.

She managed to choke down her sobs as she shoved through the door of the keep, but thoughts of Keith's hands touching her made her want to vomit. Why did lads leer at her and tease her so? She managed to find her way up the steps to the chamber she shared with all the young lasses of the Ramsay family—Logan and Gwyneth's daughters, Molly, Maggie, Sorcha; and Quade and Brenna's daughters, Lily and Bethia. She threw herself on the large bed and let her tears flow.

Gwyneth burst through the door moments later and rushed to her side, sitting on the edge of the bed. "Lina, are you all right? Och, Lina. I'm so sorry this happened to you. Did he hurt you?"

Avelina shook her head and buried her face in a pillow.

Gwyneth stayed by her side, rubbing her back.

The door opened again, and Brenna came in with her son of three summers, Gregor, and Gwyneth's son of four summers, Gavin. "Lina, Lina, I'm so sorry. Are you all right?" She sat on the other side of the bed and leaned over to hug her.

Gavin came over to the side of the bed, a sad expression on his face. "Mama, why is Aunt Lina crying?"

"Aunt Lina is sad right now. We'll just sit with her until she feels better."

Gregor ran to Gavin's side. "Dabin, I need to give Aunt Wina a tiss."

Brenna smiled at her son and ran her hands through his brown locks. "I think that's a wonderful thought, Gregor. You and Gavin can both give her a kiss."

Avelina turned her head to face her two nephews.

"Aunt Wina, I tan dib you a tiss. You will be aw bettew."

Lina smiled and reached for Gregor's wee hand. She found it so endearing how he replaced his Gs with a D sound, and Ks or Cs with a T. He hadn't spoken for the longest time, but Brenna swore there was naught wrong with him—he was just shy. She especially loved what he called his cousin, Gavin.

"Dabin will dive you a tiss, too." He nodded his head with the most serious expression on his face she had ever seen. How she loved the bairns in the family. Of course, she would love to have her own bairns one day.

She wanted to be loved, not groped; cherished, not leered at. Was it too much to hope for?

Lina sat up and reached for Gregor, then patted the spot next to her for Gavin. Brenna made room for the two lads. Once Gregor was settled onto her lap, the two lads kissed her cheeks on either side. Gregor then set his wee hand on her cheek and tipped up his head to look at her. "Bettew, Aunt Wina?"

"Aye," she whispered. "You have both made me feel much better. My thanks."

"Good lads," Gwyneth said. "Now why do you not get down and I'll find you a treat from the kitchens."

The two hopped down. Just before Gavin left, he turned toward Lina. "Would you like us to bring you a treat? Gregor and I could do that for you."

"Nay, I'm fine. But thank you." She chuckled at how talkative Gavin had become over the last year.

Gwyneth closed the door behind her.

"Do you want to talk about it, Lina?" Brenna asked softly.

Lina's head dropped. "Nay. There is not much to say."

"Did he hurt you?" Brenna reached for her hand, which was scratched from the straw in the barn.

Lina swiped the tears from her eyes before bringing her gaze up to Brenna's. "Why? Why do lads always taunt me?"

Brenna brushed back the stray strands that had fallen from Lina's plait. "Two reasons, Lina. One is you are incredibly beautiful, and the other is lads of that age are incredibly foolish."

"They all tease me. What do I do, Brenna? Why can I not seem to speak around them? I could not even scream, though I tried. He called me daft. Am I?" More tears slid down her cheeks.

"Nay, absolutely not." Brenna hugged her. "Lina, do not worry. It will come in time, just as Gregor's words came to him. Are you sure the lad did not hurt you? He tore your clothes."

Lina stared at the wall in front of her in a daze. Aye, Keith had tried to rape her. She'd heard the word before, but she hadn't realized how dirty such an act would make her feel. She rubbed her arms, wishing she could rid herself so easily of his touch.

Attempted rape was a crime her brother could decide merited many types of punishment. Keith could be flogged, sent away, put in the dungeon, or even executed. Quade was the laird, so it was for him to decide. Mayhap she should not say that the lad had attempted rape. Then his punishment wouldn't be as bad. If he were whipped, it would be all her fault.

Brenna seemed to read her thoughts, for she said, "'Tis not your fault, Lina. He made the choice to attempt to take what he wanted against your will. He must pay for his actions. Do not concern yourself with his punishment." Brenna lifted Lina's chin with her finger to force her gaze to hers. "The punishment will be decided by your laird, not you."

"But I do not..." She wanted to say that she didn't want to cause her brother trouble, but her brother's wife already shook her head.

"Nay, 'tis not your concern," she whispered. "He did not have the right to hurt you. Please forgive me, but I must ask again. Did he complete the act? Did he take your maidenhead? It would be verra painful and you would bleed if he did."

Brenna was the clan's healer, actually one of the best healers in the land of the Scots, so Lina understood why she needed to ask the question. "Nay, he did not. Logan stopped him. But he did..." She paused to gather strength. "He grabbed my breast. He tugged my bodice open and touched me..." She buried her face into Brenna's shoulder to catch her sobs.

The door flew open and Lina's mother, Arlene Ramsay, burst through the door. "Avelina? 'Tis true? The smithy's lad tried to...to hurt you?"

Lina sat up and stared at her mother, not knowing quite how to answer her other than to nod.

Lady Ramsay sat on the other side of her and wrapped her arms around her only daughter. "Lina, my wee Lina. I'm so sorry. Are you hurt? You must stop walking about alone. You are too old, and you can no longer hide in the shadows as you did when you were young."

Brenna stood up. "Why do I not get you something warm to

drink and something to eat?"

"I could not eat," Lina said. "Mayhap a drink."

Lady Ramsay said, "Get her a wee dram of whisky."

Lina decided she did not wish to talk about it anymore. She stood beside the bed and her dress gaped open from the movement. When her mother gasped, she looked down at herself and saw the bruises on her left breast. Aye, he had been rough.

"Lina, he did not finish…?

"Nay, Mama. Logan stopped him. All he touched was my breast…" Tears misted her eyes again. "Mama, I just want to sleep."

Brenna came back in with the whisky. "Here, drink this, lass. 'Twill help you to sleep."

Lina choked it down, but when she glanced at the bruise again, she turned to her mother. "A tub bath? Could I…"

Arlene gasped, "Surely. I'll see to it. Wash the monster from your sweet skin."

The whisky took effect and she felt her fine tremors subside. Aye, all she wanted to do was get clean, sleep…and then leave. She could not bear to stay here and suffer all the stares and whispers.

"Mama, I need to get away."

CHAPTER TWO

Drew Menzie stumbled toward the cottage in the outer bailey of his clan's castle. Glad that his sire was better and he did not have to act as laird anymore, he'd indulged just a wee bit too much. He'd had enough ale tonight, for sure! God's teeth, but he needed to learn some self-control. He approached the front door and knocked. A flurry of giggles greeted his ears after the last rap of his knuckles fell against the worn wood.

"Drew, 'tis you?" a young, high-pitched voice asked.

"Nay, 'tis the monster from the forest in search of a damsel who needs rescuing. Do you fit my needs?"

"Aye. Come find me, young knight."

Laughter from more than one lassie echoed through the door and he laughed as he grabbed the door handle to keep from stumbling backward. How he wished Aedan were here to join him in this eve's merriment. Unfortunately for Drew, his best friend had deserted him to marry the beautiful Jennie Grant, so he was no longer interested in fornicating with a bevy of lasses for entertainment. Ironic that at present, Aedan was the responsible laird, while Drew had been relieved of his duties until his sire needed him again.

"Oh, save me," crooned one of the lasses through the door. He barged into the cottage and pushed his way between the two buxom beauties, barely managing to find his way to the pallet in the corner. Once he fell onto the bed, he rolled over so he was lying on his back looking up at the two faces—one brunette and a lovely redhead.

The lasses giggled and teased him, grabbing him in all the right places, but suddenly his head spun a bit too much to allow him to remain in his present position. Hating to do it, he pressed away from the two soft bodies near him, forcing them to withdraw from him. The brunette had already found her way to his nipple through his tunic, and the redhead had been nuzzling his neck. An unmistakable urge propelled him up and out the door to the side of the hut, whereupon he heaved out half of the ale and whisky he had indulged in during the night.

When he finally had no more fluid left inside of him, he rubbed his forehead. His mouth felt like the hide of a boar, and the thought of another ale sent him back for one more contribution to the rocks on the side of the cottage.

God's teeth, but he had to stop. His indulgences had gotten out of hand as of late. He wiped his mouth on the sleeve of his tunic and turned back toward the front of the cottage. He groaned when he saw the two lasses staring at him, both wide-eyed with alarm.

"Och, Drew. What is wrong?"

"Naught to worry your bonny head about, sweet lassie. But I believe I'll postpone our entertainment until another night." He winked and strode past the two girls, but as soon as he was out of their line of sight, he ran into the trees to rid himself of the rest of the contents of his belly.

After he finished, he wanted naught more than to recline on the mound of soft leaves next to him, but instead he hiked back toward the keep. The reason he'd returned met him at the door as soon as he opened it a crack.

"Drew, thank the saints above. Are you sotted? You look terrible."

Drew's mother, Rhona, stood in the great hall, kneading her hands. "I'm fine. I'm going to my chamber, Mama."

"Can I do aught for you? Please let me help you." She reached for her son.

Drew pulled away from her. "Nay. I do not feel well. 'Tis late, Mama. Go to bed."

Drew headed for his chamber, barely managing to escape her reach, but then turned around to find a pallet in the hall. He couldn't handle the chamber this eve.

Hellfire, but he had to get away. Aye, he loved his mama and papa, but every time he was around them, the memories he attempted to banish bloomed to the surface. Nay, he must get away. Lately, all the ale in the world did naught to clear his memories. He would go to Aedan's. Aye, his friend was newly married, but he needed to get away from his mother, from everything.

He fell onto the pallet, closed his eyes, and slipped into oblivion.

The next thing he knew, someone was yelling his name. His sire.

"Get up, you lazy swine. Can you not spend one night away from the ale? You need to direct the men in the lists."

Hellfire, but the last thing he needed right now was to go out to the lists. He heard his friend Boyd try to reason with his father. "Word is he was heaving all over last eve."

"Boyd, if the fool drank that much, then he needs to get up off his arse and work the ale off. He's supposed to be out there with the guards. 'Tis his job to lead the men and your job to assist him."

"Aye, but I can handle them today, my laird. 'Tis a challenge for me, and I welcome it."

Drew swung his legs over the side of the bed, waited until the room stopped spinning, then threw his plaid on over his tunic and breeches. Weaving a bit on his feet, he finally made it over and stood facing his sire. "I'm coming." If he didn't go now, his father would continue throwing insults at him until his head exploded.

"Get your lazy arse out there. You need to work as they do if you plan to lead again one day."

Drew pushed past his father and out into the passageway, nodding to Boyd as he moved past him. Drew was accustomed to his father's harsh demeanor at this point in his life. He just wished he had a better way about him, especially when he was around Boyd. Drew could ignore his father's rants, but he feared someday Boyd would move on to another castle. With no family left, he had naught to hold him here, but Drew would be devastated if he ever chose to leave.

As soon as he headed down the stairs of the keep, his father's usual tirade picked up again behind him. "If you ever wish to become something other than a drunk, you must be a hard worker. You should be out there ahead of our guards."

Rather than argue, Drew stayed silent as he strode through the bailey. He'd tried so many different ways to make his sire proud of him, but it had never happened. When his sire had taken ill, Drew had taken over, working the guards in the list and leading them when the neighboring Lochluin Abbey had been attacked. His father had not once praised him for the brave way he'd fought to protect their land and Aedan's in the recent skirmishes that had broken out across the Highlands. Even though he'd suffered no injuries and lost no men, his father had told him he needed to improve. In truth, it was hopeless. He could never live up to his brothers' memories.

He strode straight for the stables.

"Drew, it's so good to see you this morn." He blew a kiss to the fair lass near the buttery, but did not slow his stride. Boyd had fallen in behind him, he noticed, and he gave his friend a nod and a smile—or as close to one as he could manage. When he passed the armorer, who was struggling to move a heavy piece of metal, he swung inside to lend a hand.

"Drew, no need to help. I'll get my son to assist me." The man in the armory was already panting from his attempts to move the heavy load.

"I'll not walk away. Boyd can help us." Boyd ran over and the three men lifted the metal and moved it to the large table in the back.

The armorer stood and smiled at Drew. "Many thanks. Would have taken us a wee bit to do it ourselves."

After trading more pleasantries, Drew and Boyd continued down the path. A lass carrying a loaf of fresh bread hurried after them. "My mama sends this for helping her the other day." She blushed and giggled after Drew accepted the loaf from her with a wink. He tore it in half to share with Boyd.

Almost to the portcullis, Drew heard the smithy yelling at the horse he was shoeing. "Ye olde beast, stop your snorting and hold still."

Drew hurried over to the old warhorse and helped calm him, talking sweetly to him and feeding him a part of his bread. The animal quieted enough for the smithy to finish his work. When the older man pulled out the stone lodged in the horse's hoof, he held it up for Drew to see. "He had a reason to be a mite ornery, lad. My thanks."

Drew spun on his heel, waved, and continued on toward the

stables.

As soon as he arrived, the stable lad tore over to him. "Drew, I'll get your horse ready for you."

Drew waved at the lad. "I'll handle it." He saddled his horse, and not long after, he and Boyd were mounted and heading out toward the area where the guards practiced. He had pushed the lads hard since the skirmishes, and he was proud of all they had accomplished. His sire followed at a distance—he could hear him yelling about something, but he wasn't interested in stopping to see what.

By the time they reached the field, Drew's father was close behind them, so Drew moved aside until his father drew up next to him. The men stopped practicing and awaited their orders. He glanced at his sire's weathered face. The laird had fought many battles, but he no longer had the strength of years past. His tales had been told so many times that most of the clansmen already knew them by heart, but they would still politely wait for him to finish.

A guard strode up to them and asked, "Drew, what move do you want us to practice today?"

Drew glanced at his father, but the older man just nodded for him to respond. He gave his instructions and dismounted. As he made his way onto the field, one guard after another ran to his side to speak with him.

"Drew, you should see how well Donnal did today. He'll be strong enough to fight with us the next time."

Another lad made his way up to him and said, "Menzie, we had five men against the winners from yesterday, and we trounced them."

Drew looked at Boyd and grinned. He had initiated a competition of strength to fire the lads up, and it seemed to be working. He patted the guard on the shoulder, but didn't stop as he continued toward his sire's second-in-command. He'd hoped his father would have given him that job, but Egan had been with his sire forever.

"Menzie, these new swords you had the smithy craft are easier to handle. How'd you know?" Egan shouted at Drew. "Brilliant design."

His father shouted, "Aye, I told Drew 'twas the way I wanted them."

Drew whirled around to stare at his father, who was still ahorse. He'd had no say at all about the swords, but now he was taking credit for that, too? Boyd gave Drew a pointed look, but continued over to a group of lads in the lists.

Aye, 'twas past time for Drew to get away for a while.

Lachlan Burnes flicked the reins of his horse, urging the beast to a gallop across the meadow just outside his sire's castle. He was eager to escape his mother's latest foul-mouthed assault.

He headed straight for his favorite place—his hideaway. The area he'd found was quite hidden, which was why he held it in such favor. He could curse, yell, holler, and throw rocks to his heart's content—or his temper's content, which was the case more often than not. When his mother and father got into their ritual insulting game, throwing every mistake he'd ever made since he was ten summers at him, he'd learned to leave as soon as possible. He'd heard all the insults before. There was no reason for him to stay to hear a repeat performance. As added entertainment, his parents had a cruel way of inciting the clansmen to chant insults at him when they joined the Burnes family in the great hall for the meal. They'd do anything at all if given enough mead.

He knew when he was almost at his special spot because the terrain became more and more laden with rocks. It was a small glen between two walls of solid rock—one much shorter than the other, which appeared to climb into the sky. Stones and moss were everywhere, and enough rubble tumbled from the walls that he didn't dare take his horse all the way in, choosing instead to tie him to a bush in the surrounding area. In all likelihood, that's why everyone else stayed away.

Once he had dismounted and hooked the reins over the branch of a nearby bush, he crept over to his spot as quietly as possible. There was a new eeriness to the glade today, one that sent a shiver up his spine, but he saw naught out of order.

His mother's voice echoed through his mind. "You lousy fool. You are of little value to the Clan Burnes. How could your father ever leave you in charge of the clan?"

Her face popped into his view, so he picked up a stone at his feet and hurled it, hitting the rocky ledge across from him. He could almost envision it hitting her right between the eyes—an image that made him smile—so he picked up another loose stone and fired it at the stone wall.

After five more missiles hit the wall, he grinned and stood back, feeling much better. Aye, that's what he needed to do. Strike the woman down where she stood. He yelled up at the sky in triumph, imagining how wonderful it would feel to hear his mother begging his forgiveness and telling him how much she loved him.

Lachlan felt so empowered he picked up a larger rock that took two hands to lift. He swung it over his head and hurled it forward, catching the middle of the wall, sending some smaller stones scuttling down the side of the glade. His blood pumped through his veins in excitement, the flush of exerting himself racing through him, making him want to do it again and again. So he did, increasing the size of the rocks until he found one he could hardly lift over his head. He laughed when it crashed against the rocky ledge, sending stones shooting off in every direction.

Finally, he stopped, panting to catch his breath, a wide smile on his face. He leaned over to rest his hands on his knees and wait until his breathing returned to normal. But a strange rumbling sound met his ears, so he picked his head up to search for the source.

Unfortunately, the rumbling almost found him first. He glanced up just in time to see a plethora of rocks shooting down the side of the glen, picking up speed and more rocks along the way, all tumbling straight for him. Covering his head with his hands, Lachlan spun around to run away, but the rocks felled him before he got very far. He hit the ground hard, cursing, banging his chin on the stones.

He curled into a ball to protect himself from the flurry of rocks still raining down on him. When they finally stopped, he didn't move for several minutes, afraid it was not yet over. Once he was certain it was done, he peeked out through his hands and stared at the ground strewn with rocks and boulders. Sitting up, Lachlan pushed the rubble away as he surveyed the destruction wrought by the shower of stones. Pain shot up his left side when he moved his legs, but deciding it would pass, he continued to test them. A sharp pain from his right toe forced him to stop. He glanced around, wishing there was someone who could help pull him out of the sea of rocks his glade had become, but there was naught.

A small squeaking noise put a stop to that train of thought. He turned his head and found a field mouse standing on its back legs on the pile of rubble next to him. The mouse's beady eyes stared straight at Lachlan, then the wee creature squeaked and began running back and forth between two different locations in the rocks. A glint of steel caught his eye next to the mouse.

Lachlan forced himself to stand, but as soon as he did, the mouse took off running, only to come to a stop directly next to the piece of steel. When Lachlan bent down to inspect it, he was surprised to see it was the hilt of a sword. The mouse sat up and squeaked at him again, his wee nose wiggling up in the air. He only moved back after Lachlan reached for the sword, though he stood next to Lachlan instead of moving out of his way.

To his surprise, the sword Lachlan pulled out of the rocks was a strange size—not even half as large as the one strapped to his back. He turned the hilt over to see if there would be some brand or sign identifying the owner, but there was not. He was immediately distracted by the gemstones on the other side of the hilt—rubies, sapphires, and emeralds. His eyes widened as he considered their value.

The mouse squeaked at him again as if it trying to tell him something. That was when the truth dawned on him.

This was the sapphire sword, the sword featured in so many fae legends. It was said the holder of the sword would be safe for as long as they held the weapon. Their clan would never be attacked, and the owner would survive all battles. He held it out in front of him, as if doing so would help him gauge whether or not it was the real sapphire sword.

He searched his recollections for any information on the sword. The size was right, and the gemstones were exactly as he'd heard. The only other thing he could remember was that it had been stolen a few years ago, but then lost. Is this where it had been all this time?

Stupefied, he couldn't decide what to do. Somehow, the landslide of the rocks had unearthed the weapon, leaving it next to Lachlan. Why, even after the rocks tumbled, he never would have seen it if it hadn't been for...

He spun around, looking for the small creature, but there was no sign of it. He sat down, and sure enough, the wee mouse came out of hiding and ran to his side again. The field mouse reared up on its hind legs and chattered to him, as if Lachlan could understand him.

"You want me to take it, do you, wee mouse? You think it belongs to me and no other? I think you have the right of it. This sword is mine now." He stood up again and found a safe place to carry the sword in his belt, securing it tight. The mouse waited at his feet, as patient as could be.

Lachlan smirked. "You wish to travel with me, wee one? I've always wanted a pet of my own." He leaned down and held his hand out. The mouse scampered onto his palm, so he lifted it up and spoke directly to it. "All right, I'll allow it, but just be careful." He stuffed the mouse into his sporran, checked to make sure the sword was safe, then climbed onto his horse to leave. The future beckoned to him now that he possessed the sapphire sword. He finally had the power he'd always wanted.

Lachlan smiled and strategized all the way home.

CHAPTER THREE

Avelina sat in the great hall of the Clan Cameron, listening to her best friend, the former Jennie Grant, now the mistress of the Camerons, discuss the menu with her cook. Aedan's mother had already gone into the kitchens to check the stores. Lina admired Jennie for how quickly she had adapted to her new role at the Cameron castle.

The door opened and Aedan strode through the door, heading immediately for his wife. He wrapped his arms around her increasing mid-section, though the change was barely discernible yet, and kissed her cheek. "Finished with your mistress yet, Cook?"

"Aye, my laird. We're finished." Cook smiled and headed back to the kitchens, but she paused to address Aedan over her shoulder. "Aye, I will have your apple tarts for dinner tonight."

Aedan turned Jennie around to kiss her lips. Lina had to admit she was quite envious of her friend's wonderful life. Would she ever have a partner of her own? How she longed to find someone to love, someone who would listen to her, someone she would be comfortable talking to in the middle of the night when nightmares stole away her sleep. Ever since the attack, she had experienced difficulty sleeping, which is why Quade had agreed for her to spend some time with Jennie.

Many, many moons ago, Jennie and Lina had been practicing archery on Ramsay land for the first annual Ramsay festival when Jennie's arrow flew astray and landed in Aedan Cameron's arse. That was not the reason they fell in love, but it did mark their first meeting. Aedan had been with a friend that day, Drew Menzie. Drew had flirted with Lina, and Lina had quite liked it. She had never seen him again, but she had dreamed of him once or twice. It had even crossed her mind that she might meet Drew again while she stayed here with Jennie.

But even if that *did* come to pass, she probably wouldn't be able to talk to him. Though she could talk to her brothers and other married men such as Aedan, as soon as she met a lad her age, her lips refused to move. The young men of Lothian apparently thought her addled. She had to do things differently here.

A loud bellow interrupted her thoughts and she lifted her gaze to the doorway, just in time to see her dream lad saunter into the Cameron keep, as if summoned by her thoughts. Her face heated instantly.

Drew Menzie and an unknown lad entered with a bang and strode confidently across the great hall before coming to a stop in front of Aedan Cameron.

"Menzie? What brings you here?" Aedan stared at his friend in shock.

"It has been too long since I've been here, Cameron. Did you not miss me?" He laughed as he clasped his friend's shoulder. "You remember Boyd, do you not?" Drew turned to introduce the two.

"Aye, I missed you, but I heard you were having a great time once all the skirmishes settled and your father was well enough to take over the lairdship again. Word has it that you were sampling every lass on Menzie land."

All three men turned to stare at Avelina, a sheepish expression of regret on their faces. Lina turned away, embarrassed to have been caught listening and a bit shocked by Aedan's comment, and found a seat at the broad table.

Alas, it would seem Drew Menzie was no longer her dream knight.

Jennie came over and sat beside her. "Pay them no attention," she whispered. "Men insist on saying ridiculous things to one another. "

Aedan's voice carried across the hall. "Either way, I'm pleased to see you. You're just in time for the midday meal. Have a seat and update me on all that's happening on Menzie land and beyond. I'm too wrapped up in my lovely wife to keep up."

The men made their way over to the table. "You recall Lady

Avelina Ramsay, do you not? Avelina, this is Drew Menzie and his friend, Boyd." Aedan took a seat next to his wife and motioned for the others to take the seats across from him. He motioned to a serving lass to bring them food and ale.

Lina nodded and tried to make her tongue move so she could greet them, but naught came out.

Drew gave her a warm smile, and his green eyes danced. "Of course I remember Lady Avelina. I would never forget such beauty." He gave her a small bow before taking his seat, and she blushed to the tips of her toes. Could he be saying the truth? Did he remember her? She certainly remembered him. Fortunately, he did not seem to take much note of her silence before sitting down and turning toward Aedan.

The men prattled on about warring, thus, Lina's mind wandered. Once she was certain Drew's mind was occupied with other things, she took the opportunity to give him a thorough assessment. That was the side benefit of being shy—few people paid her any mind at all, which gave her the opportunity to observe details others might miss.

Drew was as handsome as she recalled, with just a few changes. His white teeth and his smile still lit up his face, but his green eyes looked tired. Dark locks tumbled to his shoulder with a slight wave at the end, and it was the type of lush, thick hair that seemed to invite a lass to run her fingers through it. Her gaze followed the strong line of his jaw down to his lips. How would they taste? Or how would they feel trailing a path down her neck to her collarbone, then to her…

A nudge caught her foot and she jerked her gaze back to her friend.

There was a knowing smirk on Jennie's face. Slud, but she'd been caught. Her face heated as she realized what her friend must be thinking.

Jennie waggled her eyebrows at her, but knew her too well to say anything to embarrass her. "So, Lina, is there aught you would like to do today?"

Lina thought hard and opened her mouth to answer Jennie. Naught came out, so she simply shook her head. She had a mind to go riding, but since Jennie was expecting, maybe she would not be able to ride.

"Mayhap we could go for a stroll outside, then you can give me some ideas for a nice flower garden. I'd love to include them around my herbs. You brought seeds from your lovely garden, did you not? You have the most beautiful flowers ever, Lina. I especially love it when you use them in my hair."

Lina nodded. The serving girl brought bread and pottage out, so Jennie and Lina ate in silence while the men talked on about battles and sword-fighting strategies. She decided she could listen to Drew Menzie's husky voice all day.

Once she and Jennie finished their food, Jennie stood and leaned over to address her husband. "Lina and I are leaving to go to my garden since you are busy with Drew. I'll see you later, love."

Aedan rose from his seat and kissed her until she was breathless. The intimacy of the embrace made Lina look away. It was then, of course, that Drew's heated gaze found hers, causing her belly to do flip-flops totally out of control. If she could only talk to *him*, but she knew her efforts would prove fruitless. She turned away and strolled over toward the door leading outside, hoping to avoid another embarrassing situation.

She would not allow Drew Menzie to see her tears.

⌾

Drew's throat went dry in an instant as soon as Avelina Ramsay stood from the table. Hellfire, but the lass was breathtaking. How she had changed since that long ago day in Lothian. She had been comely then, but now...what a beauty! Somehow he'd missed it when he first arrived at the hall.

His gaze fell to the floor in surprise, but then it curved up her long willowy legs, past her perfectly rounded hips, and up to a pair of breasts that were sheer perfection. Her skin, pale and translucent, had an ivory shade that he was quite sure would be adorned with just the right shade of coral nipples.

But it wasn't just her body. Her face was strikingly beautiful, from her high cheekbones and perfectly arched eyebrows to her plump strawberry lips and green eyes the shade of a forbidden forest. Her hair was a rich sable with a touch of gold to it and was held at the base of her neck in a completely different look with tendrils free about her face, giving her the appearance of a regal queen. And her elegance was enough to stop a man in his tracks.

Unable to tear his gaze away as she made her way to the door, he made a point to lock everything about her in his mind.

He glanced to the side and noticed that Aedan was talking to his wife, who then stepped into the kitchens for a moment. Perfect, he turned back to the beauty by the door.

Hellfire, what he wouldn't give to taste her just once…

Somehow he knew once would not appease his desire for her.

"Menzie, you wee bastard," Aedan growled in an undertone, making sure Avelina could not hear him. "You're looking at her like an animal. Leave Logan Ramsay's sister alone or you're likely to be speared in your privates by him or his wife."

Drew ran his hand down his face to wake himself up, just as one of Aedan's neighbors, Lachlan Burnes, strode in through the door, as arrogant as ever. The lad was a bit of a warty whoreson in Drew's opinion, and he didn't trust him at all. Still, Lachlan's father beat him on a regular basis, so Drew tried to be patient. Every lad had their regular beatings, of course, but Lachlan had been walloped enough to leave him scarred in many places. Still, it was no justification for his coarse behavior and rude treatment of others.

"What are you two foul bastards up to?" Lachlan asked as he entered the great hall.

At first, Drew could see he hadn't noticed Avelina Ramsay standing in the corner of the hall waiting for Jennie. She was doing her best to melt into the wall. But no one in the keep could miss the moment when he did notice her. He let out a low whistle that echoed from the beams of the hall.

"Well, I'll be a horny hedgehog, look at the tits on that one."

Drew jumped out of his chair and grabbed Lachlan by the throat just as Jennie stepped into the hall from the kitchens. Drew dropped his hand while they all watched Jennie and Avelina leave.

As soon as the door closed behind the two, Drew lurched for Lachlan again. "You'll treat the lady with the respect she deserves, or you'll be wearing my fist through your teeth." Boyd jumped up next to him, ready to join in if necessary.

Lachlan smiled, showing the missing two teeth in his lower jaw. "You wouldn't be the first, or do you not recall when Hamish did the same over his sister?"

Hamish Henderson, a neighboring friend, had proven his worth to Aedan and Drew in the recent skirmishes to protect Cameron land.

Lachlan scowled at Drew. "What's she to you, anyway? I understand Hamish and his sister, but this lass is naught to you unless you're claiming her."

Drew thought hard before he responded. What was Avelina to him? Naught yet, but perhaps he wanted that to change. "She's a lady who deserves your respect and you'll give it to her."

Aedan came up behind Drew. "Aye, you'll not speak of one of my guests in such a way. Keep your base language out of my hall."

Lachlan's eyes bulged at Aedan. "Hellfire, leave off, both of you. I'll shut my mouth."

"You will or you'll be eating my knuckles," Drew ground out.

Lachlan muttered under his breath, but not loud enough for Drew to hear any words. He'd keep an eye on him. For some reason, he felt protective of Avelina Ramsay. He'd kill Lachlan if he dared to touch her.

Aedan said, "And I'll remind both of you that she is a laird's sister, and Logan Ramsay is her brother. If you value your bollocks, you'll treat her kindly."

"Logan Ramsay..." Lachlan mumbled. He stared at the floor for a few moments before his gaze flew up to Aedan's. "Och, not the one who's married to the bollocks splitter, is he?"

Aedan smirked. "Aye, one and the same. And I've had the pleasure of seeing her in action. She never touched the lad, but she had him in tears sure enough. Never seen a lass like her. Best archer in the land of the Scots."

"Hellfire, I dinna believe that. Truly? A lass? She cannot be better than all the archers in the land."

Aedan glanced at Drew and the two of them shared a grin. "Sure hope you get the chance to meet her," Drew said. "She'll spear you with one of her arrows as soon as you open your mouth, you crude lout."

Aedan added, "I mean it, Lachlan. Mind your tongue in my keep. What brings you here? I have work in the lists training my men."

Lachlan chortled. "And how will that improve aught they do? Your men are useless. They showed that when you were nearly killed in battle a few moons ago."

"'Tis my goal to see to it that they are as strong as the Grant guards. Now what's the reason behind the visit?"

Drew did not blame Aedan for being short. He had no trust for Lachlan Burnes.

"My sire's on one of his drunken rages, so I left, and I have a new problem."

"What's the problem?" Aedan asked, giving him a look of doubt. "And where did you get that sword? I've not seen it before, 'tis extra small." Aedan tipped his head in the direction of the small sword, a mite bit larger than a dagger, which hung from his belt. "'Tis not large enough to function in battle."

"Aye, but 'tis large enough to cut someone down face to face." Lachlan crossed his arms, all wounded pride. "Jealous that you have nae sword with a legend behind it like this one? 'Tis the famous sapphire sword of the faerie legends. Naught can hurt me or the Burnes clan as long as a Burnes wears it."

"What in hellfire are you talking about, Burnes? We've never seen that sword," Aedan said, scowling at Burnes.

"Nay, you have not. 'Tis because I've just found it. 'Tis mine, and all that goes with the legend." Lachlan's eyes danced with excitement.

"You believe that foolish fable?" Drew scoffed. "We have plenty of swords and daggers. We do not need one of such an odd size."

Lachlan strolled over to the table and settled onto the bench beside it, his thumbs hooked in the belt holding his sword. "Fable, aye? When was Clan Burnes last attacked? Cannot answer that, can you? 'Tis because the fae protect us. As soon as my mother set eyes upon it, she blessed herself, saying we are protected forever. 'Tis the first time she's ever been proud of me."

"When and where did you find it?" Aedan asked.

"It fell out of a landslide at my feet. 'Twas meant to be. My mother is so happy, except now she has dreams about the sword. They keep her awake at night. Blames it all on me."

"So what goes with your sire?" Drew sat on the opposite side of the table, his arms crossed.

"He's madder than a hedgehog at my mother, so I left home. My mother says the faerie have advised her in her dreams of an imminent attack on our clan if I do not find a wife, but he refuses to listen to her and I cannot watch any longer." Lachlan's head drooped.

Drew hated to ask the question, but he could not help himself. "Cannot watch what?"

Lachlan let out a deep breath. "Cannot watch him beat my mother. Much as I dislike her, I do not like to see him beat her."

Aedan sat next to Burnes on the bench. "You're stronger than your sire. Why do you not stop him from beating your mother?"

"I have tried, but he threatened to take the sword away. I know you believe 'tis naught but a foolish legend, but I'll never let this sword go. 'Twas meant to be in my hands. My mother says I must marry within two moons of possession, or tragedy will befall the clan of the holder of the sword. She tells me I have to marry soon. 'Tis all I need to do to satisfy the legend. I was hoping to find a lass here. You know I'm no good with the lasses, but Aedan, you could find me one."

"Burnes, I'll not send a lass into the middle of the fae wars, whatever they be. You'll have to find your own lass. Why not one from your own clan?"

Drew answered, "Because they all know his ways and they do not want him. Am I right, Burnes? You have a reputation of being rough. And if I recall from the fable, the lass must be willing."

"Aye, she must be willing. But I do not want one of my clan. Now that I hold the sword, I want a special lass, one of the most beautiful in the land, one that would have spurned me before. Aedan, you are the one the lasses love. Menzie's too much of a drunkard. You can help me, please. 'Tis the true reason I'm here. You'll help me, will you not? I must marry soon."

Drew was surprised to see Lachlan in such a state. "Tell us more about your mother's prediction. Things seem quite peaceful, of late. How could the circumstances change that quickly, just because you found a sword?"

Lachlan's gaze lifted to the beams of the great hall. "I'd never believe it if I hadn't heard my mother's words myself."

"What?" Drew prodded.

"My mother did not only warn us of an imminent attack. She says the faerie has predicted the end of Clan Burnes because I will not marry in time. My sire scoffs at her."

"But you just said the sword will protect you from all."

"True, but the faerie is predicting that I will not be able to find a willing wife, which is another reason my sire wants it, but I refuse to give it up. Especially because I do not trust him in his drunken spells, and he agreed 'twas safer with me." He rubbed his chin and glanced over his shoulder as if afraid of being overheard. "But my mother says if I do not marry, we will be brought down by something near to impossible, which is why my sire is so upset."

Aedan and Drew tipped their heads toward Lachlan, awaiting his explanation.

He lowered his voice to a whisper. "She says the fae came to her in a dream and told her Clan Burnes will be brought down by a lass, the mightiest in all the land."

CHAPTER FOUR

Avelina breathed a sigh of relief as soon as they stepped outside of the hall. She tugged on her plain wool gown, finally able to do her practiced move now that they were away from the lads. Several times a day she pulled on her bodice, attempting to ensure the material would not cling to her large bosom. She would do anything possible to discourage men from gazing at her chest within moments of meeting her.

"Lina," Jennie whispered. "Why are you always pulling at yourself?"

Lina shrugged her shoulders and hugged her arms around her chest.

"I've never seen you do that before this visit, but now you do it frequently."

"I know. I can't seem to stop myself, but I just want to..." Lina glanced over her shoulder to be sure they weren't being followed. "I just wish to hide my breasts," she continued in an undertone. "Lads always leer at me and I do not like it."

"Lina, you're so beautiful. Lads are such fools. Ignore Lachlan. Aedan does not like him much."

That lad's stare had made her most uncomfortable. The look in his eye had not been too different from her attacker's expression. She peeked at the others in the bailey to see if anyone besides Jennie had noticed her fidgeting with her clothing, but no one was watching them. She breathed a sigh of relief to calm her trembling hands. At least she had managed to escape the hall without revealing her shameful secret to Drew. He did not yet know that fear often gripped her vocal chords and prevented her from speaking.

While her dream knight had been kind and sweet at first, the look he'd given her before she left the hall—as if she were wearing naught but slippers—had caught her off-guard. Aedan had jested about Drew's intimacy with women. Mayhap he was like all the others.

Once they were sequestered in the quiet of the herb garden, Jennie reached for her hand and tugged her over to a nearby bench. According to Jennie, Aedan had built this bench for her after he found out she was carrying. "Lina, you told me you were attacked by a lad, but that your brother stopped it. Is there aught else you wish to tell me about it?"

Lina shook her head as she stared at the stone path under her feet, clicking her slippers back and forth, hoping to keep her eyes from misting. "Nay, there is naught to tell."

Jennie held on to her hand, squeezing it tight. "Lina, Maddie has told me about the attacks she suffered. You are not alone. Maddie believed that talking about it helped her to heal. Are you sure you don't wish to speak of it?"

Lina thought for a minute, then sighed. "Nay, Logan stopped him in time. I was just a wee bit bruised. I'd rather not talk about it," she whispered.

"But you do not seem yourself. Is aught bothering you? Why did you not speak to Drew? He is one of Aedan's closest friends. 'Tis not like you to ignore someone."

Lina fanned her face, hoping to dry her eyes, but to no avail. Tears spilled onto her cheeks, so she leaned into Jennie, hoping that somehow, in some way, her friend could help her with her problem.

"What is it?" Jennie wrapped an arm around her shoulders and pulled her close.

"I cannot..." Lina stuttered. "I cannot...it seems..." Her breath hitched several times before she was able to finish her sentence. "Every time I try to speak to a lad my age, naught comes out." She cried all over Jennie's shoulder for a few moments and then picked her head up to see how her friend was reacting.

"How long has this been happening?"

"It started sometime over the last year, but it just seems to get worse. I am tired of this. I want to answer them, but naught comes out. 'Tis as if my voice freezes. Can you help me, Jennie?" Lina gripped her friend's arms. If only she could change this one thing about herself, she was certain her life would improve. Mayhap she could fall in love and find a spouse. She was the only one in her family who was still alone. Jennie's family was connected to hers through the marriage of Quade and Brenna, and all of the Grant siblings were married as well. She just couldn't accept that her purpose in life was to be the caregiver of her siblings' bairns.

"Aye, we shall think of something," Jennie said with a big smile. "Do not worry, I am certain 'tis a reaction to your attack and all the lads who have been leering at you. 'Twill improve. I'm sure of it. Please do not fret. Mayhap Aedan can help."

Lina nodded and stared at her hands, but she was not convinced. Her world was spiraling apart and she had no control. "Jennie, you are doing such a fine job as mistress of Clan Cameron, are you not?"

"Aye, 'tis a smoother transition than I expected. I thought I would make a mess of it all, but everyone here is so willing to help."

Lina swiped away more tears, unable to banish the twisting feeling inside her.

"Talk to me." Her friend's small voice broke into the storehouse of her fears, that private part of herself that she tried to keep away from everyone.

"What shall I ever do? What skills do I have to bring to a marriage?"After wiping her tears away, she dropped her gaze to her lap and started to play with the material of her gown.

"Why, you have much to offer a lad! You have skills with flowers that I could never equal. All the bairns just love you, and some even prefer you to their parents. You'll be a wonderful mama to your bairns."

Lina's lips set in a grim line.

"What is it?" Jennie asked.

She locked gazes with her friend, needing Jennie to understand how important this was to her. "Not those kinds of skills."

Jennie's brow furrowed. "What do you mean?"

"The kind of skills that are important." Avelina stood and paced on the stone pathway. "Look at my family. Your sister Brenna is a healer, one of the most renowned in the land. Gwyneth is the best archer in the land of the Scots. None would dare go against her.

My brother, Micheil, married the laird of the Drummond clan. You are the mistress of Clan Cameron *and* a healer."

"Aye."

"What am I? I have no skills, no specialty. What can I do other than tie flowers into hair?"

Jennie frowned. "You are not being fair to yourself. You have the biggest heart of anyone. Aye, I'm a healer, but I am just learning what a laird's wife must do, just as you would if you married. What makes you think that you do not measure up to the women you know?"

"My brothers constantly speak of the talents of their wives, and I know I cannot possibly measure up to their achievements."

"But you have an unusual family, Lina. Your mother had no healing or archery skills."

"Nay, but she still runs much of the Ramsay keep, allowing Brenna the time to heal our clan and mother her bairns."

"But she learned that skill over the years. When you marry, 'twill take a while, but you will learn." She stood and leaned toward her friend, brushing the wisps of fine hair back from her face. "You are an intelligent, warm, compassionate lass who will make a wonderful wife and mother. No lad could ask for more. Look at Caralyn and Celestina, my brothers' wives. Caralyn discovered she has a talent for healing, and Celestina has developed a passion for creating fragrant oils. Both are skills you could learn. But you cannot make yourself love something. You have to find out what you love to do, which takes time."

"But you adapted so quickly to being mistress of the Cameron keep."

"True, but I have made many mistakes."

"Truly? Tell me. 'Twill make me feel better." Lina wanted to hear that she wasn't so unusual. To her, Jennie seemed almost perfect.

"Aye, there was the time I insisted Cook follow my recipe for a stew, and all the men spat it out it was so bad."

Lina slapped her hand against her cheek and giggled. "They did not. How rude of them. I would have eaten it."

"Nay, you would not have. I could not eat it myself. It tasted so sour that some of the men ran outside to heave. I was so embarrassed. Now they always jest about it, asking me each night whether Cook is using her own recipe." Jennie chuckled. "Once I wanted to pay Aedan back for something he said, so I told him I'd tweaked the recipe for the stew to make it better. 'Twas something my mother used to make, so I wished to try it. You should have seen him. He tried to come up with every excuse in the world to leave the keep. He had to go see the monks, there was a sick lad in the lists, and his mother was sending him on an errand. Finally, I made him taste it in front of all the guards. It was actually good, and his eyes bulged out of his face until the entire hall was laughing."

Lina was laughing so hard, she had to stop and take a deep breath. "Sorry, Jennie. You must have felt terrible at the time. I do not mean to laugh at you. But watching Aedan try to sneak away would have been funny."

"'Tis all right. None of us are prefect, Avelina. You'll find your way, just as I have, but your path may be anything but straight. As you know, I struggled with whether or not I wanted to be a healer, so I understand how it feels to be lost. I promise to help you. We just need to build up your self-confidence, and you will be fine."

Lina stood and hugged her friend. "Thank you. I feel much better."

"Good, and our first experiment will be with Drew. He's such a nice lad, he will not tease you at all."

Lina's stomach dropped right to her toes. Nay, anyone but Drew. She'd never be able to talk to him.

⸎

Jennie and Avelina worked in the garden for much of the afternoon. Avelina had brought many of her seedlings to share, and they planted many flowers and herbs for healing before weeding the rest of the garden.

Jennie stood up from her spot and moved over to the bench, where she plopped down with a huff. "Lina, we have worked too hard." She brushed her hand across her face to remove the sweat dripping over her brow. As soon as she did, Lina broke into gales of laughter. "What?"

Pointing at Jennie's face, she choked out, "Your face."

"What's wrong? Why are you laughing?" Jennie's eyes widened.

Lina did her best to control her giggles, and was finally able to choke out a few words. "Dirt. You wiped dirt all across your face."

Horrified, Jennie tried to wipe off her face, but she only made it worse. "I'll return quickly," she told Lina, and she raced the short distance back to the keep.

Lina removed her gloves and wiped the sweat from her brow, still chuckling over her friend's aghast expression. It had been a long time since she had laughed so. How glad she was to be here, away from home. She breathed in deep, enjoying the warm summer air as she left the garden and stepped onto the stone path. But just then a rough arm grabbed her from behind, catching her just underneath her breasts.

"You wee tease, are you not just what I have been looking for? What a delectable morsel you shall be."

Lachlan Burnes spun her around and kissed her hard on her lips. She shoved at his shoulders, but to no avail. The man was like an immovable wall. When he finally let her go, she attempted to scream, but naught came out. She had failed herself again.

"How'd it feel to taste a real man? Now you just need to agree to marry me, and I'll let you go." Lachlan grinned, apparently hoping she would be agreeable.

Outraged, Lina shoved against him and attempted to run away. "I'll not marry you, you lout." Shocked that she'd actually spoken to him, she had to force herself to focus on getting away from him.

"You think you'll get away without giving me what I want? I'll not take your maidenhead this time. You'll agree to marry me before I'm done and then you'll see. But for now, I would just like a quick feel. Be agreeable, would you? I hate having to force lasses, but I will if you make me." His grip on her arms tightened, and he pulled her in closer, rubbing his chest against her breasts.

Lina brought her boot down hard on his instep and kicked him in the shin, just as Gwyneth had taught her. His hands fell away from her and she whirled around, tearing back toward the keep.

Again, it had happened *again*. What was wrong with her? Why did lads always target her? And what was he talking about? Marry him? Never!

"Do not worry, I'll have what I want, lass. Those tits belong to me, as you do. I'll make Aedan give you to me as my wife. He's a friend of mine." Lachlan's voice echoed over her shoulder, making her move even faster. As soon as she made it through the door, she almost ran into Jennie.

"Lina, what happened? What's wrong?"

Lina grasped her friend's arms in a death grip, afraid to let go. Tears misted her eyes again. She hated crying, but she could not help it. She had been so wrong to think visiting Jennie would free her from the memory of her attack. Aye, Lachlan might not have tried to rape her, but he'd kissed her against her will and attempted to invade her private area, then had the audacity to suggest she would marry him.

How would she ever get past this?

CHAPTER FIVE

Drew didn't trust Lachlan the way he chose to run ahead of the rest of the group coming from the lists, so he followed him. He came up fast behind Lachlan, hoping he had heard wrong. "Burnes, did I hear what I thought I did?"

"What? I just wanted to get her to marry me. If she sees how good I am at kissing, then she'll agree to the marriage. Since she'll be my wife, I wasn't about to take her maidenhead. I only wanted to touch her titties. Why are lasses so stingy? Besides, have you not seen them? Hellfire, they are perfection." He smirked at Drew.

"It was Avelina Ramsay?" he asked, feeling rage gather inside him.

"Aye." He scowled at Drew and placed his hand on his sword. "What is she to you, anyway? Seems like you wish to stake a claim. Mayhap I'll claim her as mine, I need a wife, and *you* will have to stay away."

Drew balled his hands at his sides, but then he decided there was no point in holding back. The bastard deserved it, so he hauled his fist back and punched him square in the face.

Lachlan's head jerked back from the force of the blow. He swore at Drew and reached for his throat, but Drew was faster.

He grabbed Lachlan by the throat and punched him again. "The next time you touch her, I'll kill you. I warned you before." Drew's chest heaved as he forced himself to calm down.

Aedan tore down the path toward them. "Burnes, what the hell did you do now?"

"Disrespected Avelina, and I will not tolerate it. He was warned once. The bastard needs to keep his hands to himself." He shoved Burnes far away from him so he wouldn't be tempted to hit him again.

"Burnes, take yourself back to your own lands. You *were* warned once. And you are not marrying Avelina Ramsay." Aedan's eyes flashed with fury. Aedan had changed. Before, he would likely have teased Burnes or at most scolded him. He would not have told him to leave. Good for Aedan.

Lachlan growled and took off toward the portcullis.

After they watched him leave, Drew met his friend's eyes. "Being married has changed you, Cameron. For the better, I think."

"Aye, and based on the redness of your eyes and the way you reek of whisky, mayhap you should do the same. There are better things in life than drinking and carousing with a different woman each night. Find the right one, 'tis far better." Aedan's face had softened, but it was obvious he meant every word.

"Mayhap you have the right of it," Drew said with a sigh. He looked down at the ground. "I cannot say I have enjoyed what I cannot recall. Of late, I do not remember half of my antics, though I often hear of them from my sire."

"Have you an interest in the Ramsay lass, Menzie? Other than making her one of your bedmates?"

Drew jerked his gaze back to Aedan's. "Hellfire, Cameron. I would never treat her like that. I only play with maids who want to play, and I make sure to leave no bastards behind. Avelina's of noble blood, whether Lachlan chooses to acknowledge that or not, but more importantly, she's innocent and unwilling."

Aedan held his friend's stare for a long moment. "Good. I'm glad you recognize the difference. She's my wife's closest friend, and I will protect her. I want you to know that."

"Understood," Drew said.

Hellfire, why did he have an inkling that Avelina Ramsay would prove to be much, much more to him than just an appealing innocent? More importantly, why did that thought give him more hope than he'd felt in a long while?

Lina crept down the stairs and into the kitchens in the middle of the night. She had spent all night tossing and turning and was hoping to find a cup of goat's milk or a pastry, something to help her sleep.

In the middle of the worktable sat an apple pastry, so she

grabbed it and turned to leave the room. A giggle erupted from the buttery, a storage room at the back of the kitchens. Lina's mind told her to ignore it, but something else pulled her back to the sound. She made her way toward the giggles.

As she came closer, the giggles turned to moans. "Drew, you know how to please a lass, do you not?"

Drew's voice, husky and deep, echoed through the kitchens. "Aye, I do. You sure are a sweet one."

Lina couldn't help herself. She moved two steps closer and peeked around the corner of the door. There stood Drew, tall, handsome, and his hands wrapped around the bottom of a kitchen maid. He had naught but his plaid on, so her gaze followed the totally unkempt dark hair on his head down to the dark hair on his chest. The two were so intent on each other they had no idea she was there. Their arms and hands were everywhere as he kissed her deeply, causing the girl to moan.

A heat unlike Lina had ever felt before swept through her body, so she turned away and rushed out the door. Her foot knocked a stool over on her way.

"Who goes there?" Drew's voice reached her ears, but she ignored him and flew through the door and back up the stairs.

Once on her bed, she started to sob helplessly. She could never compete with a woman like that. That lass obviously knew how to pleasure Drew Menzie, something Avelina Ramsay knew absolutely naught about.

She rolled onto her side and cried herself to sleep. She'd never get married. No one would ever want her.

Drew grabbed the rest of his clothes and headed to the door, listening to his partner's wails over his shoulder.

"Drew Menzie, don't you dare leave me begging for more."

"Sorry, lass, but I must run." He ran through the door, needing to see who had caught them. He prayed it wasn't Jennie, for then he would be forced to leave Cameron land immediately. At home, they were used to his voracious appetite, but here? Nay, he could not cause any problems here. He needed to be in control. Thus, he had to know who had interrupted them.

As soon as he moved into the great hall, he caught a glimpse of a tall, lithe beauty moving up the staircase. Avelina? Hellfire, he didn't want it to be her. The lass was definitely an innocent.

He ran close enough to confirm that it was her, her cheeks dark red from embarrassment, and then whirled around to go back. Something soft squished under his foot. He leaned over to pick up the ruined apple pastry, probably the reason Avelina Ramsay had come to the kitchens at such a late hour. He cursed himself and his insatiable appetite as he thought of how it must have looked from her vantage point. How could he explain that it was because of Avelina that he had sought out the maid? She had left him wanting, yet he knew she was outside of his reach.

He returned to talk to the maid, but she had disappeared, almost as fast as his desire.

Drew headed straight out the front door into the cool air of the night, raking his hands through his hair. Normally he would not be bothered by this type of an incident, but he wished he could go back and undo what had happened. He'd been around many women at his own castle—sweet innocent ones, widows, married women—but he'd never cared about anyone in particular.

Until Avelina.

All he'd wanted to do was spend some time away from his sire's insults and his mother's clawing over protectiveness, and instead, he'd landed in a place he'd never expected.

He'd landed in a place where one lass mattered more than the rest.

∞

Lina brushed the sleep from her eyes as she sat up in bed. Someone had called to her, she was certain of it. Yet she was in the chamber she had been assigned next to Jennie and Aedan's. Her tousled hair fell around her shoulders as she stood. She hung her head as she recalled what she had seen in the kitchens. Drew Menzie, the lad of her dreams, was not the man she had hoped he was.

"Come to me. We must talk." It was a soft, female voice—one she did not recognize.

A whisper floated through the air and Lina spun in a circle to look for the source. When she could not find it, she lit two more tallows in the room.

"Come to the window, you'll see me. Trust me, I will protect you."

Lina tiptoed over to the edge and pulled the fur back to peek out into the cool night. An aura, the type you would expect to see near an angel, caught her attention under the trees near the bench in the garden. She leaned out the opening to look closer.

A wee lass with masses of golden curls dancing around her face stood there in a long flowing gown decorated with feathers and pearls. A smile adorned her porcelain face. "Trust me to protect you, Lina. I am Erena. We must speak. Please come to me in the garden. I will protect you from all lads. You'll not be bothered by the likes of Lachlan or Keith whenever I am around."

Lina glanced over her shoulder because the voice did not come from below, but above. How could that be? And how did she know the names of Lachlan *and* Keith? Mayhap it was all a dream.

"Come, Lina. We must talk. You have no idea of your own value, do you, lass?"

Lina jerked back from the window and dropped the fur back into place. She must be dreaming.

"Nay, 'tis not a dream. Come visit me."

Lina opened the door to her chamber, and noticing the passageway was empty, padded out of the room and down the stairway. As she moved toward the front door of the great hall, that same lilting voice stopped her. "Not that way. Come through the kitchens. Place your trust in me, and I will lead you."

Lina switched directions and moved toward the kitchens, tiptoeing. At first, she was afraid to go into the kitchen after what she had seen that night.

"Avelina, please trust me. Drew is not here. This has naught to do with him, just you and me."

Lina closed her eyes, took a deep breath, and proceeded through the kitchens into the cool night air. Once she stepped outside, the most beautiful aroma greeted her—the sweet scent of lavender. She inhaled deeply, and Erena's voice said, "Aye, follow my scent. 'Twill lead you to me."

A sudden sense of peace infused Lina's body. She rushed down the pathway, only stopping when the darkness of the night turned to light. There, in the center of the garden, stood the loveliest woman she had ever seen. She stopped in her tracks, waiting to hear the voice again, waiting for proof that this stunning woman was the one who had beckoned her.

Erena's ivory gown was decorated in feathers. The aroma of lavender did indeed surround her, along with something else. The garden was full of butterflies, their wings fluttering in the air.

At first, Avelina believed she was dreaming. She watched the butterflies—their wings decorated in purples, yellows, and greens—dance in the air around the woman in front of her. This was not a dream, though. This was real. Somehow, she knew. This otherworldly woman was here for *her*, and her life was about to change for the better. No longer would she be quiet little Lina in the corner.

"Hello, my dear, I am Erena, the Fae Queen of Peace and Harmony. Our purpose is to bring harmony to the land of the Scots and protect it from evil. My kind rarely appears to humans, but I have a special role for you.

"Unfortunately, you have been harmed in a way that is difficult to repair. Confused lads have injured your confidence, which must be restored before I can tell you what your purpose is in this land. You will prove to be a strong lass, but you will not believe me for some time. I shall prove it to you."

Lina stared at the vision in front of her, certain she had turned daft. Nay, this could not be true, but who would play such a cruel trick on her? What act of trickery could summon so many butterflies to one place? Could it all be a dream?

Erena sat on the bench and patted the spot next to her. "Come sit with me, and I'll try my best to explain."

Lina hesitated, but only for a moment. The vision of Erena tugged on her soul, so she stepped closer and placed her hand in the faerie's outstretched one. An immediate sense of harmony spread through her body, soothing her soul and stopping her trembling. She lifted her gaze to Erena's, still unable to believe this was truly happening to her, and took a seat next to the faerie.

"This is a verra confusing time for all," Erena continued. "After all the fighting ended on Cameron land, we thought the situation had improved, but another negative force has pushed its way to the forefront, hiding behind the face of one of Aedan's neighbors. Our council has decided to choose a human to assist us. My dear, we chose you. Though I cannot reveal what we wish you to do for us just yet, you will know in good time."

Avelina gasped, her eyes widening. "Me?"

"Aye, you are much stronger than you believe. Someday you will understand that, but we must move forward one step at a time. For now, you must trust me and do as I say, though I have few instructions for you today.

"In this land, there exists a sword, Avelina—not a large one, but one that carries certain gifts. What those gifts are does not matter at this moment, but it does matter who possesses this sword.

"Evil has found its way to the sword, and if we do not regain it, the future of the Scots will be in jeopardy. I wish we could keep the sword in our possession, but it is destined to be in human hands, so we must guide you along the way. Eventually, I will tell you how you can assist us in this endeavor. For now, I only wish for you to determine its location. The handle is encrusted with rubies and sapphires. You will know it when you see it."

Erena ended her explanation and folded her hands in her lap. "Do you think you could accomplish that?"

Lina nodded, unable to speak.

Erena stood and held her arms out from her body. A soft sound emanated from the sky as a swarm of butterflies landed on her arms. Lina could not take her eyes from one butterfly in particular—the speckles of gold on its wings matched the faerie's golden slippers.

"Whenever you spy a golden butterfly," Erena said with a smile, "trust that I am nearby. I cannot protect you from everything, but I will help you learn to protect yourself. Believe in your strength and allow others to assist and protect you as well. You will find your way."

She lifted her arms in a slow, graceful arc toward the sky, sending all the butterflies aloft but one. The golden butterfly had moved into the palm of Erena's hand, which she extended toward Lina and lifted quickly through the air. The butterfly took off and flew over Lina's head. Then the faerie placed her hands on either side of Lina's head and leaned down to kiss her forehead. "Someday, my dear, I will do the same for you. But first you must believe in yourself. Then you will be surprised by how high you can soar."

In a flash of light, Erena disappeared, and Lina found herself back in her chamber. She blinked back tears as she stumbled over to the window to look out over the garden.

Erena was gone.

As she climbed back into her bed, Avelina decided it had probably been a dream. She settled her head on the pillow and tugged the covers up to her chin with a trembling hand. Just as she was about to close her eyes, a strange sound greeted her. She sat up, then moved back over to the window, pulling the fur covering back. She searched for Erena, but did not see her. Just then a golden butterfly flew over to her, suspended in front of her face, its wings flapping for her attention. She held her hand out, and the butterfly landed gracefully in the middle of her palm before flapping its wings twice and departing. Lina watched the creature until she could no longer see it.

Even if had been a dream, Erena had given her something she had been searching for forever.

Hope.

CHAPTER SIX

Drew scowled as he stood next to Aedan in the Cameron lists, where Neil and Boyd were running two different groups through training exercises.

Aedan's brother, Ruari, joined them, having just arrived from the keep. "Aedan, may I work with Boyd today? Mayhap we can discover some new moves."

His exuberance was enough to give Drew a headache.

Aedan cast a sly glance over at Drew. "Aye, work with Boyd. Hopefully, he'll teach you something new we can use with our men. Drew is a great trainer, as well...or at least he is when his head's not full of ale."

Ruari gave his brother a surprised look, then glanced at Drew.

"Ignore your brother, Ruari," Drew hollered. "I had naught to drink last night." Drew crossed his arms and stared out at the field of warriors, not wanting to talk to anyone.

Ruari snickered as he ran off toward the training grounds.

"What has you so fierce this morn, Menzie? Couldn't find a lass last night? I told you Senga would take care of you."

"I found her and she was agreeable, but I changed my mind." He didn't glance at his friend, fearing he would spill all if he met Aedan's eyes.

"Then why are you miserable? Too much ale? Unable to perform?" Aedan laughed at the expression on his friend's face.

Drew sent a clump of dirt flying at Aedan's head, but his friend easily ducked it. Chuckling, Aedan made his way over to the group of guards practicing in the middle of the field.

"Halfwit! Nay, I said I did not drink last night," Drew growled. He stood at the side of the field, his legs planted wide and his arms crossed, daring anyone to bother him. He had intentionally kept himself from imbibing too much. While he couldn't seem to stop himself at home, it was easy to control himself at Aedan's. Though his body language was intended to repel attention, it was not as effective as he'd hoped. Aedan's guards continued to come his way. They actually lined up to speak with him.

"I heard your guards compete against one another in teams," the first asked. "Can you not do the same for us?"

Drew motioned with his head, indicating that the guard should move on.

The second one took two steps back as soon as he got a look at Drew's facial expression. "Menzie, would you be able to show us that new move you showed us one moon ago? The one that takes down twice as many guards?"

Drew growled and pointed toward the field. "Go see my second, Boyd." The lad took off running. Could they not see he had other things on his mind today? Things like plump pink lips and an innocent smile…a smile that he had destroyed with one careless action the previous night.

The third man stood five paces away. "Could you not watch us and see what we are doing wrong? That maneuver is the best we've ever tried."

"Hurry off! I'm too busy today."

Aedan had just taken a sip of mead from his skein and choked. "Too busy doing what? Acting miserable? Kicking arses?"

Drew glared at his friend and said, "Bugger off, Cameron." In truth, he was too busy trying to decide how to make amends to a certain beautiful lass for his indiscretions, and he did not have any idea how to go about it. He scowled as different scenarios played out in his mind.

I'm sorry for getting caught? Forgive me for my desires? You know I'd rather it were you?

"Arghhhh…." he yelled out at no one in particular.

Aedan laughed and strode back to him. "Hellfire, I've not seen you this miserable since you were celibate for a fortnight. What's going on? You're hiding something."

Drew just stared out over the lists, brooding in silence.

"If 'tis about your sire," Aedan said, rubbing his jaw, "he'll see your worth some day. Do not doubt it."

That was the foremost of Drew's problems most days, but not today. The worst part was that he could not confess the truth to Aedan. He couldn't explain because Aedan would either laugh hysterically or be so furious that he punched him square in the jaw.

Drew didn't answer, so Aedan sauntered off into the fields. He paused to talk to one guard after another, apparently offering them advice.

A few moments later, a lad ran up to him and said, "My laird said to tell you tonight should be better for you."

Drew stared at Aedan, wondering what he was about.

Another lad stopped in front of him. "My laird said if ye're too soft to work today, you can return to the keep."

Drew's eyes widened at the word *soft*, and his gaze immediately searched out Aedan, who was watching him from afar, doubled over in laughter.

"Bugger off, Cameron!" Drew shouted loud enough for half the men to hear him. Deciding he could stay no longer, he glared at Aedan, spun on his heels, and stalked off.

There was no reason to deny the truth any longer. The reason he was so upset was because he cared about Avelina Ramsey. Where his feelings had come from, he had no idea. But he was angry, nay, *pissed*, that Lina had seen him with the kitchen maid. And he had no idea what to say to her the next time they saw each other.

He was marching through the forest, still furious at the world, when he heard some rustling off to the side. When he glanced back over his shoulder, he was stunned to see how far he had traveled from the lists. If he hollered to Aedan, he doubted his friend would hear him.

Hellfire, he'd search out the source of the noise on his own. He moved through the trees, unsure of what he would find. In case it was a group of boars or something dangerous, he kept his hand on the hilt of his sword.

It was an animal, but a human one. Lachlan. Lachlan had a lass pinned to the ground, and he was fumbling with his breeches. He was clearly intent on molesting her.

Drew's blood was boiling in his veins before he even recognized the lass.

Avelina Ramsay's face had been punched, and she was out cold. Fury exploded inside him. He wanted nothing more than to kill Lachlan with his bare hands. He jumped on him from behind, emitting a growl that took the other man by surprise.

"Menzie, leave off. I've declared her as mine. She agreed to marry me as soon as I explained everything to her about the legend. We'll marry within a sennight as the legend of the sword goes. We're leaving soon, and I'm taking her with me since she agreed. Now go away." He scrambled to right his clothing as Drew grabbed his tunic and spun him around.

Drew bellowed, "Nay, she'll not be marrying you."

Ignoring everything Lachlan had to say, Drew grabbed him by the throat, lifted him and tossed him through the air. His back hit a tree trunk, and he crumpled to the ground. As soon as he was down, Drew fell on him and pummeled his face until there was blood all over. Lachlan tried to fight back, but his best efforts could not combat Drew's anger. Once he stopped moving, Drew went for his belly, where he landed punch after punch.

A small whimper sounded behind him, the only sound that could have stopped him, and he spun around to see if Avelina was all right. He flew to her side just as her lids fluttered open. But the only word she could mutter was, "Nay."

Drew fixed the bodice of her gown and picked her up in his arms, making his way back to the keep. His gaze traveled from her bruised face down her body, but she did not appear to be hurt anywhere else.

"Avelina? Talk to me. I'll take you to Jennie. She'll help you." His sentences were clipped since he was now running and out of breath.

Her eyes opened and she gazed up at him. "Drew? Please, I do not like Lachlan. He hurt me. Do not let him near me."

"Hush, wee one. I'll not allow him to touch you again. Jennie will help you."

Her eyes fluttered shut again as she gripped his arms, grasping him as if she never wanted to let go.

For some baffling reason, he wished she wouldn't let go. He leaned down and kissed her forehead, whispering a promise to her that he would take care of her. That he would be there for her. Odd behavior, coming from him. But he could not deny that he felt *alive* with Avelina in his arms, more alive than he'd felt in a long time—more alive than he'd ever felt at his own castle.

As soon as he reached the portcullis and the bailey, voices erupted around him, some offering to help. One of them promised to tell Jennie that Avelina was in need of help. He climbed the steps to the great hall and someone opened the door for him.

Inside, Jennie hurried toward him, giving orders along the way. "Mab, fresh water in her chamber, please. Drew, up the stairs. I want her in her bed."

As soon as they moved up the staircase together, Jennie asked, "What happened?"

"I caught Lachlan attacking her in the woods," Drew whispered.

"Where is he now?" Jennie directed him down the passageway to Lina's room.

"I left him there." Memories of Lachlan lying there unmoving gave him little satisfaction.

"He did not get up?"

"Nay." Bastard. He should have finished him off. He was almost too distracted by the thought to hear Jennie's next question.

"Why not?" she asked as she entered Avelina's chamber.

"He couldn't. I made sure he wouldn't harm her again. 'Tis twice he's dared to touch her." Drew gave Jennie a fierce look as he followed her into the room and settled Avelina under the covers.

Jennie's brow arched in response to his declaration. "Drew, you're covered in blood. Where are you hurt?"

"I'm not." Why was Jennie so calm? How could she remain this calm when Lachlan had hurt sweet Avelina?

Again, she raised her brow in question.

He forced himself to focus. "Lachlan's blood," he explained. He managed to catch his breath now that Avelina was safe in her bed and Jennie was nearby.

"Drew, do you know why she sleeps?"

Drew stepped back from the bed. "He punched her," he whispered. "How does a man do that to such a wee lass? I could not imagine taking a fist to a woman." His hands clenched into fists at his sides. He was almost afraid to move, afraid he'd go back to finish what he'd started.

"I know not the answer. Many thanks for saving my friend from that cruel man. Did not Aedan send him away yesterday? How did he get to her? She had gone to the chapel…" Her brow furrowed in thought. "I must speak with Aedan."

She moved to her friend's bedside.

Just then, the door flew open and Aedan filled the doorway. "Jennie? I heard the news. Is Lina going to be all right?"

Jennie gave her husband a bleak look before answering. "I think so, but I have not had the opportunity to check her fully yet. Did you find Lachlan?"

"Aye. A bunch of men must have beaten him."

"Does he still breathe?" Jennie asked.

"Aye, but barely. They did a fine job on him, but he deserved it. He was warned about touching Lina."

"They?" Jennie gave her husband a pointed look, then moved her gaze to Drew.

"Menzie? You were in on this?"

"Aye. I found her. When I left you, I came through the edge of the forest and heard the rustling of leaves. When I got there, Lachlan had knocked her out and was about to rape her."

Aedan's eyes widened. "I'd like to kill him myself, though you and whoever helped you did a fine job."

"Drew didn't have any assistance," Jennie whispered, returning her attention to Avelina.

Noticing Aedan's expression of shock, Drew bellowed, "Why do you look surprised? The bastard was warned to keep his hands off her on two occasions, yet he still tried to attack her. You're lucky Avelina moaned or I would not have been able to stop. But I knew I needed to get her to your wife."

Drew's gaze returned to Avelina, whose form lay still atop the bed.

Aedan made his way over to Drew's side and grasped his shoulder. "My thanks."

Jennie's house maid came through the door with linen strips, linen squares, and clean water, followed by a slew of lads carrying a tub and pails of steaming water.

Aedan leaned over and kissed his wife on the cheek. "We'll step out. Please keep us updated."

"Aye, Mab will help me wash her. I'll send her out if I need you."

Drew stopped at the door to look back at Avelina for a moment. Hellfire, but the tall, willowy beauty looked so small in her bed.

The urge to protect her...forever washed over him once more.

Lina opened her eyes and moaned. Her hand flew to her face, though touching her tender skin only made her wince. What had happened?

A sound echoed off to her side. She jerked her head that way and groaned again, for the motion sent pain shooting through her head, forcing her to hold it as if her wee hand could stop the battering inside.

"Avelina, do not move. If you move, 'twill only hurt more."

Drew yanked his stool over to the side of the bed. Her gaze caught his, and the green of his eyes mesmerized her. Before she could give it any thought, she spoke, "Please call me Lina. 'Twas you who came to my rescue, was it not?" She eased her head into a position that did not hurt. "My thanks, Drew."

"Aye," he whispered, reaching for her hand, enfolding it within his warm one. "My apologies. I should have been there sooner."

"Nay," she whispered. "How could you have known? I am forever grateful you came to my aid when you did."

The door opened and Jennie glided into the room, moving over to stand beside Drew.

"Lina? How do you fare?"

"She's sore. Her head must ache something fierce. Can you not give her something for the pain?" Drew's voice rang out in the chamber.

Lina squeezed his hand, only then realizing something. *She had been able to talk to Drew.* She closed her eyes and willed herself to continue, assuring herself that she could do this for the lad who had rescued her from that lout, Lachlan. This was an important moment for her, so much so that she closed her eyes before she parted her lips to speak. "I'm fine, Drew. 'Tis not more than I can bear."

Drew's hand reached out as if to touch her cheek, but then he retreated. "I do not wish to hurt you."

She smiled, a blush warming her insides, but somehow it did not stay her lips. "You cannot hurt me."

"Lachlan said you'd agreed to marry him. 'Tis true?"

Avelina gasped and tried to sit up. "Nay, I would never agree to marry him."

Drew reached for her shoulders. "We believe you. 'Tis just

another of his lies."

Jennie gently lowered herself onto the bed. "What happened, Lina? How did he find you?"

She stared up at the beams in the ceiling as she tried to remember. "I was on my way out of the chapel when he grabbed me. I tried to scream, but he hit me, and 'tis the last thing I recall. The next thing I remember is being on the ground and seeing Drew pummel Lachlan. Naught else is there."

"'Tis better that you do not remember everything. Shall I give you a sleeping potion?"

"Nay, I do not need it."

"If you change your mind, just say so. You may need help sleeping later."

The door opened, and a buxom maid entered. She came to a stop next to Drew and held a tray out to Jennie. "Here is the food you requested, my lady."

Jennie took the tray and set it on the other side of the bed on a nearby chest. "Thank you, Senga. 'Tis all I need for now."

Lina's gaze flew to the maid's face as the woman was the one who had been with Drew in the kitchens. She brought her gaze back to Drew, only to find him returning her gaze, a guilty expression on his face. Since she had no idea what to say, she decided to close her eyes and forget about what she had seen. Men had needs, and she had no claim on Drew.

Jennie said, "'Tis all for now, Senga.".

"Aye, Mistress. My apologies if I forgot aught." She left the room, and Jennie followed her into the passageway, leaving the door open behind her.

Lina was certain she was probably blushing a deep shade of red by now, and her inability to speak had returned. Drew mumbled something, but Lina could not understand him. Her eyelids felt heavy, so she decided she would take a wee nap. Just before her eyes closed, Drew leaned over to whisper in her ear, "Forgive me, Lina. I never meant for you to see us."

Her eyes flew open and her gaze caught his. She thought she saw regret there. But what exactly did he regret?

Drew whispered, "Truly, she is naught to me. I got caught up in something I shouldn't have. I'm sorry you caught us, but in a way, I'm glad."

"Why?" she croaked, so glad the word actually came out.

"Because I don't want her. I'm more interested in you."

She struggled to stay awake, but was losing the battle. Just before her eyes closed, he kissed her forehead. Lina fell asleep, her dark knight fresh in her mind.

CHAPTER SEVEN

Lina sat in the chair by the hearth, next to Jennie, who was sewing a garment for her wee one that was due in several moons.

Jennie asked, "Lina, I know you have not wanted to discuss your problems, but are you feeling better?"

"Aye." She was. Her head no longer pounded all day, but her fears had grown. Within a matter of weeks, she had been assaulted thrice. This last time, she had been assaulted in the chapel, no less, a place she had always believed to be safe.

Two other things muddled her mind. One was Drew Menzie, though she had seen little of him lately. She was thrilled that she had actually been able to speak with him, and she could swear he had admitted having an interest in her, but she feared every day they were apart threatened to send her back to her world of silence. The other thought that refused to leave her mind was about Erena, the faerie. She snorted and only realized it had been loud enough to be heard when Jennie raised her brow at her.

Jennie giggled. "Did that snort have a particular target? Drew? Me? The weather?"

Lina laughed, something she rarely did these days. "Nay, 'twas about… about a dream I had one night."

"Tell me about it. If it forced you to snort, I would love to hear it. You are so proper and ladylike all the time, 'twas a wondrous sound to my ears."

Lina blushed a shade of pink—would Jennie think her silly?—but she decided she could share the story of Erena so long as she called it a dream. "Surely this will entertain you."

Jennie's face lit up, prompting her to continue.

"I had a dream about a faerie visiting me."

Jennie gasped, so Lina paused to see what her friend would say. She didn't want to make herself sound foolish.

Jennie's face lit up. "One of the fae? Do tell. My mother had a strong belief in the fae. She was convinced that they guide everything we do, and that they often appear to the chosen."

"The chosen?" Lina sat up straighter in her chair, wanting to hear everything Jennie had to say about the fae. Her mother had never mentioned the fae other than when she told tales by the fire. She had to know more. Where did the fae come from, and what caused someone to be chosen? She waited for her friend to continue.

"Aye. The faeries run the land, so the tales go, but sometimes they need assistance from us. 'Tis said they will only appear in front of the strongest of all, and of course, those most likely to be able to assist them in their quests."

"Did you say the strongest of all?" Lina tipped her head closer to her friend, unable to believe this. Aye, Erena had said she would be strong, but the strongest of all?

"Aye, 'tis what my mother said."

"What type of quests?"

"My mother told me they often fix tragedies such as boats capsizing or the death of a group of bairns, and assist humans dealing with natural calamities, leadership disputes, and the like. 'Tis said they watch us all the time. Some faeries appear only near water, or during the night. Some have creatures with them. What did your fae tell you? What did she look like?"

"Her main goal for now was to help me grow strong. She knew about Lachlan and Keith, and said she would help me to grow strong against them. She told me that she had something for me to do, that there was an evil force that had uncovered something of value, and they had chosen me to help them to find it again, though she did say it was to remain in human hands. But they needed to have it in the possession of certain people. Her name is Erena, and she said she was the Queen of Peace, I believe. She was quite beautiful, surrounded by butterflies."

Jennie gasped. "The Queen of Harmony?"

"Aye, that's what she said, the Queen of Peace and Harmony. How did you know?"

"The queen 'tis the one my mother heard about from someone

she trusted. It was something about…" Pausing for a moment to gather her thoughts, Jennie chewed on her lip. Then her face lit up as the memory returned to her. "She just spoke of the fae wanting to keep peace in our land."

Lina swallowed, her focus narrowing as her heart sped up. If what Jennie said was true, then it had not been a dream at all. She had actually met a faerie, and that also meant that she was indeed a chosen one.

"Lina." Silence settled between them.

Lina brought her gaze up to her friend's. Jennie whispered, "It really happened, didn't it? You are a chosen one."

Lina nodded, scarcely moving her head, as if the truth just settled on her.

Just then, the door burst open and a large group of wee ones flew in, all racing toward her. Shocked, she turned her head to see who it was.

Her brother and his wife stood at the door. "Avelina, we had to see how you were doing. You can see everyone wanted to travel with us." Gwyneth held her arms out toward the group of young ones.

The group of *clann* surrounded her, and she wanted to hide her face, but it was too late. The boisterous group switched from loud excited voices to hushed tones. She knew why. Her nieces and nephews had all seen her bruised face and her swollen eye. Torrian, Lily, Bethia, Molly, Maggie, and Sorcha stopped dead in front of her, their expressions changing from excitement to confusion. Gavin and Gregor crept closer than the rest.

Logan and Gwyneth came up to her and clasped her shoulders, and then wee Gregor crept toward her and placed his hands on her lap. "Aunt Wina. We will help you det bettew."

"We will find who did this to you and make sure he does not hurt you again," Gavin added. His wee fist came up in a wide arc.

The door opened again, and Aedan and Drew came into the great hall, though they stood off to the side. Jennie strode up to her husband, and they wrapped their arms around each other as they watched the powerful demonstration of family love in front of them. Lina noticed Drew's look changed from one of anger to something much softer. His gaze was on her, and he watched every interaction she had with the bairns, smiling particularly at Gavin and Gregor.

Torrian, the eldest of the group, said, "I'm sure Jennie's husband has made sure Lina will not be hurt again. He will protect her."

Lily, who had grown so much in the past few years, had tears running down her face, so different from her usual animated presence. "Why must people hurt our sweet Aunt Lina?" Lily threw her arms around Lina and hugged her tight.

Gregor turned to his cousin. "Dabin, we must dive Wina another tiss."

Gavin nodded and the two clambered onto her lap, causing her to giggle at their sweetness as they leaned in to kiss her cheeks.

Gregor pointed to her bruised cheek and said, "Does it huwt you?"

"I'm much better now," Lina insisted, shaking her head. "My thanks, lads."

Once they climbed down, Gavin reached behind him and pulled out his wooden sword. "We are here to protect you, Aunt Lina."

Lina noticed that Logan had settled a hand across his mouth as he glanced at Gwyneth, totally engrossed in their son's sweet behavior. She suspected he was hiding a smile at the lad's antics.

Gregor nodded, then mimicked his cousin by pulling out his smaller sword. "Aye, we will till him if he tomes neaw you."

"Come on, Gregor. We must guard the door." They chased over to the doorway and Gavin pointed to a spot. "You stay there, and I'll stay here. Naught will get past us."

"Aunt Wina!" Gregor shouted over to her, his small sword pointed toward the rafters. "We are your 'tectors."

Avelina smiled and then hugged each of her wee nieces in turn. Drew had made his way over a bit closer, though she wasn't sure why. She had noticed he followed everything her clan had done.

Jennie and Aedan made their way over to greet their visitors, and Jennie said to Gwyneth, "I'll get some fruit and bread for you, and goat's milk for the weans. You must be hungry after your trip."

Logan added, "Molly, you and Lily can go with Lady Jennie to help bring some food out. Maggie, take the others over there, please. You can settle at that table while we speak to Avelina."

The wee ones did as they were bade.

Lina's eyes misted as she stared at her brother who had knelt down in front of her. She loved Logan so much. He was such a tough man, yet so gentle with his family. She so admired his relationship with Gwyneth.

"How do you fare? As soon as word of the incident arrived, all your nieces and nephews insisted on coming to see you. Quade and Brenna stayed back since Brenna has had some trouble with this babe, but they send their love."

She swiped at her cheek and said, "You're all verra sweet. I'm better now. Tell me about Brenna's troubles."

"She's just been nauseous with this bairn," Gwyneth replied. "She was with Gregor, too."

"We're more concerned about you. Are you sure you're all right? Would you like to talk to Gwynie alone?"

"Nay, I'm fine." Suddenly embarrassed that they had all come to Cameron land because of her troubles, she looked down into her lap.

Logan said, "Good, then I only have one question." He paused, giving Lina a chance to clear the tears from her face. Then, in the commanding voice Avelina knew quite well, he asked, "What's his name?"

❦

Drew arrived in time to see the group of children run to Avelina's side. Everything they did and said spoke to how much they adored their aunt. He couldn't imagine having that many people look up to him. If his father would just admire one thing he had ever done, he would be grateful. She deserved their affection and more, though, and he was especially grateful to the two wee lads who climbed onto her lap to kiss her cheeks. They made Lina giggle, and that was a sound he hadn't yet heard from her.

Over the past few days, he had forced himself to stay away from her. In part, he had made that decision because the sight of her bruises enraged him and made him want to finish what he'd started and kill Lachlan Burnes. But the other reason he had stayed away was he was afraid Aedan would discover how important Lina was to him. And he wasn't ready to completely admit that to himself yet, much less to his friend.

He had gone home, hoping that being away from her wouldn't bother him, but Lina was all he had thought of on his way to the keep. As soon as he stepped into his great hall, his father called him out in front of everyone eating the midday meal, accusing him of being lazy, unreliable, and untrustworthy. Since seeing his parents together only reminded him of why he would never marry, he decided it wasn't the best place for him at present. Now that he was developing true feelings for a lass, he did not need a reason to stay away from her.

His parents tended to send him in that direction.

So he turned right around and left again. His mother followed him down the pathway crying, so he hugged her once, peeled her arms away from his neck, and walked away.

He had been too worried about Lina to stay away anyway.

Now he leaned against the stone wall of the Cameron keep and watched Lina's brother. This man had the type of reputation he had always yearned for himself. Considered one of the fiercest Highlanders in the land just behind Jennie's brother, Alex, Logan was feared by most men. It was also a known fact that he worked for the Scottish crown. How did a person become so strong?

Drew decided to pay close attention to everything Logan did this week so he could model his behavior after him. Drew wanted to be important. He wanted to be respected. He wanted others to believe him fierce and noble and loyal, a man who could be counted on to fight for what was right, who would protect the innocent.

He took a few steps toward Lina, and immediately found two wooden swords aimed at his belly.

"Dabin, do no' wet him near Aunt Wina." Gregor's expression let Drew know just how much the wee lad meant it. While he could easily push them away, he decided to give into the lads' sense of honor, especially since they were bent on protecting someone verra special to him.

Gavin, the elder of the two, held his sword in two hands. "You'll not go near our aunt. We are her protectors."

"Aye. Hew 'tectors." Gregor's fierce scowl made Drew want to smile, but he managed to refrain. He knelt down in front of the laddies and said, "I promise not to hurt your aunt. In fact, I was the one who saved her from the bad lout who hurt her."

Gavin raced to Lina's side, Gregor right behind him. "Is that true, Aunt Lina? Is he the man who saved you?" Gregor bumped into him from behind.

Gavin turned to his cousin, clearly irritated. "Gregor, you're supposed to be watching that man while I talk to Aunt Lina." He used his sword to point at Drew.

Gregor tore back over to Drew. "I will teep him hewe." The laddie's wooden sword quickly swung back toward Drew's belly.

"Gregor, 'tis this man who saved me. Let him be," Lina said. "His name is Drew Menzie."

Gregor let his sword arm fall to his side and headed back toward the door, Gavin close behind him. They both nodded, stepped back, and held their swords pointed toward Lina so Drew could pass safely.

Drew headed toward the hearth, nodding to Lina as he came closer.

"Is this true?" Logan asked, now leaning against the hearth. "You saved her?"

Drew nodded and tried to make eye contact with Lina, but she stared at her hands, kneading the linen square there.

"My thanks." Logan grasped his shoulder. "You have my deep gratitude. If you ever need aught, let me know."

Gwyneth, who stood next to her husband, added, "You have my gratitude as well. We are all verra devoted to Avelina. She is a treasured member of our clan."

Drew nodded. "I can see that."

Turning back to face Lina, Logan said, "You still have not answered me. Who was it? Someone you knew, someone from Aedan's clan?"

Drew crossed his arms, never taking his gaze off Lina. "It was a lad from Clan Burnes, actually the laird's eldest and only son. He will not be back. I convinced him to leave."

Speaking directly to Logan, Aedan said, "My apologies that this happened on my land. 'Twas my job to protect her."

"Lina's beauty is known all across the land of the Scots," Gwyneth said. "Unfortunately, such a reputation oft becomes a beacon for unseemly sorts."

Lina blushed and twisted her skirts in her lap, probably wanting this discussion to end. Lina was not one that liked being the center of attention, of that he was certain. The topic alone would be difficult to discuss with a brother. The weans looked upset again, so Gwyneth said, "Why do we not sit down for something to eat?"

Logan nodded. "We'll talk later, Cameron." He strode over to the table, and Aedan and Jennie and the rest followed, leaving Drew alone with Lina.

Drew sat in the chair next to hers, deciding this was as good a time as any to make amends with her. The bairns made enough noise to ensure that no one would overhear them.

"Lina, I know I apologized to you the other night, I just would like to be certain you heard me. You were verra sleepy. The issue in the kitchens, please forgive me. I no longer have any interest in that kind of passing relationship."

Lina gazed into his eyes, and it was as if she hit him with a sledge hammer. Hellfire, between her innocence, her beauty, and how adept she was with those young ones, the lass was mighty enticing to him. Damn, but she had the most kissable lips he had ever seen. This was not a simple case of blood rushing to his groin… He would do aught he could to protect her and prove himself to her.

Suddenly, he felt a bit like the lads with their swords, wishing to stand in front of her at all times.

Lina whispered, "I recall. My thanks for the apology." She fingered her linen square before she continued. "Drew." She reached up and touched her fingers to his lips, silencing him. "But you do not need to apologize to me. I am aware that men have needs." She dropped her hand from his lips, and he caught her hand with his.

"It was a mistake, and it will not happen again. I like you." He paused, not knowing what else to say. He rubbed his thumb across the tender skin on the back of her hand. This was not the time to confess that he had sworn he would never marry or that Lina was making him question everything he had ever believed in. He just didn't know yet. But what he did know was that everything about him was changing and mostly due to the lass who sat before him. But he needed to say something. "I know you're an innocent, and a lad should not subject a respectable innocent to such things."

She pulled her gaze from his. "Mayhap I am tired of being innocent."

Drew didn't know what to say to that.

CHAPTER EIGHT

Lina tiptoed down the stairway toward the kitchen. One of the luxuries she'd enjoyed while at the Cameron keep was a chamber of her own. She had quite liked it. But now that her family was staying at the keep, she was back to sharing her bed with the lassies, though Sorcha and Maggie were with Logan and Gwyneth. Molly, Lily, and Bethia were all with her. She enjoyed it when they all huddled together to keep warm and told stories until they fell asleep, but she was oft awakened by movement, especially Bethia, who wrapped herself around Lina.

As soon as she stepped into the kitchens, she froze. There, next to the table in the middle used for chopping, stood Drew Menzie in just his plaid, no tunic or breeches or boots. Her mouth went dry as she stared at his chest, the sprinkling of dark hairs she wished to touch. He didn't notice her at first, but then his gaze caught hers.

All she could think about was the maid he'd been with the other eve. She knew there was a room off the kitchens somewhere for the maids to sleep, if they so desired. Was he here to meet another maid? As soon as the thought entered her mind, she spun around and headed back toward the door.

A strong arm caught her from behind, wrapping around her waist. "Please stay. I'm not here for another, just for food. But since you're here, can we not talk?"

His breath warmed her neck, and she caught the aroma of apples from him. Aye, the old Lina would have pushed against him and run away. But the new Lina was surprising her.

The new Lina wished to stay. Now that she trusted him enough to talk to him, she wished to get to know him better. Or perhaps find out a wee bit more about what he'd been doing with Senga.

She whirled around and smiled. "Aye, I'll stay." She glanced at the apple pastry in his hand. "That is, if you're willing to share your pastry. 'Tis what I came for, and it appears to be the last one." Lina couldn't believe how bold she was being. A blush that had started at her toes had continued up to her face, but she didn't care. It was just the two of them, and she wanted more—anything at all from Drew Menzie.

His mouth quirked at one side, and a challenge danced in his eyes. His arm fell from her waist, and he reached for the pastry in his other hand, broke off a wee piece and held it out for her to taste. She hesitated for just a second, taking in everything about him—his scent, his heat, and the sheer animal magnetism arcing between the two of them.

Her tongue darted out to take the piece of pastry. She closed her eyes and inhaled the scent of apple, breathing deep enough to send the sweet taste shooting to her pleasure centers.

Embarrassed by the slight moan she released, she fluttered her eyes open, worried she would find him laughing at her. But Drew's gaze was dark and focused, and it was aimed at her and her alone. A bolt of lightning shot straight to her core. His free hand reached for her hair, his fingers running through the silky strands before he pulled her close. His mouth descended on hers with an intensity she could hardly have imagined, and she found herself completely entranced in the taste and feel of Drew Menzie. His lips were warm and soft at first, but they turned possessive as he angled his mouth over hers. Her lips parted and his tongue swept inside, causing a soft mewling sound to build in the back of her throat.

Wanting to be even closer to him, she twined her arms around his neck, and he tugged her to him until every inch of her body was pressed against his. The full length of his hardness melded against her, and she wished that she could tear his plaid off and run her hands over his skin, his muscle, feel his strength under her fingertips.

He ended the kiss and her knees buckled, but he caught her and held her against his heat. She buried her face in his shoulder, wishing the moment wouldn't end. Forcing herself to move away from him, she licked her lips and stepped back. "What happened to the pastry?"

He chuckled. "Seems I did not much care about it. 'Tis now on the floor." His fingers grazed the line of her jaw, and he reached up to tuck her hair behind her ear. "I have never seen you with your hair down before. 'Tis beautiful, as you are."

She smiled, but turned away from his close perusal. This was all so new to her—kissing, touching, being close to a man whom she liked. A painful memory broke through her thoughts, so she pulled away from him.

His thumb brushed her cheek. "Does it still pain you?"

She shook her head, tugging her night rail closer.

"Are you leaving? Is that why Logan has come? To take you home?" He wrapped his arm around her waist to keep her close to him.

"Aye, 'tis his wish to take me home, but I've requested to stay. I'll not go home unless he forces me." While his closeness made her a wee bit uncomfortable, it also gave her a boldness she'd never experienced before. Just the way he gazed at her spread a heat to her core that she didn't fully understand.

"Why not? Would your family not comfort you after everything you've been through? Your nieces and nephews adore you."

"Aye, because I spend all my time with them. I do love them, but I feel like I have a chance to grow up here. There are things here…" She took a deep breath and paused. "I have a difficult time explaining myself sometimes."

His finger lifted her chin, forcing her eyes to his. "Am I fortunate enough to be one of those things?"

She grinned, unable to lie to someone this close to her. "Aye," she said in a small voice. Then, summoning up all her courage, she squared her shoulders and lifted her chin with confidence. "Aye, I'd like to get to know you better. You make me feel like an adult, not a young lassie. And I like it."

"Have you expressed this feeling to your brother?" He tugged her closer and kissed her forehead, then each cheek, and wrapped both arms around her waist. "I'd like to get to know you better as well, but I do not wish to incite his anger."

Lina nodded and leaned into him, wanting just to stay as she was at this moment—protected, special, beautiful. She didn't wish to break the spell cast upon them, and she just now realized another thing about him.

He hadn't tried to touch her breasts once. But there was

something more about him, a sweet vulnerability that she wished to explore. She knew little about him, his clan, or his castle, yet it seemed he was often at the Cameron keep. Why? She found she wanted to know. But the sincerity in his apology, the way he'd been there for her during the most recent attack, just made her want more. At first Drew's looks had drawn her to him, but there was much more to Drew Menzie than a handsome face.

Aye, she was falling for him, and she liked it.

Logan and Gwyneth left less than a sennight later, guards and bairns all in tow. They had continued to try and to convince her to go home, but in the end, they had acquiesced to her wishes.

Logan had also given in to the promise from Aedan that he would deal with Lachlan should he ever return. Drew had believed Burnes would never return, but Aedan wasn't so sure. Lina hoped Drew was right, she never wanted to see Lachlan Burnes again. The whole issue of marriage had escaped her. He had told Drew they were to marry, but yet Lina had no memory of Lachlan discussing marriage with her.

True, women were little more than possessions in their land, but the woman had to agree to the marriage.

She certainly did not agree.

Gwyneth had taught her a few more moves to protect herself. One day, when Logan wasn't around, she had pulled Avelina aside for a private talk. "'Tis much different for you here, aye?"

Lina nodded. "In my family, I will always be the youngest, the wean. Here, I feel older."

Gwyneth hugged her and said, "I understand. Your brothers all treat you like you are still five summers, and you are shy because of it. They are too protective, especially Logan and Quade. Micheil is a mite bit better. Mayhap you could visit him. I'm sure Diana would love to see you."

Lina had considered her suggestion, but then rejected it. "I like it here. Jennie is my closest friend, and she understands me."

"You're growing up, and your brothers have to allow you to do that. I'll help your mother understand, as well."

"My thanks, Gwyneth." She loved her brother's wife because she was so strong, so different. Gwyneth was always patient with her, even when she had taught her to use a bow and arrow. But being attacked was something different, something she wasn't comfortable discussing with anyone in her family. She was just too embarrassed.

Throughout their visit, Gregor and Gavin had sandwiched her in kisses multiple times, as they were wont to do, and she'd loved every minute of it.

Right before they left, wee Gregor had run over to say a final goodbye. "I wuv you, Aunt Wina."

"I love you, too, Gregor."

"Aunt Lina!" Gavin hopped over to her side. "If you need protecting again, we will come back for you. You know Gregor and I are the best protectors."

Gregor chimed in, "Aye, we are da best 'tectors."

Then off they had gone. Her heart felt a wee bit empty now that her family had left, but that sense of hope that had bloomed inside her the night she'd seen—or dreamed—the faerie had not left her.

Jennie sat down next to her at the table not long after the others rode off. "Lina, have you seen the fae again?"

Lina shook her head. "Sometimes, I think I imagined it all."

"Nay, not if what you said matches what my mother told me. 'Tis true. I believe it. What else did she tell you?"

Lina was about to tell Jennie everything when a loud commotion erupted in the bailey. Jennie gave her a puzzled look and got up from her stool. Lina followed her as she made her way to the door, curious to see what had transpired outside.

Jennie opened the door and stepped out, but then twirled back to face her and said, "Go back inside."

Now she was more curious than ever. She peered over Jennie's shoulder at all the horses in the middle of the bailey, trying to understand what all the shouting was about. As soon as her gaze stopped in one spot, it felt as if a fist had punched her in the gut.

Lachlan was back. Lachlan and a man who had to be his father, accompanied by several guards still on horseback, were arguing with Aedan, Drew, and Neil, the head of the Cameron guards. She tried to listen, but Jennie pushed her back inside. As she wasn't interested in seeing Lachlan ever again, she turned toward the door readily enough. Then one word caught her attention.

Sword. They were arguing about a fabled sword. Now, she had to stay. She gave Jennie a pointed look, and her friend's eyes widened.

Lachlan's father shouted the loudest. "Someone stole my son's sword! Possession of the legendary sapphire sword came to him fairly, and now it's disappeared. Lachlan had it when he came over here, and he didn't have it when he returned. It had to be a Cameron who stole it. You all want it."

"His sword was not stolen by anyone on Cameron land, Burnes. Take your daft son and go home, or I'll hold him in my dungeon for attacking a lass on my land." Aedan's face, usually calm, was furious at the Burnes laird.

"Nay, we'll not leave without the sword of the fae. He came by it honestly. 'Twas destiny, destiny that would protect our clan for years into the future. Now, I do not know who stole it, but we expect you, Cameron, to do a search of all those that were here when Lachlan was knocked out. That's when it was taken, and we need to get it back. By all rights, 'tis our sword."

Lina listened intently, not wishing to miss a word of the exchange. A sword? Stolen from him? A fabled sword…just like the one Erena had described. And for some reason, she could actually picture the sword hanging from Lachlan's belt, its hilt encrusted with jewels. Her fingers rubbed her forehead as she tried to force her mind to function.

Could Lachlan be the evil force that held the sword? The very sword she was supposed to watch for?

She couldn't take her eyes off the action unfolding in front of her. Lachlan's face had not completely healed from Drew's beating, but then neither had hers. Lachlan's face was a mix of bruises from before and some fresh ones. From where? She didn't care.

"There she is!" Lachlan pointed his sword at Lina. "Mayhap she stole the sword."

Drew yanked him off his horse and punched him again. "You beat the hell out of her, you filthy swine. How could she have stolen aught from you? I found her lying on the ground and there was naught in her hands."

"Then mayhap you stole it, Menzie. You were the last to see me before I awoke. Where is it? Where's my sword? It belongs to me. It protects me and my clan. You all know the fable of the sapphire sword." Lachlan's misshapen face was covered in spittle he was so riled up.

His father brought his horse next to Drew. "We'll hang you for stealing what's ours."

Aedan and Neil, the head of the Cameron guards, came up on either side of the Burnes laird. "You'll not do aught to him. He's on my land, and your son was on my land when he committed his crime. You'll get no assistance from me. In fact, I banned him from Cameron land, so if you do not leave, I'll throw him in our dungeon and he'll pay for his crimes here."

"Against a whore?" Hogan asked. "All women are sluts. She asked for it. Who wouldn't want the son of Hogan Burnes?"

Drew reached for the daft man just as an arrow flew through the air and embedded in the flesh of the man's thigh. He bellowed and reached down to protect his private parts.

Gwyneth had galloped into their midst with her bow and arrow, but she stayed a distance away. "Take yourself away or this time I'll split your bollocks in two." She nocked another arrow.

"Get the hell away from her. She's the one they told me about." Lachlan covered his bollocks as he spoke.

Drew held his sword to Hogan's throat as Aedan held his to Lachlan's. "I suggest you leave. Your sword is not here."

Hogan Burnes motioned for his men to leave. "This is not over."

Lina tore into the keep and rushed up the staircase to her chamber, Jennie right behind her. Once inside, she closed the door behind her and rifled through her clothes in the chest, looking for something. Bits and pieces of Lachlan's attack were returning, and she struggled to keep searching rather than to throw herself on the bed and sob as she wished to do.

Jennie finally reached past her and found the sword at the bottom of the chest. "I put it here. 'Twas in the pocket in your gown the day he attacked you. I knew not what it was, so I hid it. Honestly, I forgot about it until just now. I was too worried about you to think on it again. Is it Lachlan's?"

Lina picked up the silver sword, turning it over to view the bright red rubies and the deepest blue sapphires embedded in several places on the hilt, along with two emeralds.

Jennie stood over her shoulder, murmuring. "Lina, 'tis such a beautiful sword. I've never see the likes of it anywhere. Who would not wish to keep it? And the gemstones are verra large."

Lina fell down into a nearby chair. "Aye. I remember now. He grabbed me in the chapel and turned me around. I saw the glint of the rubies and sapphires as soon as I faced him. 'Twas just as Erena had described it to me. I had no intention of touching it until he hit me. We struggled and I grabbed it, but he did not seem to notice. He hit me with his fist, and I saw stars and fell to the ground, but I hid the dagger in the folds of my skirt, never once letting it go. I think I passed out then. When I came to, I had just landed on the ground in the forest. He turned his back on me to pish, so I hid the weapon in my pocket first, then screamed. He punched me again and that's the last I remember until Drew came to save me.

"Oh my, Lina." Jennie stared at her with wide eyes. "You've done what the fae told you to do. Surely she will come to you again."

"Nay, I did not. She told me to merely observe it. I *stole* it." She stood up and stared at the sword as she paced the room. "I'm not a thief, but I was so angry with him that I wanted to get back at him, so I stole it. What do I do now?" She flung her arms in circles as the gravity of the situation dawned on her. Hellfire, what had she done?

Jennie reached for it and put it back in the chest. "Naught. You'll do naught for now until we take some time to think on it and decide our next move."

"But they're wrongly accusing Drew of being a thief. I cannot let that go on."

Jennie reached over and hugged her friend. "Lachlan was trying to force you. He does not deserve to get it back. You must hold onto it. The fae queen will come to you again. I'm sure of it. Then we'll know what to do."

CHAPTER NINE

Drew was so upset, he didn't know which way to turn. Jennie and Lina had gone up to one of their chambers. He was desperate to see how she fared, but he knew he would have to wait, so he returned to the table in the great hall where Aedan, Neil, Logan, and Gwyneth all sat.

"My lady," Neil said to Gwyneth with the utmost respect. "You do fire a fine arrow."

Logan wrapped his arm around his wife, tugging her down on his lap before he kissed her cheek. "Finest lass in all of England and the land of the Scots."

"Logan," she giggled, "I'm hardly a lass anymore. I have four bairns."

"You'll always be a sweet lass to me."

Drew wondered what it took to be a couple so in love with each other. They were a far cry from his parents. He especially loved watching Logan support his wife in her unusual endeavors. He'd learned much from observing the man.

Aedan glanced from Logan to Gwyneth. "Why did you return? You had already taken your leave."

"Word reached us before we were far that a group had been seen. I guessed it was Clan Burnes, though I'd hoped to be wrong," Logan answered. He kissed Gwyneth's neck, making her giggle. "My Gwynie loves the element of surprise. Daft men never suspect a lass of aught. She got them again."

"Rode right past the Burnes men with my mantle over my shoulders." She shouted the Ramsay war whoop, though in a decidedly feminine voice.

Drew became totally caught up in watching the interplay

between the husband and wife. He couldn't imagine such a situation. Logan had allowed her in front of him to ride past those dangerous fools.

Drew finally dared to question the man. He had to learn from them, did he not? "You did not worry about your wife being so close to them?"

"Nay, I never worry about my Gwynie, though I'm never far behind her. She can take down any man she pleases. She's a fighter. You do not want to be opposite her dagger either."

"But she's your wife. Most women do not fight. How did that come about?"

Drew glanced at Aedan, and from the puzzled look in his friend's eyes, he could tell he was asking himself the same question.

"I met Gwyneth after she'd been attacked by the Norse on a ship headed off to sea. There were many women on the boat, but there was one difference between Gwyneth and the others."

"What was that?"

"She may have had a bruise or two, but she was already intent on revenge. I learned one thing that day."

Gwyneth spun her head to give him a puzzled look. "What?"

He stared into his wife's eyes. "That naught would ever crush your spirit. I knew right then that you were the strongest lass I would ever meet. And I wanted you for myself."

"Your family never questions what your wife does? You have bairns, do you not?" Drew asked, so interested in understanding this unusual couple and this man that he wished to emulate.

"Aye, I knew our children would be the strongest in the land. She has given me a beautiful lad and a beautiful lassie, and we adopted two lassies. Her brother Rab raised her to hold a bow. He taught her well."

Gwyneth leaned back against her husband, and he wrapped his arms around her. "Thank you, husband, for being different."

"Which lad is yours?" Drew asked.

"Gavin is ours; Gregor is Brenna and Quade's son. The two of them together are wee terrors. But we love them."

"Speaking of the lads," Neil said, "where are your bairns and the rest of the guards?"

"We left them in a cave not far from here. We promised to be back before dark, so we'll head out to join them soon. But what think you of the location of the sapphire sword? Who could have taken it?"

"Hellfire, I surely did not," Drew barked. "I may have been the last to see him, but my attention was on Avelina. She was barely moving. I left Burnes there and anyone could have come along."

"Do you recall seeing the sword on his belt?" Aedan said.

Drew thought for a moment before answering, "Nay, I do not think so, but I was too upset about finding him on top of Lina to think clearly. It could verra well have been there."

A servant brought out some food so they continued to discuss the sword, but came up with naught. There were no guesses as to its location.

A short time later, Logan said, "My thanks for the food, but Gwyneth and I must return to our bairns."

Drew said, "May I walk with you for a moment?" He needed to learn as much as possible from the man. The opportunity was there, so he decided to pursue it and ask more questions.

"Aye, of course," Logan gave him a confused, questioning look, but nodded.

Gwyneth said, "I have a few things to do, I'll meet you in the stables, love."

Logan nodded, then proceeded out the door through the bailey. As they walked outside, Drew could *feel* the unrest of the Cameron clan. The skirmishes that had almost ripped them apart had not ended that long ago, and they had just watched a crude group of warriors dare to threaten their keep.

"You will watch over my Lina, lad?" Logan asked, clasping his shoulder. "She is my only sister, and you can see how much she means to my clan."

"Aye, of course. I'll do my best to protect her. May I ask a question?"

Logan nodded.

"How did you get your reputation?"

"I may not be able to answer that question," Logan said with a booming laugh. "But I can tell you that I have always followed my gut, not the reasoning or the advice of another man or woman. I do what feels right to me."

"And what was the best thing you've ever done?" Drew

watched the expression of this strong warrior in front of him as it changed to something inscrutable. Was it happiness? Pride?

"Without a doubt, marrying my Gwynie. A strong lass will only make you stronger."

Drew's puzzled face must have struck a chord with Logan, because he grasped Drew's shoulder, chuckled, and said, "You'll see, lad. Hard to believe at your tender age, but someday you'll see the truth of it."

CHAPTER TEN

Lachlan Burnes paced the great hall of the Burnes castle. Finally, the stars had aligned for him. He would get his just due from his clan, from his parents, from all the Scots in the land. He could see it clear as day. He just had to make sure his plan was sound.

His mother sat at the table next to his sire.

"Fool. I knew you could not be entrusted with something so valuable," his mother yelled loud enough to shake the rafters.

"Mama, who was the one to find the blessed sword? Not you, not Da, but *me*. 'Tis time to give me some respect. I may have saved our clan from some unknown tragedy. Thanks to me, we are safe."

"Mayhap you would get some respect from me if you still had it in your possession. But you lost it. What a fool! Find it again, and I'll think about treating you better." His mother drummed her fingers on the tabletop as she oft did when she was annoyed.

Lachlan ignored her and continued to pace, pausing to curse every once in a while.

"You need to go back there and get it," his sire barked at him, not for the first time.

Lachlan stopped to glare at his parents before continuing his pacing.

He needed to strategize. Now he had two very different goals, but if he planned it right, he could accomplish them both at once. First, he had to retrieve the legendary sword and return it to its rightful owner—himself. Second, he would have Avelina Ramsay. Aye, Menzie had stopped him, but he was still eager for a taste of her. She would be a fitting bride for the holder of the sapphire sword. Someone from his own clan would not be appropriate. He wanted someone special, someone every other lad would want for themselves. Aye, that was it. He wished to make every other lad in the land of the Scots wish to be him.

Now that he had seen Avelina up close, he had to admit there were none he would rather have. In fact, he would make sure never to beat her face ever again; she was just too lovely. The plan had other benefits. The marriage would tie his family to hers, raising his status in the Highlands tenfold. Quade Ramsay was laird, and Logan Ramsay worked for the Scottish Crown. Avelina's other brother, Micheil, was married to the Drummond laird. Aye, it would be a good match.

If he managed to find the sword and steal Avelina away, he could sweet talk her into marrying him. Then all would revere Lachlan Burnes and his beautiful wife.

Last time, he had simply jumped at an unexpected opportunity. This time, planning would be everything. They were on to him now, and he would not get onto Cameron land easily. Finding the sword would help him achieve his other missions; he was certain of it.

Who the hell had stolen the sword, anyway? It could only be Drew Menzie. He'd have to find him and torture the truth out of him. Why, then he'd be almost as powerful as the King of the Scots. He could imagine himself riding in the royal burgh, Avelina seated in front of him, as peasants lined the pathway to see him with his beautiful wife. He'd carry the sword everywhere.

His mother bellowed again, "Why can you not do something so simple as hang on to a sword? And now Menzie says you attacked a lass on his land? You cannot find a lass here to satisfy your urges? Everywhere you go, you soil our good name. In fact, I recall the time…"

Lachlan sighed. His mother would go on for hours now. Once she got started, she would never stop. She loved to talk about all the foolish things he'd ever done. He was so tired of his parents' lies and accusations; he could not bear to listen to them any longer. He needed to leave again. Still pacing, he moved toward the opposite end of the hall.

They'd see. All he needed was a bit of time to prove his worth. He'd find the sword *and* sweet-talk Avelina Ramsay into marrying him. His parents would finally love him, and they'd be proud to tell everyone he was their son. Aye. His plan was sound, and his world was about change—all for the better.

He opened his sporran to give his pet mouse a wee bit of cheese, then closed it before anyone noticed.

Just as soon as he changed his direction, a fist struck his left eye, making stars dance in front of both of his eyes.

"I'm talking to you, lad, and you'll learn to answer me." He turned in time to see his sire's other fist aimed right at his jaw.

Lina had lain awake in her bed for most of the night. Guilt raced through her, something she had rarely dealt with before.

Avelina Ramsay was a thief, a common criminal. If anyone found out, Aedan Cameron would have her flogged, or thrown in the dungeon, or left to the elements. Jennie would never be allowed to associate with her again. Such thoughts had tormented her most of the night, and she had yet to find a resolution. Her soul was doomed to hell. She needed to tell someone, but whom? The chapel was an option, but Aedan had said she couldn't go there without an escort, which meant that at least one person would overhear her confession.

Mayhap she could trust Drew to help her out. Nay, he would insist she give the weapon back, and she couldn't do that. It would risk offending the Fae Queen.

What to do, what to do. She wrestled with this decision for more than half the night before the unmistakable scent of lavender wafted into her room. She sat up in bed and swung her legs over the side, waiting to see what would happen next. Could the Fae Queen be nearby?

"Come to me, my dear. I will await you in the garden. 'Tis my favorite place."

Lina peered out of the window, and as soon as she noticed Erena's glowing aura, she slipped her feet into her slippers and headed out the door, careful not to awaken anyone. When she finally reached the garden, she paused for a moment to enjoy the scene in front of her. Erena was seated on the bench in the garden, a wee puppy in her lap. "She lost her mama," Erena said in her tinkling voice. "I will care for her unless you would like to."

A sad set of puppy eyes peered up at Lina when she sat down

beside the faerie. Erena set the dog on the ground, and the wee beast limped over to Lina and sniffed her feet. As soon as she did, her tail wagged softly against Lina's leg. How could she ignore such a thing?

She picked up the tri-colored dog, mostly black with a white face and tan markings. The puppy licked her hand.

"I thought you might like her," Erena said. "She has also been mistreated, but no more."

Lina picked the puppy up so she could look at her face. "Awww. What's her name?"

"Whatever you wish it to be. She's a collie. She'll work hard for you, and she's accustomed to eating scraps."

Lina settled the pup onto her skirts and the wee dear rested her head against Lina's lap with a contented sigh. "Abby. I think I'll call her Abby." Lina patted the dog's head and then glanced up at Erena, hoping to find answers to her questions.

"You have been busy, have you not, Avelina?"

"Aye." Tears filled her eyes and she turned her ahead away, ashamed to admit she had failed in her quest.

"Why do you cry?" Erena reached for Lina's chin and turned her back to face her.

"Because I failed you."

"You failed me? 'Tis impossible."

Erena's warm smile encouraged her to continue. "But I did something I shouldn't have." Her gaze fell to her lap, and she rubbed the puppy's head a bit faster.

"Ah, you believe you have wronged me in some way because you found the legendary sapphire sword."

"Aye. Did you not tell me to simply be aware?" Lina's hands were clasped together, and she squeezed her fingers together so hard, it was a wonder she did not break a finger. What would Erena think of her once she knew?

"Aye, I *asked* you to be aware."

"Well, when I found it, I took it, as if I were a plain thief." A tear slid down her cheek and she brushed it away.

The fae's voice softened. "I'm sorry I was not here to protect you from Lachlan."

"You did not need to protect me. As you said, I must learn to protect myself." Tears flooded her face now and her breath hitched in her chest.

"I'm sorry you had to deal with Lachlan, but you did find the sword." Erena brushed a soft strand of hair away from her tears.

"Aye, 'tis true, but…" She met Erena's gaze—afraid to see derision there, but unable to look away. "Mayhap I will make a mess of everything. I know not what to do. Please help me." She hiccupped as tears continued to run down her face.

"Tell me this, please. How did you feel when Lachlan felt your breast through the wool of your gown?"

Lina stared at Erena in shock, hardly able to believe she had been so blunt. "Terrible, angry. I wished to lash out at him," she whispered. "I hate it when the lads look at my breasts and try to touch them. You are the fae. Can you not just get rid of my breasts? Make them smaller, so I won't be the center of attention? I bind them and it does not diminish them at all. 'Twould be easier for me if they were just gone."

"Do you think your mind was functioning normally while you were being attacked?"

"Nay," she choked out. "But what does that have to do…"

"Were you able to give careful consideration to the possibility of securing the sword before you grabbed it?"

"Nay, he was…I was…" Her breathing had become so uneven that it was difficult for her to speak. "I did not think. I just grabbed it."

Erena covered Lina's hand with hers. "Of course not, my dear. You were upset and distraught, two conditions that prevented you from thinking properly. I do not fault you at all for your actions. In fact, what you did tells me we were right in choosing you. You are so strong, Avelina."

"Truly? I will not burn in hell for taking what was not mine?"

"Nay, lass. *You* were wronged, not Lachlan. There is evil in him, though it is not entirely his own fault."

"So how do I get him to leave me alone? I do not want him touching me again. Help me, please?"

Erena set Abby on the ground and pulled her into an embrace. "Ah, child, sometimes we must live through many trials in order to learn about ourselves and others. There are many here who would protect you now. Lachlan holds no power, and you must not let him convince you otherwise. 'Tis you who holds the gift. He should fear you. He will come to understand that soon."

Lina breathed a huge sigh of relief and leaned down to pick Abby up again and settled her back on her lap. "See, Abby. Everything will be all right." Abby sat up and wagged her tail, and Lina giggled in response to her. "You're just too cute. What should I do with Abby?" she asked, turning to look at Erena. "Are you giving her to me for a reason?"

"Aye. Someone else will need her love soon, but not yet. You'll know when it's time."

Lina thought about this for a moment, scratching Abby's head. Who would benefit from a puppy's love?

Erena added, "However, your possession of the sword does bring up one small complication."

Lina jerked her attention back to Erena. "What complication?"

"I'm afraid 'tis part of the legend."

"What is it?"

"Whoever holds the sapphire sword must marry within two moons, or tragedy will befall their clan."

Lina gasped, startling wee Abby. "Marry? Are you certain of this?"

"Aye. Avelina, we couldn't be happier that you now have the sapphire sword. We feel 'tis finally in the right hands. 'Twas destiny. But you must marry soon, or you will lose it."

She'd have to marry within two moons. Somehow, she felt there wasn't a chance that she'd find a husband that quickly. Again, she was doomed. But this time, she was forewarned, and she had a little time to do what she must.

Erena reached for Abby and set her on the ground, then tugged Avelina up and wrapped her arms around her. "Aye, you will be tested along the way, but I have faith you will find your husband. Tarry not, my dear." She spread her arms wide to the heavens and disappeared.

Avelina sat staring into empty space. She had no idea what to do now.

Since he had promised Logan Ramsay to watch over his sister, Drew was heading home to tell his parents of his duty before returning to Aedan's keep. He had no desire to go, but he only thought it right. How he wished he could just yell across the

Highlands and they would hear him.

He hummed to himself all the way home until he arrived at his own gate. Slud, but he hated coming home. The guard waved to him as he passed. "'Tis about time you got your lazy arse back here, Menzie. Get to work."

Drew smiled and ignored the lad. He was oft teased about his supposed laziness because his sire so frequently ranted about it in front the clan. As he dismounted near the stables, a lad ran out to assist him.

"My lord, I promise to take good care of your horse. I'll give him a fine rub down." The lad's eyes lit up with excitement.

Drew reached over to ruffle the lad's hair. "Now do not be too nice, or he will not want to ride with me again."

Moving through the courtyard, he greeted his clan members as he passed.

"Glad to have you back, Menzie."

"Calm your sire down, if you please."

"Your sire's been on a rant again."

Drew sighed and made his way up the steps to the keep and inside his great hall. As usual, the hall was dark and gloomy. His mother sat crying in a chair near the hearth.

His sire sat beside her and hadn't even noticed his arrival. "Would you stop your blathering, woman? 'Tis bad enough our only son stays away. If you'd cease your caterwauling, mayhap he would return."

She did her best to slow her tears, mopping at the corners with her linen square.

"I'm sure our first born would have treated us better. Or mayhap the second, James, he was a strong lad. He would have comforted us in our time of need."

Drew sucked in a deep breath and said a silent prayer for strength. Aye, it was true his mother had birthed three lads before him and all had been taken away, but must he listen to it on a daily basis? He had begged them to stop clinging to the past for years. They still did not listen, often arguing over who would have been the best son.

His eldest brother, Tomas, had died from the fever. James, their second, had fallen from his horse when he was seven summers and snapped his neck, and their third son had died only a week after his birth. Aye, he understood their natural need to protect him, since he was the only one left, but he would not let it keep him from living his life.

At the age of ten and five summers, he'd finally told his parents that he would no longer live as a prisoner in his own home. That's when he and Boyd had first gone to Aedan's keep and learned how different life could be. Ever since, he had stayed away as much as possible, even though his mother clung to him. When he was home, he could barely handle the painful memories that ruled life at the keep, so he wallowed in ale and whisky as much as possible.

Aye, he tried his best to make his sire proud, but he knew he could never measure up to Saint Tomas or to Saint James, as he oft called his brothers. His parents could never let go and see the son standing directly in front of them.

Drew sat in the chair across from his father's near the hearth, and announced his intentions. "Da, I've been charged by Logan Ramsay to do a job, so I leave now to complete my mission." He needn't explain what the mission was, just that he had to do it. "I know not when I will return."

"Hmm," his father scratched his chin. "Logan Ramsay. Aye, he's an important man, if I recall. Does he not work for the Scottish Crown?"

Drew nodded, surprised his sire's head was clear enough to recall that piece of information.

"I thought so. Well, do as he tells you, and do a good job so I have reason to be proud of you."

His mother's sniffling told him she had overheard. He stood, shook his father's hand, then moved over to kiss his mother's cheek and say good-bye. When she clutched him and wouldn't let him go, he said, "Mama, I'll be back. Do not worry, but I have work to do." He loved his mother; he just couldn't stay here with her. It was too much for him.

He walked out the door, not looking back. Visions of green eyes haunted him. This could be the best job he'd ever been asked to do. Yelling to Boyd who stood in the courtyard talking, he headed straight for his horse, feeling as if he'd been assigned an important duty.

He would be guarding the true treasure of the Highlands.

CHAPTER ELEVEN

As soon as Lina had a chance, she dragged Jennie up to her chamber to tell her what Erena had said. She needed advice, and she needed it now.

"Lina, you have been upset all morn. What has happened? And is that a dog I hear?"

Lina tugged her onto the bed next to her, "I saw her last night. And aye, she gave me a puppy." As soon as she spoke, Abby came out of the corner to sniff the new arrival.

"Erena? Why would she give you a puppy?" Jennie could not contain the excitement in her voice. As soon as she noticed Abby, she bent over and held her hand down as Abby scampered over to her, her tail wagging. "Aww, she's so cute, Lina. I want her. You know I miss my dogs from home."

"Do not concern yourself with the puppy for now. She said I'd know what to do with her later."

Jennie scooped the dog up and settled her on her lap as she sat back onto the bed. "All right, though she's awfully cute. I'll just keep her warm while you tell me everything. But what did she say about the sword?"

"Erena was not upset about me having it, and it *is* the gifted sword they are seeking."

"Gifted? What gifts does it have?" Jennie asked, clutching her friend's forearms in a death grip.

"I do not know, and it does not matter. It is something else that I must share with you."

"What? Tell me…tell me." Jennie bounced on the bed while she held Abby in anticipation of Lina's news.

"I must marry," Lina whispered.

"What?" Jennie shouted, her brows knitting into a frown.

Lina shushed her. "Do not let anyone hear us."

Jennie's voice lowered into a harsh whisper. "What do you mean you must marry? Why? How can she force you to marry? You are not ready yet."

"I know that, but 'tis part of the legend of the sword. Whoever possesses it must marry within two moons."

"Then return it." Jennie said, rubbing Abby's soft fur around her neck.

"I doubt that would work. 'Tis a simple solution, and Erena never mentioned there was a way to escape the mandate. She just told me I must marry. What will I do?" Lina prayed Jennie had sound advice because after contemplating her situation in her chamber for the remainder of the night, she had come up with naught.

"And what will happen if you do not?"

Lina took a deep breath and stared at the ceiling while kneading her hands in her lap. Telling Jennie was making the situation feel much more real. "She said if I do not marry within two moons, then tragedy will befall my clan in some way, and I will lose the sword."

Jennie gasped.

Saints above, what was she to do? She could tell from the expression on her friend's face that she had no suggestions.

"Do not worry, Lina. We'll think of something."

They both stared at the floor, Jennie's lips pursing as she worked through what Lina had just told her. "I have thought of a solution." She lifted her gaze to Lina's, a tentative look on her face.

"What?" Lina asked, trying not to cry.

"I believe you should marry Drew Menzie."

Lina didn't respond to her declaration, but not because she was disinterested. She didn't *know* how to respond. Should she admit that Drew was the only lad she had ever met that she had any interest in marrying?

A long moment passed, and Jennie finally asked, "What say you?"

Lina nodded slowly. "Drew is the only man who interests me, but I do not know if he would consider me. I cannot ask him!"

"Nay, you cannot." Jennie set Abby off to the side, then rolled onto her belly on the bed and rested her chin in her hands. Abby proceeded to clamber all over her, sending her into a fit of giggles.

Lina hugged her knees to her chest as she watched Jennie. She had forgotten how Jennie's brother had given her puppies when her parents had passed. Clearly still an animal lover, Jennie had a difficult time ignoring Abby.

Then her friend's expression changed. She knew her friend well enough to recognize when she was scheming.

A few moments later, Jennie grinned and sat up opposite Lina, crossing her legs beneath her. "You have to make Drew think of it or 'twill not work."

Lina just stared at Jennie, baffled by her declaration.

"We have work to do," Jennie said with a mischievous wink. "We must flaunt all of you in front of Drew Menzie *and* make him jealous at the same time."

At dusk the next day, Drew and Boyd dragged their feet as they returned to the inner bailey from the lists.

"Did you learn anything new, Boyd? Anything we can take home?" Drew stretched his back, attempting to pull the soreness out of his muscles. For some unknown reason, he welcomed the physicality of all they had done today. His mind had cleared of the ale and whisky.

"Aye. I can tell Aedan has brought new maneuvers back from the Grants. My shoulders ache from all my swings," he said, wiping the sweat from his brow.

Drew stopped his progress toward the keep. Aedan was not far behind him, talking to his brother, Ruari. He glanced over his shoulder at his friend. "You planning a feast, Cameron?"

He noticed the servants were carrying the tables from the great hall into the center of the courtyard.

"Aye, Jennie wants to entertain tonight. 'Twas her idea."

"And he always agrees to his wife's wishes," Ruari added, a smug grin on his face.

Aedan smirked and glanced at Drew. "Aye, I do. 'Tis worth it for me. You should try falling for your own lass, Menzie."

"Why did you not warn us? I'm all sweaty from the lists. We cannot go as we are. The lasses will run from us all, most of all

Boyd." He laughed and shoved his friend.

"Aye, I won't deny it," Boyd said.

"We have a small loch not far," Aedan said, pointing in its direction. "Go jump in if you're worried about the lasses. Ruari and I would most appreciate it as well." Still smirking, he rubbed his fingers under his nose.

"Meet us there, Cameron. We'll see how strong you are." Drew and Boyd reversed their paths to head toward the loch.

"Aye, but first I must see if Jennie needs any assistance," Aedan called out from behind them. "I'll join you in a bit."

Drew snorted, knowing his friend wouldn't join them, not when he could instead use the special tub he'd had made for his wife. Women made some men go soft. "Don't expect to see him," Drew said to Boyd as Ruari ran up to join them. "He'll not leave his wife."

Ruari laughed. "Aye, 'tis true. But I like my brother much better as a married lad. He's happier."

Later that eve, as soon as the crowd began to gather in the courtyard, Drew made his way into the bailey to seek out his friends. He'd taken a ride on horseback to dry himself off after his swim, then found a spot under a large oak tree to take a wee rest. He'd dreamt of bronze colored hair and a set of sweet hips.

But even that didn't prepare him for the vision in front of him. He halted on the periphery of the crowd, his eyes wide as he stared at Lina. Hell, but she was gorgeous. Her hair fell in soft waves down her back and she'd tucked a pink flower behind one ear. He took a step forward in order to get a better view of the true length of her hair. It had been too dark in the kitchens for him to see. It fell to the top of the round globes of her bottom, a place he'd dreamt of touching with no cloth to stand between them.

His eyes widened as she turned, giving him a full view of her from the front. The bodice of her gown pulled tight around her breasts, exaggerating them even more if that were possible. He closed his eyes and turned away, hoping to calm his manhood, now at full attention. Shite, his reaction had been instantaneous and his plaid told everyone around him. His mouth went dry as he remembered how she'd felt in his arms in the kitchens.

You cannot marry, you cannot marry, his mind chanted, but his heart and the blood in his veins did not listen to him at all. *If you touch her again, you'll need to marry her.*

He groaned at his thoughts, then opened his eyes and ran his hands down his face, as if that small movement could erase the sight of the lovely lass.

A voice sounded behind him. "Trouble, Menzie? You do not appear verra happy."

Aedan. He swung around to face his friend. Jennie was on Aedan's arm, and both of them had huge grins on their faces. The hell with them. He changed his position so he could keep an eye on Lina to see what she was doing. After all, Logan Ramsay had asked him to protect her, had he not? He was only doing his duty. "Nay, no trouble. Why would you ask, Cameron? Excuse my manners. Lady Jennie, you look lovely tonight."

Aedan's smirk was begging for Drew to put his fist through it. Only his wife's presence saved him.

Jennie replied, "Thank you, Drew. Though I for certes cannot compete with Lina Ramsay tonight. Do you not agree? You have seen her, have you not?"

Drew glanced off to the side and sighed involuntarily, chastising himself as soon as he heard his own voice. "Nay...aye...she is lovely."

"Do you know I've already received two offers for her hand tonight?" Aedan said.

Drew swung around to stare at him. "What? Who?"

"I do not recall their names," Aedan replied. "Hmmm...do you, wife?" He turned to look at Jennie, but Drew ignored them. Giving a low growl, he left them and headed straight to Lina.

His protection duties should extend to shielding her from any young lads trying to take liberties, he decided, including those who hid their true intentions behind promises of marriage.

As soon as he found his way to Lina's side, he noticed Jennie was calling for the kitchen maids to begin serving. Ignoring the fact that Lina was speaking to another lass, he ushered her toward a nearby table, one large enough for only two stools. He decided it would be best if they were alone. He did not wish to have to argue with any lads during dinner.

"Drew," Lina craned her neck back in surprise. "I hadn't seen you yet."

"I did not mean to startle you. My apologies. Would you mind sitting here with me?" He moved her so quickly, she almost tripped. "Forgive me, but you are aware that I promised your brother to watch over you."

"My brother asked you?"

"Aye, he did. So I'm doing what I promised him." He gazed into her eyes and his mind turned to mush. Hellfire, the light blue gown she wore was striking. "My lady, you are lovely tonight."

"My thanks." She gazed at her hands as she flushed a soft shade of pink. "And my thanks for protecting me."

"I also would advise you against speaking to any new lads tonight. I take the pledge I made to your brother seriously." Drew cleared his throat and glanced around him to be sure there was no one close enough to listen to them. Jennie and Aedan sat at the table in the middle of the courtyard, a good distance from them.

"You do not need to worry about that, Drew."

His brow furrowed. Had she no idea of her appeal? "I don't? But why?"

Lina blushed again and cast her eyes downward. "'Tis no reason to keep it a secret any longer. I have difficulty talking with lads I do not know."

His eyes widened and his heart leaped within his chest. "You do?" Holy hedgehog, the lord had blessed him again.

"Aye." She brought her gaze up to meet his.

"But you speak to me."

"Aye, 'tis true. Though I could not speak to you when I first saw you at Aedan's."

The serving girl set a trencher of mutton in front of them, so Drew took his dagger out to serve some meat to Lina. She wasn't his wife, but it seemed right for him to serve her as husbands normally did.

Lina took a small morsel and chewed slowly.

Drew just stared at her, thinking back to that day in the great hall. It was true, he realized; she had spoken to no one. Nor had he noticed her speaking with any other lads this eve.

"What has changed?" Drew was so curious, he could not contain the question. The lass in front of him could have any lad she chose, yet she feared speaking to them?

"I'm not sure, but…" She lifted her chin and stared off into the trees. "I think mayhap 'tis because you rescued me from Lachlan. I was able to speak to you because I was so appreciative of what you had done for me. Otherwise, I probably would not have been able to say a word. Mayhap a wee elf ties my tongue, I know not."

He noticed her eyes misting as she spoke. It shocked him that someone who carried herself as she did, someone was so comely and kind, could have such deep-rooted fears.

They had something in common.

"Lina, do not be too harsh on yourself. We all do things we are not proud of."

She swung her gaze back to his. "You? What have you done?"

He gave her a sheepish look. "I've done much to shame myself. You can ask my sire, and he'll tell you tales aplenty."

She giggled, covering her mouth with her hand. "Tell me one thing you regret."

"All right." He thought for a moment and said, "About a fortnight ago, I drank so much ale and whisky that I had to leave a cottage in a hurry to heave my insides outside."

She laughed again, her shoulders shaking as she tried to contain it.

"Aye, 'twas mighty embarrassing. Here I was trying to impress a lass, and I heaved all over the stones to the side of her cottage."

"Have you seen her since then? Are you attached to someone at your castle?" Her voice cracked a wee bit. "Are you betrothed?"

"Nay," he shook his head, hoping what he'd heard in her voice was just a touch of jealousy. "I'm not attached or betrothed, 'twas a while ago, and I do not wish to see her again. I'd be too embarrassed."

"Why? You could not help it. 'Twas not apurpose." She was doing her best to make him feel better, for which he was truly grateful.

"And as long as we're being bold and honest, 'struth is, I had to run into the forest to heave again after I left her."

"Mayhap you drank too much?" Her eyes sparkled, making her face even more stunning, if that were possible.

"Aye, I'll admit I did. And I'll admit I have not had much to drink since then."

She giggled again and said, "Drew, you humor me so."

Drew watched her laugh and play with her food. What he wouldn't give to have someone like Lina to look at every morn instead of his parents.

Then he scowled, realizing he'd just given himself a solid reason to marry, and he could come up with no argument against it.

Lachlan Burnes had fed his sire as much whisky as he dared— any more, and the man would turn into an abusive mule. He couldn't help but smile at the sight of him so impaired.

"Look what you did to your mother. She's asleep at the table, snoring for all to hear." He guffawed and slapped Lachlan on the back. "I'll not holler at you for it. 'Tis good to see your mother like that. She's been in such a lather over that sword you found. You found it, 'tis ours, and we're to be blessed forever."

His father's head tipped from side to side a few times before he settled it on his arms on the table. Muttering something incomprehensible, he closed his eyes and huffed out a deep breath.

He loved how his sire often forgot important facts when he was drinking, such as the fact that Lachlan had lost the sapphire sword. He believed it proved one thing about his father, he really did love his only son. Lachlan smiled at this thought, a warm spot in his heart for his father. It didn't change what he had planned for the eve, but it did give him a much needed good feeling.

While he couldn't say the same about his mother, he believed his father did indeed carry special feelings for his son. He just seemed to forget them when his wife was around. Lachlan glanced over his shoulder to be sure that the few who remained in the hall were asleep, all drunk on ale and whisky, and then opened his sporran. He held his palm open and his pet jumped into his hand. He set him on the table and said, "There you go, wee one. 'Tis plenty around for your dinner."

Lachlan smiled as he watched his new pet scuttle back and forth across the table. He sniffed the laird before running off in the opposite direction.

Lachlan chuckled, "Me thinks 'twas a wise move, my pet. 'Tis never good to make an enemy of my sire, especially when he has been at his drink. The only thing I'll tell you is 'tis easy to avoid his fists when he's drunk. You'll be too fast for him."

Lachlan reached for his father's pocket, but then jumped back when his sire's head shifted. After waiting a few moments more, he reached into the pocket again and pulled out the purse, which he emptied into his hands. "Och, Da, you had many coins today." He laughed and made a clucking noise with his tongue.

The wee mouse ran back down the table toward him, his nose wiggling at Lachlan.

When Lachlan held his hand out, the mouse scampered onto it. Lachlan placed him carefully into his sporran again. Then he stood and bowed to his father first and then his mother. "Papa, Mama, this has been a pleasure."

Lachlan strode out the front door, talking to his pet as he walked. "Mama is finally proud of me. I cannot believe how happy she was to see the sword in my hand. She actually patted me on the back that day, do you remember, wee one? Now she's in another dither because 'twas stolen. If I do not locate it in my travels, I'll be forced to hunt it on my own."

He strutted through the bailey and the portcullis, noting that it was mostly deserted except for the one guard he waved to on his way by. Once outside, he headed for a small grove of trees behind a big rock. He set his mouse atop the rock and started digging in the dirt behind it.

While he dug, he would lift his head occasionally to explain things to his pet. "You see, we'll be able to do whatever we wish in the Highlands soon. We'll have so much coin, I swear 'twill be more than the King of the Scots."

The mouse moved over to the side of the rock and watched him pull the heavy bag out of the dirt. Lachlan held it up in front of his friend. "No one ever believed I had a brain in my head, but who is the smart one now, my friend? Hmmm? Look at all the coin we have. I know, it took me a verra long time to accumulate this much, but somehow, I knew 'twould be necessary someday. First I'll find the sword, then I'll marry Avelina Ramsay. All will kiss my feet once that happens."

He added the new coin to the bag and buried it next to the other full bags. "Won't be long now, my friend. Just you and me...and Avelina Ramsay."

CHAPTER TWELVE

Drew awoke to a racket. He'd had a bit of ale, though not as much as he usually imbibed at home, and he and Boyd had decided to sleep on pallets in the hall. In the middle of the night, a pounding noise roused him from a deep sleep, and he noticed a lithe form carrying a satchel bolting down the stairs and heading for the door, a puppy fast at her heels.

"Lina?" He sat up and brushed the sleep from his eyes, hoping he hadn't really seen Lina running down the stairs, headed out the door. Perhaps he'd enjoyed more ale than he remembered. But nay, it was unmistakably her. He watched as she attempted to open the heavy door three times, failing each time because she only had one free hand to open it. She wouldn't give up. Finally, she dropped her satchel on the floor and used both hands, bracing herself to pull the door open with all her might. He forced himself up from the pallet and reached her just in time to stop her from running outside.

She whirled around and swung at him with her fists. "Nay, leave me be. Do not touch me."

Drew guessed she was remembering Lachlan and all he had put her through. Hellfire, but she seemed mighty strong for a lass her size. "Lina, stop. 'Tis me, Drew. I'll not hurt you."

As soon as she recognized his voice, she stopped flailing her arms and leaned into him. Lina gasped for breath, her chest heaving as though she had been in a battle.

"Lina, what is it? What has you so upset? Where are you headed?" He ran his hand down the middle of her back and tucked her head under his chin.

"I must go, please, Drew. Help me. I must go to Gregor."

"To Gregor? Your brother Quade's son? Lina, 'tis the middle of the night and you must have had a bad dream. Come over by the hearth and slow down, just for a moment, please."

She allowed him to lead her to a bench near the hearth. After he sat down, she moved to sit next to him, but he pulled her onto his lap instead, turning her sideways so she could rest her head on his shoulder. The puppy scampered over and curled up at her feet.

"Is that your puppy, Lina?"

"Aye, but do not concern yourself with her. There are more important concerns at the moment."

"All right. Tell me, what happened in your dream?"

"I think 'twas Gavin who came to me first. He begged me to come home. He told me that Gregor is ill, so he needs his Aunt Lina." Her face dropped into her hands and she let the tears fall freely, flooding her gown. "I have never had such an awful feeling. What would I do if aught happened to him?"

He wrapped his arms around her and held her close. "But 'twas just a dream. I'm sure Gregor is fine. We'll send a messenger to your family in the morn."

Once her tears slowed, she gripped his forearm and stared at the hearth. "Lily. Lily came to me next. She told me that Gregor needs me, and he will not get better if I am not there. Lily was as gaunt as she used to be when she was a wee bairn. She and Torrian were ill for many years until Brenna came along and discovered the source of their sickness. I have not seen Lily like that in many, many moons." Her fingers played with his tunic. "What if the dream is real and someone was trying to tell me something? What if Gregor needs me?" She lifted her gaze to his. "I could not bear it if he did, and I did not come."

Drew did his best to ignore her sweet lips and stay focused on the situation. "Is your brother's wife not the most renowned healer in the Highlands and part of the Lowlands? You do not trust that she could heal her verra own son?"

"Aye, nay...you do not understand."

He wiped the tears from her cheeks. "I'm trying my best, Lina. You were asleep, aye? Your dream about your nephew woke you. You dreamed he needed you to get better, but his mother is a skilled healer." He had to help her see the truth of the situation. God's teeth, she could not just go running out into the forest in the wee hours of the night searching for her nephew. Especially not given the current situation with the Burneses. "What could you do for him that his mother could not?"

"I do not know." Her tears started fresh again. "But I must go to him. I *must*. Will you help me, or do I need to find my own way?"

Her audacity stunned him. "Lina, you're but a wee lass. How could you get yourself to Ramsay land safely?"

She frowned at him, and he changed his direction. "I am not trying to offend you, lass, but there are many rogues out there who would love to find such a pretty lass alone in the woods. Do you understand my meaning? And you must be aware of the discourse with Clan Burnes. You saw how upset they were about the sapphire sword. We have no idea where they are or what their intent is once they left here. 'Tis not safe for you outside the castle. I promised your brother I'd look after you."

"Aye." She looked down at the floor for a moment, then glanced back up at him with flashing eyes. "But you can take me there... I must go. Do you not see? What if aught were to happen to Gregor, I could never forgive myself. I cannot explain, but I must go."

Drew took one look at her pouty lips and lively eyes and leaned forward to touch his lips to hers. Hell, but she tasted of apples and everything sweet, no matter what time of day. She parted her lips for him and he groaned as he invaded the cavern of her mouth with his tongue, teasing her until she tentatively brought hers out to meet his.

And then he was lost. He tugged her to him, angling his mouth over hers so he could get even closer if possible. He'd wanted to do this in the middle of the courtyard the other eve. It had taken all his self-control not to take her into his arms. His hand cupped her cheek and then his fingers wove through the silky strands of her hair. He would kiss this woman forever if given the choice. Her response to him was so innocent and passionate that it built a fire within him, but he would not take advantage of her vulnerable position right now. He heard someone clearing his throat and guessed it to be Boyd. He ended the kiss and leaned his forehead against hers. "Avelina Ramsay, you know how to drive a man daft. I cannot think clearly with you in my arms."

She giggled, a sweet sound that made him smile. "Then take me to Gregor. Please, Drew? My brothers will repay you. We must help him."

Drew stared off into space, thinking of what to do. "All right. We'll talk to Aedan in the morn. He will send as many guards as he can spare to travel with us. Boyd can accompany us, too."

"Nay, not in the morn. We must leave *now*. If we wait until morn, it could be too late."

God's teeth, but he shouldn't leave with her now. Still...he had promised Logan Ramsay to watch over her, had he not? Somehow, he knew he was seeing a different Lina. She was changing in front of his eyes from a timid lass to one who was much stronger than he would have guessed possible. "You'll find a way to go without me if I turn you down. 'Tis true, is it not?"

She nodded sheepishly. "Please understand, I must do as my heart demands of me. And it's telling me I must go to Gregor now."

Boyd stood up and said, "I'll see what I can find in the kitchens to take with us."

Lina jumped, clearly surprised the lad was so close to them. Then she blushed and turned away from the newcomer.

He saw her reaction to Boyd, and recalled what she had told him during the feast. Mayhap she would not like it, but Boyd would travel with him. He'd try to get her to understand. "Boyd rides with me everywhere, he's my best friend," he explained. "He's always there to help me. I do naught without him."

"Naught?" she whispered in his ear and hopped off his lap, giving him a sly smirk over her shoulder. "Come, we must go soon," she said, heading for the door.

Aye, Lina Ramsay was changing. That smirk could have caused him to pull her back onto his lap and finish what he'd started, but he knew this was not the right time.

While Lina and Boyd had gone to the kitchens to pack food for their journey, Drew had gone to Aedan to inform him of what had transpired. Surprised by his response, Drew followed Aedan down the stairs and listened to his inquiry of Lina. Aedan apparently needed to determine for himself that Lina would act without them, so it was best for them to provide guards for the trip. This was another example of how Aedan Cameron had changed as well. Prior to his marriage, he would not have been pulled out of bed by a headstrong lass. Now he understood that he was responsible for her and acted accordingly—just as Drew had done when he'd been in charge.

His intentions were sound. He reminded himself he was doing exactly what he had promised Logan Ramsay he would do. Wasn't he?

❧

Lina rode in front of Drew with Abby nestled in her lap. Aedan had insisted on sending five guards in addition to Boyd and Drew, so they were well protected. It usually took just under two days to travel from Cameron land to Ramsay land. At the verra last minute, Abby had bounded out behind them, and Lina had insisted on bringing the small pup along.

Leaving in the early morn had been a wise decision, as they had not run into anyone on the path. Lina, feeling quite comfortable in Drew's arms, leaned against him and fell fast asleep. At one point, she awoke only to realize she was about to drool all down his arm, but he just grinned at her.

A few moments later, he leaned in and whispered, "I'd have been happy to taste that. No need to be shy around me, lass."

Lina blushed a deeper red, but she did not try and answer him. There were too many other men in their vicinity, and though she could easily talk with Drew, she found she was still shy around other men.

The dream about Gregor had taken her mind off her need to find a husband, but in the daylight, the memory of her newly assigned quest returned to her. She had stuffed the sapphire sword in her satchel just in case, but in case of what, she did not know. A part of her feared she was not ready for marriage. Those two lads had handled her so crudely...

But then memories of Drew's lips on hers invaded her mind. She had enjoyed their time together in the courtyard, and always enjoyed being in his arms. She reached up and touched her fingers to her lips, and as if he could read her mind, he whispered in her ear, "I have sweet memories, too, lass."

She ignored him and rearranged her bottom in the saddle since it was getting a little sore, but then he leaned down again, his heated breath warming her to her core. "And those wee moves will only send waves of temptation through me."

She didn't know what he meant at all, but did not dare to ask.

Sending waves of temptation through him was a good thing, she hoped. She peered over her shoulder at him, and the heavy-lidded gaze he gave her confirmed as much. Drew was a handsome lad, more so than any other lad she had met. His beard was a wee bit rough, but the angle of his jaw enticed her, making her want to use her fingers to trace the lines of his face down to his lips and then kiss him in her own way.

Everything about him puzzled her. When had she ever wished to touch a lad's face? Never before to her recollection, but Drew called to her—particularly to her sense of touch, something she hadn't paid much attention to before. She wished to touch him everywhere, to feel the heat of his skin under her fingertips, and she wanted Drew to touch her everywhere, as well. She shivered and tucked in closer to his heat. Drew ran his hand down her arm, causing her to shiver again.

"Are you cold, lass?"

She shook her head, but did not speak. Her tongue still felt stuck in her mouth, though she knew she would have been able to speak without hesitation had it only been her and Drew present.

One step at a time.

After a full day of being tortured by Lina's round bottom pressed so close to him, he was certain to be sainted. Even her scent roused his desire. He'd gone back and forth between having a hard on and not, depending on how she rubbed against him, which had caused him a considerable amount of pain at times.

But other than the pain of the unwanted erection, he had to admit he quite liked having Lina in front of him on the horse. She was so soft and sweet.

"Tell me what it was like growing up with so many siblings," he said once she had awakened.

"Well, Quade was the eldest, but Logan was the bossiest. He was always telling everyone else what to do. But he is still like that today. Micheil was always the most agreeable. He rarely argued with our brothers."

"So how long have you been afraid to talk to lads?" He whispered in her ear to be sure no one could overhear, wanting to be sensitive about her feelings.

She sighed. "I'm not really sure. 'Struth is my brothers

protected me so well I was rarely around strange lads when I was younger. The only ones I recall are the Grants, but I was around them so much, I was never afraid. And there was the time Jennie and I ran into you and Aedan in the forest." She shrugged her shoulders and peeked at him over her shoulder, a sly grin on his face.

Drew laughed. "How could I forget such a moment? Jennie sent her arrow straight into Aedan's arse. What a fine shot she was."

"I do not think Jennie has used a bow since then. We were practicing for a competition, but after that experience, she refused to participate."

"I haven't seen Aedan that upset since then. 'Twas destiny, for certes. I like to tease him about it every now and again. He swears to put an arrow in my arse every time I mention it."

"So you and Aedan were the only ones outside of my brothers and cousins. I was not allowed to chat with the lads in the clan much, only the stable lads and they are much younger."

"That makes sense." Drew couldn't imagine being so restricted, but then again, he *had* been restricted as much, but in a different way.

"Why? It makes no sense to me."

"Because if you had no experience with strange men, how could you be comfortable talking with them, especially once you reached the age of five and ten. 'Tis a difficult age. The keep likely has more women than men. You may have been afraid of them for a long time without realizing it."

"I never had anyone to be afraid of until…"

He filled in for her. "You mean until Lachlan?"

"Nay, until Keith. He tried to attack me at my keep, and I could not even scream. I was frozen. 'Tis why I came to Jennie's. I begged to be sent away."

"Ah, Lina." He leaned his cheek against her head and tugged her close. "I promise you that will never happen again while I'm around."

Lina rubbed her hand across the hair on his arm. "I know. I feel much safer with you."

Later on that day, they rode through a glen with rocks and hills on one side. A loud bird chirp echoed through the trees, and Avelina jolted to attention in the saddle.

"What is it?" Drew asked.

She held out her hand to hush him, so he slowed his horse. The same sound came three times in quick succession.

"Lina?" he persisted, his voice lowered this time.

"I'm quite sure 'tis Logan. 'Tis the bird call he uses among the clan." She pointed toward the hills and said, "Head that way."

Drew hoped she was right and they weren't heading into a trap. The sound echoed again, closer this time, and she nodded. "Aye, 'tis my brother. I'd know that sound anywhere." They moved around some rock formations by the creek, eventually reaching a waterfall. Lina dismounted, listening intently for any sounds, and Drew pulled out his sword, ready to attack anyone who came out at them.

He'd been searching for any sign of Clan Burnes as they traveled. He hadn't mentioned it to Lina, but he knew Lachlan to be sneaky. Fortunately, he hadn't seen any evidence of them, but his gut churned at the thought of being caught off-guard. What would he do to protect Lina? She was riding in front of him, so if a horse came directly at them, its rider wielding a sword or a bow, she would be in danger. The thought made him quite ill.

How did Aedan handle being married? Drew couldn't stand the thought of Lina being hurt in front of him, and they were not even wed. It was surely a telling thought, but he ignored it, forcing himself to focus on the task at hand.

He breathed a deep sigh of relief when Logan stepped out from behind the waterfall and waved to her. She took off in a fury, Abby tucked up on her hip. Drew begged her to watch her step, but he could tell she was barely listening.

CHAPTER THIRTEEN

Something was wrong. Lina could tell from the look on her brother's face, and besides, her family should have reached Ramsay land long ago. Setting Abby on the ground, she did what she needed to do most. She ran straight into her brother's arms, and Logan wrapped her into a tight hug. "How did you know?" he whispered into her ear in wonderment.

She pulled back. Rather than answer, she said, "Gregor? How is he?"

"Come lass, I'll bring you to him. He is not well. Gwyneth has gone for his mother. But since Brenna is carrying again and you know she's had difficulties, she may not be able to travel."

"And Gavin?"

"We've all been sick in one way or another, though we know not why. Gwynie is the only one who has stayed healthy. Gavin and Maggie are improving, and the rest of us are better now, but we don't dare travel with the wee one still so sick."

Lina followed Logan into the deep cave behind the waterfall, which was surprisingly warm. She felt a comforting hand on her lower back, and when she looked over her shoulder, she saw that Drew had joined her. He had a strange expression of disbelief or wonderment in his gaze as if amazed to see her dream had proven true, but he was here to support her, and that realization sent a welling of warmth through her.

Gregor lay unmoving on his side in a pile of furs. They knelt down beside him and Logan moved his hair back from his forehead. "Gregor?" He leaned down to kiss his forehead. "He's got a terrible fever. His temperature rages, and he talks nonsense much of the time, but he seems to know we're here. We cannot get him to eat or drink anything. He asks for you, Lina." Questions danced in his eyes, but Lina could not take the time to explain.

She peered down at her wee nephew, his hair plastered to his face, his body much thinner than usual. "Gregor? 'Tis Aunt Lina."

Unable to lift his head from the fur pillow, he tilted his head to look at her. "Aunt Wina? You tame for me. Aunt Wina." His arms reached for her, but then they fell back onto the pallet. He was too weak to hold them up.

Abby had followed her into the cave and was sniffing out all the bairns who sat a distance away from them. It was Lily who came to Lina first, her arms outstretched for an embrace. "Please help him, Aunt Lina. He's so sick."

Torrian followed Lily. "Aye, we've all been sick, but none as bad as Gregor. He reminds me of the days when Lily and I were too sick to get up from our beds."

Gavin held Torrian's hand. "Please, Aunt Lina? Make him better."

"I'll try my best." She gave them each a quick hug before returning her focus to Gregor. Their sad expressions and their lack of movement told her more than words. Her loved ones had been through a most difficult time.

Lina picked him up and settled him on her lap, cuddling him close. "I'm here, Gregor. Will you drink something for me?" Logan brought over a cup of broth. "Gregor, you must eat something. Try this broth." Abby followed Logan over and sat down at Lina's side, her tail wagging. The wee pup leaned over to sniff Gregor's toes.

"Is that a puppy, Aunt Wina?"

"Aye. I brought a friend for you. Her name is Abby."

Abby licked his toes until he giggled. "I want a puppy, too."

"Well, if you get better, she may stay with you." Erena's meaning about finding a home for the puppy suddenly became quite clear to her. Abby kept her gaze on Gregor as if she'd chosen her next master. He reached over to pet her, and could barely hold his hand up, but it was long enough for Abby's tail to wag again and to bring a smile to Gregor's face. "See. She would like to help you get better. But first you must drink some broth."

At first he shook his head, his mouth turned down at the corners, but after Abby nuzzled his hand, he finally opened his mouth and swallowed just a bit.

Abby pushed at the broth, so Lina continued to slowly feed the broth to Gregor, and to her relief, he seemed to perk up for her, especially since Abby wagged her tail every time he had a taste. Logan stepped back and spoke to Drew, though she could hear their conversation.

"While I'm most grateful she's here, why is she flying across a glen with only seven guards, especially after the troubles she has had with Clan Burnes?"

"Well, your sister is a wee bit stubborn, as you likely know. She insisted that Gregor needed her." Drew's gaze caught hers, and he gave her an almost imperceptible nod of confirmation for what she had done.

"How could she possibly have known that?" Logan asked in disbelief.

Drew hesitated, so Lina offered the answer. "Gavin and Lily came to me in my dreams. They both told me that Gregor needed me."

It was obvious Logan was taken aback by her explanation, but she did not care to discuss it any longer. "'Tis more important that I am here, where I am needed."

Logan didn't push the issue, which she appreciated. She needed to keep her attention fixed on Gregor.

"Wina, will you tay with me? Pweez?" His hand patted her arm in a steady rhythm.

"Aye, Gregor." She kissed his forehead. "I will stay with you just as long as you need me."

Lily came over to sit beside her. "Aunt Lina, I'm so glad you're here." She hugged her and leaned her head against her shoulder. The other children fell in around them—Torrian, Bethia, and Sorcha on one side, Molly and Maggie on the other.

"We will all help you to get better," Gavin said. "And I'll hold the puppy for you."

Logan said to Drew, "My thanks for bringing her here. As you can see, she has a special bond with the bairns."

Lina hummed a song and they all relaxed around her. "Drew, would you fetch the satchel with food?" she asked. 'Tis on your horse, is it not?"

"Aye." Drew nodded.

Once he left, Lina said to Logan. "We thought our trip would be longer, so we brought quite a bit. We had no idea you were so close or we would have been here long ago."

"Aye," he said. "I'm glad you brought food. We could use something fresh if you have enough to share."

───

Drew and Boyd returned with the satchel full of food. They shared oatcakes and a loaf of bread and cheese with the Ramsays, then Drew positioned himself where he could watch Lina with Gregor. He was absolutely fascinated watching the relationships between Lina and her family. He'd never seen such strong bonds before.

It made him realize how verra much he had lost when his brothers had passed—how his parents would enjoy such a loving family. This is exactly what his mother mourned every day of her life, he decided. Not that his family would have been the same, but they would have been a family of four just as Avelina was one of four siblings. Had they the opportunity to grow and marry, their family could have been similar.

All along he'd sworn to never marry. He did not want a relationship as his parents had. But would everything have been *so* different if his brothers had lived?

He eventually fell fast asleep in an upright position.

The last thing he recalled was wondering how Lina would look with their bairn on her lap.

───

Lina knew the moment Brenna arrived in the middle of the night. A slew of guards were everywhere, and a slight form dismounted and ran toward them. Lina handed Gregor over to his mother as soon as she came inside the cave. Brenna gave him a powder in his food and rubbed a salve on his wee chest, but mostly held him, soothing him any way she could.

"Is there naught you can do for him, Brenna?" Lina asked. She had hoped Gregor had improved, but he looked no better.

"There is little I can do at this point," she said, tears in her eyes. "I hope what I put in his broth will help, but he must fight this himself."

Lina kissed Brenna's cheek, then made her way outside the cave to relieve the tension in her shoulders from her fears. Drew followed, and she was pleased. Too worried to sleep, she didn't wish to converse inside and bother the sleeping bairns.

Logan and Gwyneth followed them. As soon as Logan drank from the skein of ale Brenna had brought, he said, "Lina, you'll travel home with us, aye?"

Before replying, Lina glanced at Drew, then at Logan and Gwyneth. "I am sorry," she finally said, "but I cannot." Though she tried to think up an explanation Logan would accept, she came up with naught.

Logan glared at her, then asked, "Why not?"

"Because there are things I must do."

Drew moved over to her side in a silent show of support. There was so much they did not know about. Jennie was the only one who knew she possessed the sapphire sword. She could not share that truth with the others, nor could she tell them she had been chosen by the fae. They would believe her daft if she did.

Logan's eyes narrowed at her. "What could be more important than your clan? Your family needs you, can you not see that?"

Lina shook her head. "I cannot return yet. My apologies, Logan."

"I do not care what you think. You *will* go home with us. I'll not allow you to do otherwise." He spun on his heel and stalked off into the trees.

Lina chased after him. "Please listen to me. I must stay. I cannot explain, but if I walk away, the consequences will be severe for all of us."

Gwyneth strode forward to join her husband. "Lina, you need to come home. Please. I have to agree with Logan."

Her sister-in-law's defection caught her off-guard, but it did not change her mind. "I'll not go with you."

Logan moved toward her, towering over her tiny frame. "If I must carry you or tie you to the horse, I will. I do not like what has been happening on Cameron land, so 'tis my judgment to remove you."

"If you do," Lina whispered, "the situation will be worse." Her hands settled on her hips. "I must do what is right for all, not just for my close family."

"What are you talking about? What has fostered this change in you?"

Lina stared up at her older brother, her lip quivering. She would not yield, but should she tell him everything? Perhaps it was her only chance. She was not strong enough to fight Logan. She glanced at Drew, who stood directly behind her, but she knew she had to make her own decision. Mayhap it was time for them to know the situation, Drew included.

Silence reigned in the forest. The guards were a long distance away, the bairns were all tucked inside the cave with Brenna. Naught was said for a long time while Lina tried to decide what to say.

Logan finally whispered, "Lina, come home with us where you'll be safe. What could be more important than that?"

A lone tear slid down her cheek. "I cannot go with you."

Logan came closer and reached down to brush the tear from her cheek. "Lass, if you do not tell me why, I'll not consider it," he said, his tone gentle now. "You must have a reason. You would not be this insistent if you did *not* have one."

"You must promise not to tell anyone but Quade and Brenna."

"You have my word." He waited.

Lina stared at the ground for a long moment, then took a deep breath. "I cannot go home with you because I hold the sapphire sword the Burnes men seek." She waited for the impact of her words to hit.

"Saints above!" Gwyneth said, her hand coming up to her throat.

"Lina!" Drew sounded the most shocked of all, and she could hardly blame him.

Logan took two steps back. "And how did that come about?"

"It was when he attacked me. I just did not remember until…until the day Lachlan came to the Cameron keep with his sire. Something about it made the memory return to me. I took his sword and hid it in my skirts. I knew it was the one." She hesitated, wondering if she should reveal the rest.

"The one?" Logan prodded, his hands settling on his hips.

"You must swear never to reveal this to anyone outside of our family." Lina's hands flexed in her skirts.

Brenna crept out of the cave from behind the waterfall, her arms wrapped around her sleeping son. From the look she gave Avelina, she had heard everything.

"I swear, Lina. Now tell me what this is really about." Logan ran his hand through his hair and mopped the sweat from his forehead.

"The fae. The Queen of Harmony came to me on two occasions. There is evil in the land of the Scots and the fae have asked for my help. They wanted me to locate the sword. But the queen has not told me what I must do with it yet." The words came out in a rush, but no one stopped her.

No one moved after she finished her explanation. Lina searched each of their faces to see if they believed her. The expression on her brother's face was one she had never seen before. Was it fear? Confusion? Gwyneth had stepped closer to her husband and laced her fingers with his, Logan responding with a tender squeeze.

Though Lina was afraid to look at Drew, she needed to know how he was reacting. When she finally peeked at him, his gaze was already fixed on her, his eyes wide, but she thought she could also see a sense of pride there. She clung to that thought, hoping the others would feel the same way.

Then Brenna stepped toward Lina, her arms outstretched. Gregor was still not moving, and his skin had taken on a dusky hue. "Take him," she said.

Lina stared at her brother's wife, confused by her request. "What?"

"I said *take him*."

Lina stared at her, confused by her fierce expression and harsh tone. "I do not understand, Brenna. You're frightening me."

"Take him, Lina. He is near death. He will be dead in less than an hour. I can tell by the sound of his breathing. Please take him." Her voice rose an octave as she spoke, becoming almost shrill. "Take him. He needs your embrace."

"Brenna, nay." Tears tracked down Lina's cheeks. "He's your son. You must hold him if he's dying."

"Nay, you, Lina. Do you not understand? 'Tis why you had that dream. He was calling for you. Please, I beg you."

Lina did her best to absorb what Brenna was trying to explain to her, but there was too much in her mind.

"Gregor knows, don't you see? He called for you because he knew you were the only one who could save him. Bairns know things we do not." Brenna took two more steps forward and thrust Gregor into her arms. "Take him or he will die."

"I do not understand." Lina caught Gregor and cuddled him against her heart.

"You. 'Tis you," Brenna whispered.

"What?" Logan barked, finally finding words. "Brenna, what are you saying?"

Brenna pointed to Avelina, not looking away from her. "*She* is a chosen one." Then she spun back to face Lina. "You are a chosen one. My mother told Jennie and me about this fae queen, who could choose a human when necessary to help her save the Scots. She told us any chosen by the fae would have special energy. 'Tis you, and only you can cure my son. Please, Lina. Focus your energy on him. I beg you."

Lina's arms trembled as she held Gregor close and leaned her cheek against his forehead, pouring her attention and love into the nephew she adored. Oh, how she loved this lad, and she hated to see his lips so waxy and dry. Warmth stole over her body, and she closed her eyes and said a prayer over wee Gregor. She heard a light fluttering, and when she opened her eyes, her little nephew's color had gone from gray to a light pinkish hue.

Logan gasped and whispered, "Saints above, 'tis true." He wrapped his arm around his wife, tugging her close.

Lina lifted her gaze first to Brenna, pleased to see a look of hope on her face. Then she shifted her attention to Drew, whose face lit up with wonder. They locked gazes and he gave her an almost imperceptible nod, clearly pleased with her newfound talent.

The others had all moved back from her, Lina noticed, probably due to the bright, buttery gold light surrounding her. She heard a fluttering next to her ear, and a golden butterfly flew down onto Gregor's chest.

Erena. Lina smiled as the butterfly flapped its wings a few times before it flew away, but not before landing on her shoulder for just a moment, as if to pat her.

Gregor opened his eyes and placed his hand on Lina's arm. "Aunt Wina, is my mama hewe? I dweamed she was." Lina nodded, unable to speak because of the joy in her heart and the tears lodged in her throat.

Brenna came to her and picked up her son, tears flooding her cheeks.

"You awe hewe, Mama, I wuve you. I'm hungwy."

Brenna leaned over and kissed Lina's cheek, whispering, "My thanks." Then she answered her son. "Come, I'll find you a piece of bread."

CHAPTER FOURTEEN

Drew glanced up at the sun trying to peek out through the clouds overhead, still unsure of everything that had transpired in front of him the night before. He wouldn't have believed it if he hadn't seen it with his own eyes. They all believed Lina to be a chosen one, something Brenna's mother had heard about. The tale was that every fifty years or so, the fae would come against an evil so strong, they would choose a human to help them. This chosen one would be blessed with special gifts and would be asked to fight evil in the name of the Scots. It was difficult to accept—he had always believed the fae to exist only in stories and in Lachlan's ramblings—but what other explanation could there be for Gregor's miraculous healing and that golden aura that had formed around Lina?

He stood by the horses, having finished packing all the belongings up. The bairns were all deemed strong enough to travel. He'd grabbed Lina's things because he knew she was exhausted, she hadn't slept much since they'd left Cameron land. Now he waited for Lina to say her farewells, then they would return to Aedan's castle.

She made her way over to her family, all on horseback and headed home. "Do not get down. You have the wee ones situated." She headed toward Logan first, Gavin on his lap. "Thank you for trusting me." Drew stood behind her, ready to say his own farewells.

Logan squeezed her hand. "I know not if Quade will believe me, but we have enough witnesses to convince him. Mayhap pen a note to our mother? You know how she shall worry. And Menzie? I'm counting on you to protect her, which will be a harder job than we thought."

"I will, I promise." She moved to Brenna, Gregor and Abby on her lap. Tears misted in her eyes, and Drew knew she was thinking of how close they had come to losing her sweet nephew.

"Aunt Wina, if you need a 'tector, Dabin and I will help you. Tank you for my new puppy." He leaned over to kiss the top of Abby's head.

Lina grinned. "My thanks, but I have Drew to protect me now. And you take good care of Abby. Hang on to her so she doesn't fall." Brenna had created some contraption to hold the puppy on the side of the horse so she could be close to Gregor.

Brenna leaned down to kiss her cheek, Gregor giggling as he tipped to the side and Abby licked his hand. "You have a different path ahead of you. My mother told Jennie and me many tales of the fae and their chosen ones. Believe in yourself. You *are* special. You are a strong woman and I am proud of you and forever grateful for your help."

Gwyneth rode behind Brenna and had Sorcha on her lap. "Fare thee well, sister. We trust your judgment, as should you. Do not doubt your path. 'Tis as special as are you."

Torrian and Lily followed, Bethia riding with Torrian. They all said their farewells, and promised to pen her a note together to show how much progress all the bairns had made with their letters.

As soon as the Ramsays and their guards rode off, tears started coursing down Lina's face. Drew came up behind her and wrapped his arms around her waist, allowing her to lean up against him.

A cloud of dust erupted across the path, and within moments, Logan was stopping his horse in front of them. Still cradled in his lap, Gavin giggled at how fast they had traveled. "Remember 'tis my sister you are touching, lad," Logan said with a fierce stare. "Do not forget that I will find you if you do her wrong."

Drew dropped his hands from her waist and nodded to Logan, who then flicked his reins to return to the head of the line behind two guards. Once he was gone, Drew helped Lina onto his horse, then mounted behind her.

A few hours later, Lina turned to Drew and said, "If you don't mind, I need to stop."

Drew pulled on his reins, but waved Boyd and his guards ahead, pointing to an area for them to stop. He guessed that Lina needed a private moment. After he helped her down, she made her way into the woods, but she returned quickly. She leaned against the horse and stared at him for a moment, then said, "I liked your hands on my waist before. Mayhap I am too forward, but you have distanced yourself from me. Is aught wrong? Is it because I am a chosen one?"

Drew took her hands in his. "Nay, but I'd be a fool to try to steal a kiss from Logan Ramsay's sister in front of him. That man scares the hell out of me."

Lina laughed. "So 'twas not because of the sword and all that happened to me?"

Drew took a deep breath and rubbed her hands inside his. "I admit it took me aback at first, but the more I think on it, the more sense it makes. If I were the fae, I would want someone trustworthy and honest to assist me—someone like *you*. But Lachlan will continue to search for the sword. I think we need to come up with a plan with Aedan and Jennie."

Lina nodded. "Mayhap you are correct. We must include Aedan."

Drew's thumb brushed her cheek, making her gasp. "You have the most beautiful skin I have ever seen."

Lina's gaze caught his just before he lowered his mouth to hers.

All Drew could think of was that it had been too long. How he had suffered last night—lying so close to Avelina without being able to touch her was akin to torture. But God's teeth, he would not have dared to touch Lina, especially not with Logan and Gwyneth both nearby. He savored her lips now, taking it slowly, teasing her with his tongue until she parted her lips. His tongue darted in to taste her, and hers wove with it. She pressed her body against his, so he reached down and grabbed her hips, tugging her against his hardness. He groaned, knowing he couldn't finish the act, but he wanted her more than he had ever wanted anyone.

She ground her pelvis against his, and his need roared to life. He pulled away and trailed a path of smaller kisses down her neck. "Lina, I want to taste you everywhere, but I do not want to rush you." His breath came out in soft pants. "I want to feel your skin in my hands, but not until you are ready."

Lina nodded. "I want you, too. I want you to touch me."

Drew worked on the ties of her gown in the front, and she helped him until they were loose enough to allow his hand inside. He reached in and cupped her breast. All he could do was moan, "Your skin is the softest I have ever touched." He rubbed his thumb across the tender bud, bringing it to a soft peak. Her gaze stayed locked with his, and she grabbed his wrist as if she never wanted him to stop.

"*More.*"

It was the only word he heard, but it was enough to spur him on. He kissed a path down across her creamy mound and into the deep valley between her breasts, finally returning to her nipple and taking it into his mouth. He teased her with his tongue and then scraped his teeth across it before taking her fully in his mouth and suckling her until she cried out with pleasure.

His erection threatened to burst out from under his plaid, but he stopped. There was an audience ahead, and besides, he could not disrespect her by taking her maidenhead here.

He cupped her breast again, "Lass, you are sheer perfection, and your passion incites a fire in me like no other, but I cannot do this now." He tied up her gown, doing his best to ignore the desire in her eyes. Hell, but she was a passionate one, and he would love to see her underneath him. Once he fixed her clothes, he paced in a circle around the horse in an attempt to bring himself back under control.

He helped her mount her horse, then mounted behind her, a heavy sigh escaping him as he rode up to the others and motioned for them to continue.

He chastised himself for allowing it to get this far. In fact, since he had no intention of marrying, he should never have kissed her in the first place. To marry would be to risk becoming like his parents. They had never overcome the pain of losing three sons, and their sorrow had washed over their only living son for years. He could not bear to become like them, or to wound his own bairns the way his parents had wounded him.

But could it be different for him, especially with someone like Avelina Ramsay? Watching Lina with her family, he had seen a different world—one he'd never been a part of before. Love and support, happiness and forgiveness, emotions he'd ached for his entire life, were evident in everything they did.

And Aedan, how he had changed since marrying Jennie. Knowing she carried their bairn had affected the way he dealt with his men, his friends, and how he spent his time. He'd never seen his friend so fulfilled and joyful. Was it possible to hope for those same things for himself?

The lass in front of him had affected him more than he had ever thought possible. He tugged her closer, just at peace to have her near. Yet even though he felt more serene with Lina pressed against him, he did not stop searching the area for Burnes. He'd never allow that monster near her again. Protectiveness and possessiveness had inched their way into his cold heart. God's teeth, if he wasn't excited about it.

But this is exactly what he had sworn his entire life to avoid. How could everything change in one day or with a couple of interludes with one person? Why was he allowing this emotional nonsense to change his mind? And when had he ever been emotional? This was unfamiliar territory for him. Drew ran his hand across his face, squirming in his seat. He had let this go too far. He had no claim on her, and he couldn't allow two days to change everything he had promised himself for years. He'd vowed never to marry, never to have bairns. He reminded himself of his promise. There were still too many doubts. What would he do if he and Lina lost a bairn?

"Drew, have I done something wrong?" she whispered, clearly sensing the change in his mood.

"What? Nay. *I* have. I should never have allowed things to go that far."

"But why?" She glanced at him over her shoulder. "I liked it. I like you. I want us to get closer."

"I cannot, Lina. I just cannot…no matter how I feel." He had planned to wait, but since she had brought the subject up now, he might as well tell her the truth. She deserved to know how he felt.

"I do not understand. You do not like me? Is it the way I kiss? You can teach me. I'm not verra experienced." She hung her head, and the slump of her shoulders showed how defeated she felt.

"Nay, none of that. Your kisses *are* too good. You make me want to bed you right away." He noticed her blush. "Sorry, I shouldn't have said that."

"I am glad to know 'tis naught I have done." She stared straight ahead, apparently not wanting him to see her face.

"It's not you. I..." He paused to think how he wished to say this. "I promised myself I would never marry."

"What?" Lina turned to face him as best she could since they were traveling at a decent pace on horseback. She could not have heard him correctly.

"I promised myself a long time ago that I would never marry."

"But why?" It felt as if that one statement would crumble her whole world, but she did her best to hold it all together. "Why would you not want to marry? You are heir to your land. Do you not want a lad to carry on your name?" What possible reason could he have to have made such a foolish vow?

"My parents lost three sons before me, and they suffer for it every day. I could not bear to live like they do. I do not want an heir."

A sense of hopelessness overtook her, so she turned back away from him, not wanting him to see her expression.

Drew peeked at her face. "I know I have done wrong, but I have not led you to believe we would marry, have I? Trust me, Lina, if I were to marry, it would be you and no other."

"Nay, it's only..." She swiped at the tears threatening to spill down her cheeks.

"What is it?"

"The Queen of Harmony said that since I am in possession of the sword, I must marry within two moons or tragedy will befall my family. There is a connection between us, so I had hoped you would consider marrying me. More than a fortnight has already passed. I do not have much time left."

Drew stopped his horse. "Does anyone else know this? Your brothers, Jennie or Aedan?"

"Only Jennie. She is the only one I have told." She sighed, sorry she had said anything at all. She had her answer from Drew Menzie. He would never marry. Now what was she to do? Like it or not, she would have to marry another lad. After seeing poor Gregor so near to death, she could not bear the thought of anyone else in her family suffering.

They spoke little for the rest of the afternoon. When they were but a short distance away, dark clouds closed in on them.

Drew motioned for the guards to stop. "Lass, I'll not risk riding through the storms that are headed this way. There's a cave not far from here. We can spend the night there and arrive by midday tomorrow. I do not wish to travel in heavy rains in the dark."

Lina nodded, not caring what they did. She didn't want anything else from Drew Menzie. He had dashed all her hopes with one statement.

Now she would have to marry a lad who did not interest her. What matter did it make who she chose? Her marriage would be loveless—a sad fate she needs must accept. As soon as she dismounted, she took care of her needs and walked into the cave, not stopping to speak to anyone.

Paramount in her head was the wish that this was all one big, horrible dream. If only she could awaken and return to her old life, she would not complain or wish for more excitement or love or anything. All she wanted was to be free of the sword, the butterflies, Erena, and Drew Menzie.

Drew had placed his plaid on the hard stone for her, so she thanked him, grabbed her satchel to rest her head on, and lay down for the night. She faced outward so she might watch the rain as it fell.

Drew moved closer behind her, so she tipped her head toward him and said, "Please do not."

"Do not what?"

"Do not touch me," she whispered.

"Lina, I'm sorry…"

"And stop saying you're sorry. You do what you must. I was the fool to think we might be more to each other."

"I wish to give you my warmth, and whether or not you wish to be near me, I will continue to protect you."

She turned her head away from him, focusing instead on the dance of the storm outside and the claps of thunder reverberating through the cave. The lightning that had started to fork down from the sky lent a mystical feel to the night.

"Did you know that Aedan loves to sit out at night and watch the thunderstorms?"

Lina vowed to ignore him.

"Did you know that Aedan can tell you the shapes made by the stars and identify which ones are there all the time, and which are more transient?" His warm breath heated her neck, soothing her in spite of herself.

"Nay." It came out as a whisper, but he heard her.

"Jennie and Aedan like to sleep under the stars on warm summer nights. They lay flat on their backs and gaze at the twinkling bodies, trying to recognize patterns in the sky."

"I am not surprised."

"Why not? It surprised me," Drew replied. "I had never heard of such a thing."

"Because Jennie and Aedan are in love. They enjoy doing things together. 'Tis a passion of his, is it not? So she does it with him. And in return, he does things for her. Did you know he bought her a famous volume from the east about healing?"

"Aye, he did tell me that." His hand reached for her hip and settled there.

The heat from his hand warmed her. But she didn't want him to tease her, torture her, or torment her. Why, she could hardly talk to any lad outside of Drew and her family. How could she find another if she could not *talk* to another?

She fell asleep, Drew's hand on her hip and tears in her eyes.

CHAPTER FIFTEEN

That night Lina experienced another dream, but this one was even worse.

The dream was about a wee lad a bit older than Gregor and Gavin. He kept shouting her name and begging for her help, but no matter which direction she traveled, she could not find him. By all appearances, it was a keep, but an unfamiliar one, and she never passed the great hall.

She called to him over and over to come to her, but he said he could not. He told her he was unable to move at all because someone hated him and would not let him leave.

He shouted and pleaded, and she followed his voice, chasing through passageway after passageway trying to reach him, but to no avail. After what seemed like forever, she managed to get closer.

She reached a heavy wooden door, and from the sound of the lad's voice, she could tell he was in the room that lay beyond it. Grabbing the handle, she pushed and pulled with all her might. She was only able to open the door a crack, but it was enough for her to see the true problem.

The lad was tied to the bed. He screamed and screamed, yanking at his bindings to no avail, and blood ran down over the side of the bed where the hemp had scraped his tender skin.

Drew shook her shoulder. "Lina, Lina, wake up. What is it?"

She screamed. Drew's voice broke through her haze and she grabbed him, clutching him as if he were the only thing that was keeping her from drowning in the sea.

"Lina," he said softly, wrapping her in his embrace and waving the guards back as they came to check on her.

Waiting to catch her breath, she kept her head nestled against his chest. She was safe, and there was no lad screaming for her help…but that didn't mean there wasn't a lad who needed her. Something told her this dream was as real as her last had been.

Drew caressed his hands through her hair and massaged her neck. "What is it, Lina? 'Twas just a dream. You have naught to fear. I'm here to protect you."

"A lad needs me," she whispered, still not wanting to move away from him.

"Who?" he asked with a furrowed brow. "There are no lads here. Was it one of your kin?"

"My dream. There was a lad screaming for me. He called me by name and asked for my help."

"What did he want you to do?"

She sat back and gazed into Drew's green eyes. "First, he begged for me to find him. I searched and searched…" She paused for a moment to catch her breath. "It seemed to take forever, but I finally found him."

"Where was he?" His hands held hers, and even the mere warmth of them offered her comfort. "Did he give you any clue as to his whereabouts or what land he was on?"

"Nay, he was in a chamber alone, one completely unfamiliar to me."

"Did you know the lad? Is it someone you could find on Cameron land?"

She shook her head.

"Someone on Ramsay land? I'll take you there if need be."

She shook her head again. "Nay, nay, I could not even see his face. 'Twas too dark. But Drew, I must find him. I must. Will you help me?"

"Of course. When we return to Cameron land, we'll find a way to determine the identity of the lad."

"Aye, we must. 'Tis urgent."

Drew's brow knitted together. "But why? You did not say he was in danger."

"Because…" Lina clutched his hand to her heart. "You do not understand."

Drew arched a brow at her.

"The lad was tied to his bed, and his wrists were raw from

trying to free himself."

Drew's jaw dropped.

Drew sat in Aedan's solar awaiting Jennie and Avelina. After hearing about Lina's dream, he swore he would never be able to sleep again. He was not sure how she would handle this dream. They had no idea where to go, yet she was distraught over the possibility that a lad existed out there and needed her help. He had no idea how to help her. Pacing the side of the room, he found a linen square on the side table and mopped the sweat off his face. What could he do?

He had already informed Aedan of Lina's dream about Gregor, of the lad's illness and how she had healed him. Aedan had decided on his own that it was Brenna who had healed Gregor, not Lina, apparently not wanting to believe Drew's story about faeries. He'd scowled at Drew as soon as he'd shared the idea of Lina being a chosen one by the fae.

Aedan had stopped him before he finished and asked, "You are expecting me to believe that this faerie would come out for Lina's troubles, but not for all the problems with my wife and the issues with the Abbey not long ago?"

Drew had no answer for him, so he'd decided to wait for Lina and Jennie to arrive before he told Aedan the rest of the story. In fact, he would allow Lina to tell it herself. He could not argue his friend's point, but who understood the working of the fae?

Neil and Boyd had come to the solar to seek direction for the day's activities with the guards, and they were still there when Jennie and Lina entered the room.

"Good morn to all," Jennie said.

Lina gave Boyd and Neil a quick nod before immediately moving as far away from them as possible. Remembering what she had said about her shyness around lads her age, Drew decided to do what he could to help her get past her troubles. He led Boyd over to the wall where she stood. Turning to his friend, he asked, "Boyd, did you get a look at Lina's puppy? She had the cutest wee dog named Annie."

"Abby," Lina interjected, then covered her mouth instantly.

Drew locked gazes with her, hoping she could continue.

Boyd said, "Aye, she was nice. I heard you gave her away, but to whom?"

Lina's gaze dropped to the floor. A long moment passed, but she finally lifted her gaze to Boyd and said, "Gregor." A surprised smile crossed her face, and she continued in a more confident voice. "My nephew needed him more than I did."

"Aye, I knew you gave him to your family because I missed her on the way home. Your nephew will enjoy her."

Lina peeked at Drew and said, "Aye, he will."

Neil had been speaking with Aedan, but he walked over to join them. "Come," he said to Boyd, "we have our instructions for the day." The two men nodded to Lina and left.

Drew reached for her hand and gave it a soft squeeze, a look of satisfaction on her face. Though he wanted nothing more than to kiss her senseless, they needed to speak with Aedan.

Aedan rose to greet his wife as soon as Boyd and Neil took their leave, kissing her soundly enough to make both ladies blush.

"Aedan, please, we have company," Jennie said.

Aedan chuckled. "I cannot help myself if I cannot get enough of you, sweet one." He motioned for Lina to sit next to Jennie, then addressed her directly. "My wife shared with me while you were away that you have the sapphire sword in your possession. Please do not be upset with her for telling me, but she is most concerned for your safety, Lina, and I could tell something was amiss with her. But it seems more has happened on your journey than I am aware of. Would you share the rest of your story with me, Lina?"

Lina sighed and stared at her hands. "Aye, I'll tell you all, as I would like your assistance."

Hellfire, the lass looked so beautiful this morn. Her hair color was almost a bronze. She wore it in many different styles, all of which he liked, and today it was held loosely at the base of her neck, but with long strands down her back and tendrils free around her face. A single flower was tucked into one side. How she had found the time to fix her hair, he had no idea. And there was something else…her aura was today stronger than it had ever been. If he had to guess, he would say that this entire episode had given her confidence. He noticed she sat up straight in her chair, her chin up, and did not waver from Aedan's gaze.

Aedan coughed, so Drew turned to look at him. His friend was glowering at him. He scowled back and returned his attention to

Lina, only this time he *listened* to her as well as stared. Hellfire, he couldn't help it if her beauty was distracting.

"So Gregor struggled until his mother arrived in the middle of the night."

Aedan interrupted her, "And so Brenna was able to give him something to help him recover? Your sister is a renowned healer."

Lina gave him a puzzled look and shook her head. "Nay, Gregor worsened after she gave him a potion. Later Brenna asked me to hold Gregor, because she believed I was one of the fae's chosen ones. She said if I focused all my energy on Gregor, I would have the power to heal him."

Jennie had tears in her eyes as she listened to her friend tell her story. Drew decided it was time to step in to support Lina's claim. "Had you been there to see what transpired, you would never doubt again that Lina is a chosen one, the gifted one, or whatever you wish to call it."

He had Aedan and Jennie's complete attention, so he continued, his gaze never leaving Lina's. "As soon as she held her lips to Gregor's forehead, a golden aura surrounded her, and Gregor's color turned from gray to pink in a matter of moments. He awakened a bit later and told his mother he was hungry. I've never seen aught like it before. 'Twas as if the lad came back to life in front of our eyes. A golden butterfly alighted on Gregor's chest and then hopped onto Lina's shoulder before flying off into the night."

Aedan stared at Lina, taking it all in for a moment.

"Aedan, you can have your doubts, but please listen to the entire tale before forming your opinion," Jennie whispered. "I believe my friend, and my mother believed strongly in the fae."

Aedan moved over to his wife and kissed her cheek before returning to his chair. "For you, I will."

Drew didn't wish to question his friend about trusting him, but he couldn't help but notice that Jennie had quite an influence over her husband.

Aedan pursed his lips and took a deep breath. "So let's assume I believe you are a chosen one. Jennie has already shared with me about her mother's belief in the fae, and I know many of our elder clan members believe strongly in their existence. Please tell me exactly what your instructions were from the queen and how we can be of service."

Lina nodded and squared her shoulders. "She told me that there was a strong evil force in our land. She was pleased to find out that I had the sapphire sword in my possession, but she has not told me what to do with it yet."

Lina paused. Jennie reached over and grasped her hand to give her encouragement, then nodded her head.

"The queen told me that whoever possesses the sapphire sword must marry within two moons or else lose possession of the sword."

"And?" Jennie prodded.

"And if I do not marry, tragedy will befall my clan."

"Lachlan never mentioned this to us." Aedan glanced at Drew and paused. "Or did he?"

Drew nodded. "Aye, he did mention that his mother said he had to find a wife. 'Twas not clear his meaning, but 'twas mentioned. And his mother knew the fable."

"Where did Lachlan get the sword?" Lina asked.

"He found it. 'Tis all we know," Aedan replied. "How much time remains to you?"

Lina heaved out a huge sigh. "One moon. I have one moon left to marry."

Aedan burst out of his chair and began pacing. "So we need to find you a husband right away. Is there anyone you are willing to consider? And Jennie mentioned something about a lad tied to the bed?"

"One question at a time, Cameron," Drew said. "She needs a husband. 'Tis the most important matter presently. You must have someone in mind. She's a lovely woman. I'm sure many would be happy to wed her."

Aedan stopped in front of his friend. "Aye. And the first one I would ask would be you, Menzie. What say you?"

"Cameron, you know that I have always sworn never to marry. I have explained as much to Avelina and she understands. Find another." He glanced over at Lina, embarrassed to be asked such a question in front of her. She refused to look at him, and had already flushed a deep shade of red. God's teeth, but he felt like a lout.

Aedan tried—but failed—to hide his smirk. Drew scowled,

wondering what his friend was about. Whatever it was, he would not budge. He would not marry.

Aedan returned to his chair. "What about Boyd? He's a fine lad."

"Absolutely not," Drew said, bounding out of his seat. "He is totally unsuitable."

Aedan quirked his brow at his friend. "He is? Why? I thought him to be your close friend."

Drew stuttered, "Errr...well...he needs to be by my side. He runs the guard when I am unable. I cannot do without him."

Aedan gave him a sly look, but he acquiesced soon enough. "All right. I'll find another." He rubbed his chin in thought. "Ervin is a fine lad. What about him? I know he is ready to marry."

"That pimply faced lad?" Drew all but shouted. "I think not. He's too young for her. Have you looked at Lina? She deserves a much more handsome lad."

Drew sat back down to await Aedan's next suggestion, doing his best not to look at Lina to see how uncomfortable she was listening to their discussion. If he did, he'd be too tempted to wrap her in a warm embrace.

"Craig is a nice looking lad. Do you not agree, Jennie?"

Jennie nodded, about to speak, but Drew interrupted.

"Please, the lad cannot hold up a sword with one arm. How could he possibly protect her? She's a chosen one, so she must marry a strong warrior, one who is willing to fight for her. Craig will not do." He glowered at Aedan to get his point across, truly exasperated by his friend's ridiculous suggestions. None of the fops and louts that Aedan had suggested were at all suitable for Lina. And he noticed that poor Lina appeared to be near tears.

Aedan glanced at his wife, then tipped his head toward Lina. Taking the hint, Jennie stood up and held her hand out to her friend. "Come, we'll go for a stroll outside. 'Tis stifling in here." She held her hand across her growing belly. "The babe wishes to move about."

Lina nodded to Aedan and Drew before she left.

As soon as they closed the door, Aedan said, "What in hellfire is wrong with you?"

"Me? There's naught wrong with me. What is wrong with *you*?" Drew fired back.

"Every name I mentioned did not suit you. Why are you being so disagreeable?"

"Because they were all so wrong for her. Can you not see that?" He swung his hand toward the chair Lina had vacated. "You made her cry with all your foolish suggestions."

"You silly fool," Aedan bellowed. "She's crying because she wishes to marry you and you denied her. Why are you so daft? I know your parents have soured you on marriage, but you must get over it."

"I cannot waver. My parents have made their lives and my own a misery. I'll not do that to a bairn."

"What makes you believe your marriage to Lina would be anything like your parents' relationship? Or that you would lose a babe? She's a strong woman, and besides, she has the *fae* on her side. You could not ask for anyone better. Did you ever stop to consider that the reason all my suggestions did not suit you is because you're jealous?"

"Jealous?" Drew stared at his friend, frozen by the accusation. "What a foolish notion. I am not jealous of those lads."

"Aye, you are, and it's time you admitted it to yourself. You need to overcome your problems and marry the lass. You were meant for each other. Otherwise, if you do not and you wish for me to support your story, then I am forced to find her a match. Are you willing to watch her with another? Your reactions tell me otherwise. In fact, I'm willing to predict you will be miserable, regardless of her choice."

Drew glowered at Aedan and stormed out of the chamber. "I'll not marry!" he bellowed at his friend as he stalked off.

He hated to admit that his friend was correct. It wasn't just that he was jealous.

He was in love with Avelina Ramsay.

CHAPTER SIXTEEN

As soon as she made it through the courtyard, Lina ran. Tears were blinding her vision, but she just had to get away. She had never listened to something so cold and calculating in her life. The two men had discussed her as though she were horseflesh they planned to sell.

"Lina, please stop!" Jennie's voice echoed behind her.

Lina spun around to face her friend, managing to force out, "Jennie, go back. I just need some time alone." When Jennie's steps slowed, she sped up through the gates.

All she needed was a few moments to cry in isolation, without any witnesses to her breakdown. Even though she suspected a couple of guards would follow her, they usually kept a good distance away. Once outside the gates, she headed toward the forest, not stopping until she reached a narrow path in the trees with lavender-colored flowers draped overhead, the branches making a canopy. The scent wasn't lavender, but the beautiful spot reminded her of Erena, and she was desperate to speak with her now.

Sobs wrenched through her body, and she crumpled to the ground and rested her head on a mound of leaves. Drew cared about her so little, he was willing to send her off with a strange man rather than marry her himself. Aye, he had refused a couple of suggestions, but he hadn't even looked at her or acknowledged her presence while he was discussing her future.

Aedan had not been much better, but she could not fault Jennie's husband for attempting to help her. Once her sobbing slowed and she was able to control her breathing enough to speak, she sat up and stared into the branches overhead. Silently, she wished for Erena to appear, but naught happened.

"Please, Erena. I know not who to turn to for help. My family knows naught of the fae, and Jennie does not know much more."

She waited a few more seconds, plucking the leaves and dirt from her gown. Before she knew it, a rustle came from the end of the path, and she jerked her head up in time to see a swarm of butterflies overhead. An odd purple-winged one sat on her knee. At other times in her life, she would have been fascinated, but not now, not here. She just did not care anymore.

A gentle voice called to her. "Avelina, my dear, what troubles you so?"

Lina lifted her gaze to watch as the Queen of Harmony, adorned in a pale blue gown, glided toward her through the thick trees, a smile on her face.

"You came for me," she said in a small voice. "I was beginning to think no one cared at all."

"Ah, wee one, you still do not know your true value, that I can see, but you will. You must be patient. Some things take time."

Tears slid down her cheeks again as she listened to the lilt of Erena's voice. "Take it, please."

"What did you say?"

Lina lifted her chin to stare up at the beautiful queen in front of her. "I would like to bring the sapphire sword to you. I no longer wish to have it in my possession."

"My dear, I cannot take it. The sword is meant to be in human hands because it represents all that is good with your people, but in the wrong hands, it can wreak havoc. 'Tis your people it governs, not ours. Do you wish to tell me why you no longer want it?"

Lina nodded and struggled to speak through the tears coursing down her cheeks. "I cannot find someone to marry. You must take it. Please? I cannot have aught fall upon my family. I love them too much."

"'Tis too soon. You have not given yourself enough time. Do you not believe in destiny?"

Lina swung her head back and forth. "Nay, I do not."

"Well, you must trust me. I will not allow you to live a life burdened with pain and disaster. I promise you much happiness, for the most part. But you must fulfill this prophecy on your own by following your heart."

Lina fingered the gown in her lap. "I cannot. No man wants me."

Erena tipped her head to the side. "Or is it that the lad you want has not offered for you?"

Swiping the tears from her cheeks, she said, "He does not want me. He has sworn never to marry."

"Then you must give him a good reason to marry."

Avelina cocked her head toward the faerie. "What?"

"Some men are foolish, but when they meet the love of their life, they will give up that foolishness for her. You shall see. But they must be encouraged in the right direction. Sometimes they do not recognize what is directly in front of them. You must make him desire to reach for you and claim you. He has good reason to fear marriage. You must help him through this, and you have everything you need to see this accomplished. He can put his belief behind him, but he will not do this alone."

Desire me? Lina wasn't quite sure what she meant by that, but decided to give it some thought. "I fear for my family. What if I fail to do my part? What if I make a mistake? Then they will suffer for my actions. 'Tis not fair."

"I would trust you to act responsibly if you were my family. You have certain inherent qualities, or you would not be one of the chosen. My dear, handing the sword to me will not help you. You must complete this quest on your own. Your spirit is meant to soar. I am here to help you learn this truth, but it will take time."

"Will you promise not to hurt my family until I find my destiny?"

"Some things are simply a part of life. Just as your father passed on, so must your mother some day, but there are reasons why things happen as they do. I cannot guarantee you that you will never experience pain in your life. 'Tis quite impossible. Do you understand?"

Lina nodded.

Erena swirled around, sending the butterflies soaring.

"Wait, please."

"All right. How else can I help you?"

Lina heard a gasp behind her, and glanced over her shoulder to see Jennie standing behind her.

Erena greeted her immediately. "Hello, Jennie. Thank you for being such a fine friend for our chosen one. She struggles, but she will fulfill her destiny."

Jennie could only stare at the vision in front of them as she stumbled to a stop at Lina's side.

"Erena," Lina said, her voice insistent, "a young lad appeared in my dreams. He is in danger, but I cannot determine who he is or where. All I know is he is tied to his bed. How can I help him? When do I know to act on my dreams? Will I always carry this gift of sight?" Lina stood, brushed the leaves from her dress, and moved to stand in front of Erena. "Help me save him. 'Tis a child."

"You will know his identity soon. Have faith in the fae."

"But I cannot rest with the knowledge this is happening somewhere nearby and only I have the power to stop it. You have given me the gift of sight for these children, so I must use it to save them."

"But what you do not understand is that sometimes these visions that come to you are not in the present or the future. We send to you what you need in order to act, 'tis what the dreams are designed to do—help you in your quests."

Lina rubbed her forehead, trying to absorb this information. She glanced at Jennie, but her friend seemed as confused as she was.

"Sometimes—" Erena grasped Lina's hand in hers, "—what you see is not in the present or the future, but in the past. The lad you see in your dreams will come to you, and you *will* be able to help him. Understand he is not in danger at the moment. Just do not give up on him when you recognize him. He's depending on you."

Erena waved and held out her arms, a gesture meant to beckon the butterflies. Once they had all settled, she lifted her arms toward the sky, sending them into flight. The one golden butterfly stayed near Lina, fluttering around in front of her.

Erena said, "Hold out your hand, Lina. She wishes to visit with you."

She did as Erena suggested, and the golden butterfly landed on her hand. Waves of calm seemed to descend into her body from the points where its wee feet touched her hand. Lina smiled, then turned to Erena for further direction.

"Now send your friend off to soar to the skies." She demonstrated how to do it, and Lina copied her, watching as the butterfly flew so high she could barely make it out above her.

"Soon, you shall do the same." Erena lifted her arms and disappeared.

"Oh my, Lina. You are quite special."

Lina reached over and hugged Jennie. "I'm so grateful you were here to see her. Sometimes, when I awaken, I believe 'tis all a dream. But she is so real, is she not? Do you believe in her?"

Jennie stepped back and tipped her head back to stare at the sky. "Aye, I do. She is exactly as my mother described her. What do you suppose she meant about the lad who cries for you, the one tied to the bed?"

"I think she meant he is no longer tied to the bed. But if that were true, why would he need my help now? I cannot make sense of her words."

"Did you ask her who you should marry?"

"Nay...but how I wish I had." Lina stared up at the clouds and shouted, "Who should I marry, Erena? Please tell me."

Naught but silence greeted them.

A cold wind whipped up out of nowhere, so Lina reached for Jennie. The wind appeared to come from nowhere, as there were no storm clouds nearby. As they turned back toward the keep, the wind moving through the trees sounded almost like a voice echoing two words.

"Your destiny."

Drew committed an act so outside of his character that he apologized immediately afterward. He yelled at the stable lad.

"Get him ready, fool," he had screamed as soon as he neared the stable. The lad had raced into the stable, grabbed his horse, and brought the mount out as quickly as possible. But the lad looked so crushed, Drew felt horribly ashamed. "Sorry, lad. Didn't mean to be so gruff." He tossed him an apple and left, not waiting for Boyd and the rest of his guards to join him. They'd catch him if they had a mind to do so.

He'd finally had enough. As he tore over the countryside toward his land, all he could think about was how unfair it was that his parents had influenced every aspect of his life. Aye, he knew it had been tough to lose his brothers. Why, he had been with James when he tumbled from his horse and snapped his neck. He had been around five summers when his older brother had died instantly. Even now, his father's desperate screams echoed in his ears. How horrible it had been to realize his beloved brother wasn't moving.

Aye, his parents had reason to grieve, three times over. But they should not have taken it out on him. His life at home had become a misery that he could only escape through too much drink and too many loose women.

He could take no more. His mind was made up. There was finally someone in his life who had made him want more—Lina. He was developing strong feelings for her, and she reciprocated those feelings. Under no circumstances would he allow his parents to ruin this for him. This trip would put an end to their meddling and controlling forever. He knew what he needed to do, and if it meant his father would ask him to relinquish the lairdship, he would. It was the only way he could make a break with his past and move forward, wherever it would take him. It remained to be seen whether that would help him conquer his fear of marriage, but at least he would no longer be trapped.

Once he arrived at his castle, the guards waved to him and opened the gates. He rode past the stables and through the courtyard, heading directly to the great hall. This was it. At the last minute, though, he turned around and ran back to the smithy's building. "Gus, have you any whisky? Just give me a touch, enough to get me through what I must do."

He'd poured a touch down his throat, but not enough to get sotted.

As soon as he entered the great hall, his mother leapt out of her chair. "Drew, I'm so happy to see you."

"Mother. You probably won't be happy to see me once I've said my piece. Where's Da?"

"He's out somewhere. What's bothering you? Why is my son so upset?"

Drew refused to look in his mother's eyes, because he knew if he did, the pain he saw there would draw him away from his purpose. He ignored her and continued onward. It was time to take charge of his life. He tore up the stairs, taking them two at a time, and then ran down the passageway until he reached the tower room.

His room. At least it had been for years. The sight of the lock on the door stopped him in his tracks. This lock had meant torturous days of loneliness, of forced imprisonment, all for what? Fear. His parents were so afraid that the same horrid fate that had befallen his brothers was in store for him that they had committed unconscionable acts.

No more. It was time for the past to be put in the past. He spun around and headed back down the passageway, down the staircase, and out the front door, ignoring the pleas of his mother. He headed straight for the smithy.

"Gus?" he panted, wiping the sweat from his brow with his sleeve.

"Aye, my son? How can I help you? You're always helping me when I need it. Have you need of more whisky?" Gus stood with his hands on his hips, awaiting direction.

"Nay, no more whisky. Your axe. I must borrow your axe."

Gus's smile left his face as he reached without hesitation for the axe hanging on his wall.

The look on his face made Drew suspect the older man knew what he was about. Could he possibly have guessed his intentions?

"Been a long time overdue, lad. Do what you need to do. We'll all support you."

Drew was confused, though the man's support meant a great deal. Had they all known?

He grabbed the axe and spun on his heel. Pausing for a moment before heading back to the keep, he stopped and yelled over his shoulder. "My thanks."

The time had come.

He threw his shoulder into the front door, which opened with a percussive bang, then sped past his mother up the stairway. He raced through the passageway, but then paused when he was nearly there, stopping only for long enough to take the deep breath that would give him strength to finish what he must. He swung the axe over his head and then brought it down hard on the latch and the lock, springing it open with a clanking loud enough to wake the dead.

He reached for the door, but then decided it was not quite destroyed enough. He used his momentum to arc the axe just right so it landed in the wooden door with a thwack, embedding itself right in the middle. Pausing to stare at his handiwork, he rested his hands on his legs and wiped the sweat from his brow and stared at what he had done.

He smiled as his sire came barreling down the passageway toward him.

"What in hellfire are you doin', Drew? Have you lost your mind? You've destroyed my door." His father's expression of shock did not deter him.

It only fueled his ire. Yanking the axe out of the wood, he grasped the tool to swing it again. "I'm doing what I should've done many, many moons ago. No more, do you hear me, Da? No more," the axe struck again, "ever," and again, "ever."

"Lad, what we did, we did out of love. You understood that. Your mother could not tolerate the fear of losing you. You were always safe inside those walls. Stop, will you not?"

"Nay, I will not stop until 'tis destroyed." He would complete this no matter how long it took. This was something he needed to do.

His mother's footsteps echoed through the passageway. "Drew, are you daft? Please stop what you're doing now before 'tis too late." Her hands flew up to either side of her head. "Aye, you've lost it, you have. Arthur, stop him. He's addled."

"Stand back." When the door was splintered enough for him to walk inside, he moved into the large room and headed straight toward the bed.

He squeezed his eyes shut to stop the tears that threatened to fall at the sight of the cursed thing. How many times, how many days…visions ravaged his mind, forcing him to do the only thing possible. He swung the axe over his head attempting to cleave the bed in two.

"Drew, there's naught wrong with that bed. Leave it be, son."

"Aye, there is much wrong with it." He swung the axe again. "And 'twill never be used again."

"Lad, we had it special made," his mother whispered. "Just for you. You were such a busy lad, and we could not keep you in one place. You were everywhere. We were forced to do something. 'Twas the only way we knew you would be safe."

"Aye, I know, 'tis why I'm destroying it." He swung the axe again, sending splinters of wood flying everywhere. "I know your intentions were good," he panted. "But it cannot happen again. To anyone."

His parents stood in the doorway watching, his mother with her hands held over her ears.

He continued to heave until the bed was in pieces, then he pulled back the fur on the window opening and tossed the pieces out.

"Why, Drew, why?" His sire stared at him.

"*Why?*" Drew thought his head would explode. He dropped the handle of the axe to the ground, flinging it away from him. "Because I could not live with the thought that it might ever be used for another. That another wee lad might be tied up and kept prisoner in this room."

His mother wailed. "Drew, 'twas the only way we could be sure not to lose another. I made your sire do it. I could not bear to lose you, too. Please, do not be angry with us. 'Twas the only way I would not go daft. Four beautiful bairns and three dead. Oh my sweet bairns." She sat on a stool and hung her head in her hands, sobbing.

His father strode toward him, his hands on his hips. "Look what you've done to your mother. She's been tortured enough. Can you not see we did what we had to?"

"Da, you tried to lock me up in here after I had grown. Look me in my eyes and tell me 'twas right." His breath heaved as he spoke. "I've had enough. I'm sorry for your losses, but they were my losses, too. They were my brothers." He wiped his sleeve across his face to clear the sweat away. "I'm done with grieving. 'Tis time for me to live my life, and if you wish for me to do that somewhere else, I shall. I'll not put myself in a position to be locked up again, but before I left, I had to be sure you would never lock up another."

He headed out the door, but stopped for a moment next to his sobbing mother. "Mama, I'm sorry, but 'tis over. I could not abide by having these reminders here anymore."

Boyd rushed into view and stood in the passageway, wide-eyed and breathing hard, but there was a sense of satisfaction in his expression once he realized what was happening. He knew better than most how much Drew had suffered in this room.

"Where are you going now?" Arthur Menzie asked. "When will

you return this time?"

Drew turned around to answer his sire. "I cannot answer your questions, because I do not know. I may never be back."

His mother stood and beckoned to him, so he leaned down to kiss her cheek. "I'm sorry, Mama. I love you both, but I need to get away."

He strode down the passageway, but then stopped and turned to look at his sire. "I know you needed to spend your time grieving. My only wish is that you had also spent some time with the son who survived."

A weight lifted off Drew's shoulders as he made his way down the stairs and out the front door of the keep. He lifted his face to the clouds, wishing the sun would shine through.

Boyd put his arm around his friend's shoulder. "Needed to be done, Drew. They'll deal with it."

Drew nodded to his friend, grateful for his support at this difficult time. When he lowered his gaze again, he paused, surprised to see the path to the stable was full of his clan members.

"Drew, 'twas right, what you did."

"Come back to us, Drew. You are the one we need."

"Drew, we'll support you in whatever you do. You're the backbone of our clan."

Drew's brow furrowed as he walked past his friends. How could that be true? His sire had always been the leader of the clan— except for the one time he'd been ill. They had never looked up to him. He was the one who was always drunk, the one who could not help but make mistakes. Wasn't he?

His steps slowed as he heard further confirmation.

"Drew, do not leave us forever. Do what you must and come back. We understand. You were a great leader when you took over for your sire."

"Glad you threw it over the edge."

"We'll miss you, Drew."

When he finally made it to the stables, the lad flew over to him. "You'll not leave us forever, will you, my lord?"

"My lord? You've always called me Drew." He ruffled the red hair atop the lad's head.

"Aye, but you seem different today. You look like a lord."

Drew smiled and climbed onto his horse.

Boyd mounted next to him and said, "Mayhap Avelina Ramsay is meant for you. Have you changed your mind?"

"I'm still uncertain at this point. I'll give it some thought, mayhap see how I feel around Lina now that I have righted that wrong." The next thought in his mind was whether or not he could confess the truth to Lina about the lad in the bed. It had been him, without a doubt. But it didn't answer his question. Why would Lina dream about something that had taken place years ago?

CHAPTER SEVENTEEN

Lina lay on her side in the huge bed, waiting for slumber to overtake her, but sleep would not come. She rolled onto her back and stared up at the ceiling. Drew had disappeared after his argument with Aedan two days ago, and she was certain he would not return. She had not seen Erena since their visit under the lavender flowers, when she had been advised to be patient.

She was not patient.

Every lad she saw or heard about became of interest to her. She scrutinized everyone, but found naught to admire. She had to concede that Erena was probably correct. Drew was the only lad for her.

Her eyes grew heavy, so she turned onto her other side, deciding to think about the last time Drew had kissed her in the hopes that it might give her pleasant dreams.

Many hours later, she was awakened by someone shaking her shoulders, and by the sound of her own voice screaming. She was still disoriented as she peered up into Drew's green eyes. It was another nightmare, she realized. About that poor wee laddie in the bed.

"Lina, Lina, wake up!" Drew said. "What is it? What could make you scream so?"

Her first coherent thought was that she was imagining things. But then she searched his gaze and realized she wasn't. Drew Menzie was very much in her chamber, leaning over her in her bed, his own hair and clothing in total disarray.

Suddenly, she realized something…something that changed everything. Shoving away from him, she flew out of bed and backed up to the wall, her eyes wide.

"Saints above, 'twas you, Drew Menzie." They were the only words she could get out at that moment.

"Of what do you speak?" He stepped back and leaned against the table next to the other wall.

"My dream." Tears slid down her cheeks and she swiped at them with the back of her hand. "The lad tied to the bed. Everything makes sense now. You. *You* were tied to a bed. You came to me in my dream asking for my help."

His shoulders sagged and he sat on the edge of the bed. "Aye. 'Twas me."

Lina rushed to his side. "I'm so sorry. How horrid. How could anyone treat their son like that?" She sat next to him and grabbed his hand, not even thinking of what had transpired between them before this night. "But why? What had you done?"

Drew kissed her hand, then stood and started to pace the room, pausing only to wipe his sweaty palms across his plaid. She sat on the bed and waited, wanting to give him the time he needed. Now she saw him in a completely different light. How could he have come through such an ordeal? Had it only happened once? Multiple times?

"I had three brothers. Tomas was the eldest, then James, and Robert was my other brother. Tomas died from a fever at two summers, James was around seven when he fell from his horse and snapped his neck, and Robert died at birth.

"It started when I was around five summers. James died instantly in the accident. My problem, according to what my parents and others have told me over the years, is that I never kept still as a bairn. I was verra curious and never thought about the possible consequences of my actions, so I would run to do something as soon as it popped into my mind.

"I recall my mother often telling me to sit still, but I just could not. When James was still alive, my sire assigned him and one of the guards to protect me. James could keep up with me, but no guard could. I would always find a way to lose them. I do not know why, but after James died, I worsened. I could not sit still. Once my mother found me in the stall with the wildest horse, another time she found me walking across the ice on the loch before it was completely frozen. Once I sneaked out the portcullis to follow my sire when he and his men were going hunting. Another time I was caught trying to get stew out of a huge pot hanging over the fire." He stopped pacing and sat down next to her. "I don't recall these things, but my clan members will tell you I was known as Drew, the wee demon."

"Oh, Drew. I feel terrible for you." She reached for his hand.

"Once my brother died, they believed they had no way to contain me, so the safest thing they thought they could do was lock me in my room. I also believe they were overcome with such grief that they couldn't watch me. They had others watch me, but I was always able to get away from even the best. As I grew, I discovered ways to get out of my room, so they started to tie me to the bed as well.

"They tell me it would only be overnight or for part of a day, but for a bairn, it seemed an eternity. I hated them for it, and my mother would often get so upset that she would hug me and not let go. It was torture for me because I preferred to be moving all the time.

"The older I got, the more dependent they were on this method of containing me. My mother became so addled over the possibility of losing their last son that she tried to talk my sire into leaving me in that room all day."

"Drew." She shook her head and a tear tumbled down her cheek and into her lap. "I know not what to say."

He squeezed her hand. "Just listening has been helpful. You do not need to say aught. You had naught to do with it. 'Twas all my parents. My clan members knew about it, and many tried to talk them out of what they were doing."

"They did not try to keep it a secret?"

"Aye, they did, but apparently I was quite a screamer. Gus, the smithy, told me I would scream for hours on end. Once, someone went to my father to complain of how my parents were treating me. My sire had the complainer whipped, so no one dared to try to help me again."

"And how long did this go on for?" She reached for his hand.

"A long time. Even when I was past twelve summers, my father would have his guards lock me in the room whenever he went off fighting because I had tried to follow once and was almost captured by reivers. The last time he tried to lock me up was because I was going to help the Hendersons, but I refused to back down so I held my sword to his throat and left. Fortunately, I believe he understood that I needed to help my neighbor to be honorable, but my mother was beside herself during the entire situation."

He clutched her hand in his, and she noticed his hands were scraped and raw in spots.

"Drew, what happened?" she asked, gently running her fingers over his injured ones.

He sighed with satisfaction. "I did something I should have done long ago."

She lifted her eyebrows at him in question, almost afraid to hear his answer.

"I took an axe to the lock on the room and then to the bed. They had it made special just for me with boards for my arms. They wanted my arms to be held away from my body in case I had a dagger, so they were straight out sideways."

"And you destroyed it?"

He laughed and his eyes lit up. "I did. All of it." He reached for her and tugged her onto his lap. "I broke down the door and smashed the bed into small enough pieces that I could throw out the window. 'Tis gone."

Lina gazed into his dancing eyes, realizing anew how much she loved him. "Is that why you spend so much time here at Aedan's?"

"Aye. I need to get away from them. Every once in a while, I feel stifled, like the walls are closing in on me, so I leave. Whenever my mother walks toward me, I have that old fear that I'm about to be locked up. I find myself running from my own mother."

Her voice dropped to the merest of whispers. "Does this have something to do with why you do not wish to marry?"

"Aye, for two reasons. One is that I could never do what my parents did to me, what they did to each other, and if I lost all my bairns, I fear I might go daft, too."

She stared at his lips, wanting so much to touch him, to run her fingers across his jaw line, to feel the muscles in his upper arms. His hair was a mess and she loved it. She reached over and threaded her fingers through his locks. "And the other reason you do not wish to marry?"

"Because what if my son is the same as me? I do have trouble keeping still, and I cannot control it. Plus my fear is that my mother would try to do the same to my son when he was just a bairn."

His gaze darkened as he stared at her, and all she could think of was being in his arms. "I can understand how difficult this is for you." She reached up and ran her finger across his bottom lip, exactly where she would taste him if she dared. The man's lips were so tempting…

His mouth descended on hers and she moaned in satisfaction, letting him know how much she wanted him. He ravaged her lips, tasting her, claiming her in a way she had never experienced. His tongue swept inside her mouth and found hers, and he teased her until she moaned again.

Drew broke their kiss and leaned his forehead against hers for a moment before he kissed a path down her neck. "Lina, do you want this as much as I do?" Hellfire, she was sweet. Every taste of her delicious skin was better than the one before.

"Aye." She held his forearms in a vice-like grip, as if she would never willingly let go.

He kissed her again, sucking on her bottom lip, and she went utterly still in his arms. Pulling back, he gazed into her eyes and the passion he saw there almost undid him.

"I cannot make any promises to you, but I've never wanted another lass as much as I want you. Do you trust me? Do you believe what I tell you?"

"Aye," she whispered, running her fingers across his bare chest, teasing him by getting close to his nipple, but then moving away.

His erection pushed against her belly, so he moved away just a bit to keep himself from finishing in seconds like a laddie. His hands fumbled with the ribbons on her gown. "May I see all of your beauty, Lina? I wish to taste you everywhere."

She lay back in the bed, giving him access to all of her ribbons. He moved to pull the gown down over her shoulders, but she surprised him by stopping his hands, then tugging the gown off and throwing it on the floor. Then she reached for his plaid, so he tossed it on the floor next to her gown.

His gaze ran down her body, and he followed it with his fingers.

She was so incredibly beautiful, he could find no words. His fingertips ran down the center of each breast, grazing each nipple enough to make her start, arching her back into him. Then he leaned over and ran his tongue over the same path, settling over one nipple. He took the pink bud in his mouth, teasing her with his tongue. Her fingers threaded in his hair, then gripped him tight when he finally took her full in his mouth to suckle her. She bucked against him, a soft sound of desire coming from her throat.

Her hand left his hair and found its way down his belly until she had him gripped in her hand. Watching her, he held his breath, afraid he would lose it completely. Her fingertips floated across his tip with the lightest of touches.

"Tell me what to do." Her innocent gaze found his.

His voice came out deep and husky. "I like what you're doing now. Do not stop."

His lips found hers again and she surrendered to him completely, letting go of him so she could align her body against his, the soft buds of her breasts teasing his own nipples. She clutched his shoulders and moved her pelvis toward him, teasing him as if she'd been doing this forever.

He was about to enter her, but something stopped him. He stilled. This was wrong, so wrong. He could not finish this. Cupping her face, he gazed into her eyes, "I'm sorry, but I cannot do this."

Dazed and confused, Lina stared at him. "What? Please do not stop. I want this. I want you."

Drew could not bear to see the disappointment in her eyes, but his honor would not allow him to continue. "Lina, I love you, but I am still unsure about marriage. I cannot do this without promising marriage to you. 'Twould be wrong, and you know it." Hellfire, but he hated his rotten conscience. *Finish it! You want her! Just finish it!*

But he could not. "I'm sorry, Lina." He climbed out of bed and fixed his plaid before disappearing into the night.

When he ran down the stairs, all he could think of was how right it had been to hold Lina in his arms. The astounding part was that he had confessed all to her, something he had never done before, and she had still accepted him. She did not seem to care that he could not keep still, that he still was often compelled to keep moving. He had also confessed a truth he was only just acknowledging.

He loved Avelina Ramsay—more than anything else in the world.

CHAPTER EIGHTEEN

Lachlan Burnes didn't move a muscle as he stood in the middle of his great hall. His parents, Hogan and Effie, were both ranting and raving at him in front of most of the clan as they paced the dais. Aye, he was once again being ridiculed in front of peons who should be kissing his feet. Aye, he was of noble blood, not them. He would be laird someday, not them. So how dare they sit and stare at him as if he were worthless?

Because his own parents had just told them so.

"Fool!" his mother yelled. "You are a lazy, daft fool! You lost the sapphire sword and you cannot find it? We could have been protected for life if not for your foolishness. Och, what am I to do with you?"

He mumbled, "Just remember, 'tis I that found the sapphire sword. You knew naught of it. 'Twas my abilities that found it." Unfortunately, his parents were so loud that no one heard a word he said. They never did. Never...ever. His hands clenched at his sides, wanting to rid himself of their cruel words so much, yet he had no idea how to stop them.

His father filled in any gaps in her rant with ranting of his own. "Your fault, wife. You coddled the lad when he was young. I told you your coddling would cause him to be weak. Now look at him!" His father's arm swung in his direction, then settled on his hip. "He's daft. He has not moved since the meal began."

Lachlan *couldn't* move. He wanted to kill them. Nay, killing would not be enough. He wanted them to suffer like they were making him suffer.

"Get out!" his mother screamed, loud enough to shake the timbers above.

For some reason, this particular comment registered with him, pulling him out of his vengeful thoughts.

Mothers were supposed to love their children, were they not? Well, Lachlan's mother had never loved him.

She pointed her finger at him, coming closer. "Get out, I said. You've lost the sword and placed a curse on all of us. You've had a fortnight to find it, and you have not."

"Effie, have some consideration for him. He is our only son, and if you give him time, he'll find the sword and return it. If you send him out, he'll not even bother to look for it. 'Tis our chance to be blessed as well. Suppose he finds it again, the gift will not be ours if you send him out." His father turned to face him and added, "Your mother hates you for what you've done to us, lad."

"Aye, Hogan. You have the right of it, except I don't hate him. He's had his chance to make amends. And what has he done? Naught! My stomach flips over at the sight of him for fear of the fae. Get him gone before the curse settles on us. He found the sword and then lost it, so the curse should be on him, not the entire clan. 'Tis all his fault and the faeries know it. Be gone before you cast your spell upon all of us." She waved her hand as if it were that easy to rid herself of her son.

Lachlan hung his head, unsure of what to do. Where would he go? He had met a few unsavory sorts after the Cameron skirmishes, but many had been English. Still, some had been Scots who hungered for coin. They spent their time stealing and raping. Mayhap he would join them.

"Get your things and get out!" his mother bellowed, startling him out of his daydreaming. "Please leave before you bring the wrath of the entire faerie world down upon us."

There were many voices shouting to him, he realized, begging to be heard above his parents. His clan. They were all yelling at him, raising their fists at him. What were they going on about? Ah, the sword, the wonderful sapphire sword. He had been protected when he held it, but now it was gone.

"Leave, Lachlan," his mother barked. "Do the right thing. Take yourself away and never return. 'Tis our only chance to prevent the prophecy from coming to fruition." His mother's loud voice riled up the rest of the clan.

"Aye, 'tis the only thing that will save us," one person shouted.

"You must leave," another added. "And stay away forever!"

Now out of their seats, they all turned to face him, chanting, "Leave, Lachlan. Leave, Lachlan. Leave, Lachlan."

His hands reached up and held his head, the only thing he could do to stop the pounding that shook his very insides.

Lachlan whirled around to find his parents standing directly behind him. His sire's face crumpled. "I hate to do it, lad, but you must leave to save all of us. Forgive me, but I must join the others in asking you to go."

His mother sneered at him. "I told you that you were a halfwit." She joined the others in their chant, all of them scorning him. "Leave, Lachlan, leave."

Lachlan did the only thing he could.

He took his sword off his back and plunged it into his mother's black heart.

When her eyes caught his, he sneered and winked at the fear and surprise he saw.

His father whispered, "Thank the saints above. God be with you son, but go. They'll tear you limb from limb. Now go."

Lachlan stared at his father, nodded, then turned and ran out the door.

A plan twisted its way into his heart as he rushed to the edge of his land. He had buried a bag of necessities there, along with all of the coin he had stolen from his da over the years. Part of him had always feared this day would come.

He shook the heavy weight of the bag in his hand, smiling. This was exactly what he needed. He had coin enough to buy all the reivers he needed. Now he had one mission, and one only.

He would find that sapphire sword.

And then he would kill the person who had stolen it from him.

CHAPTER NINETEEN

I love you.

Those three words had echoed in Lina's mind ever since Drew had uttered them. Though she worried she might have heard him wrong, she knew in her heart that she was not mistaken.

She loved Drew Menzie. But he was still unsure if he wanted to marry, so her heart was lost, or so it seemed at the moment.

Seated at the hearth in the great hall, she placed a stitch in the garment she was about to finish for Jennie's bairn. *"You must be patient, my dear."* Was that not what Erena had told her?

But how much longer did she need to wait? At this moment, she wished to tear every hair out of her head.

Jennie glanced at her over her needlework. "At least you know he has fallen in love with you. 'Tis a huge step for Drew Menzie. In my mind, 'tis a step forward and he will never turn back. We just need to convince him to marry."

Lina sighed. "I know not how to do such a thing."

Jennie bit her lip as she concentrated on her fine stitches. "I must speak to Aedan. He is the closest to Drew. Mayhap he can convince him 'tis time to settle down. And for the good of all, it must be soon." Jennie lifted her gaze to peer at Lina, but then dropped it back to her work. "I wish there was something I could do."

The door burst open and Aedan moved over to them, a messenger behind him. Lina did not like the look on Aedan's face. He sat down by Jennie's side, taking her needlework from her and setting it on the nearby chest.

Jennie stared at her husband. "What is it?"

Aedan cleared his throat but did not speak. Lina had a bad

feeling in the pit of her stomach. Something had happened. Something was not right.

She held her breath as she waited for the messenger's information to be brought to light. Aedan nodded to the messenger, who reached inside his sporran and pulled out the letter, which he handed to Jennie.

Jennie's nimble fingers shook as she took the parchment, her gaze catching Lina's as she unfolded the message.

Jennie,
We're sorry to have to tell you that your sister Brenna has lost the babe she carried.

Jennie's hand flew to her mouth at the same exact moment that Lina gasped, dropping the garment she labored over onto the floor. Her gaze returned to the parchment in Jennie's hand.

Brenna is fine, as are all her bairns, but she has asked for you, so we would like to request that you return home for the blessing of the bairn by Father Rab. If Aedan cannot free anyone to escort you, we will come for you. She would also like Avelina to return so we can have some time with all the family present. Quade is sending the same message to Micheil and Diana. We have not decided about the rest of the Grant clan. Please advise the messenger of your need for escorts.
We wish many blessings on you and Aedan, as well as Avelina.
Logan Ramsay

Aedan took the parchment and set it on the chest, then wrapped his arms around his wife. "I'm so sorry, Jennie. I would be happy to escort you both back to Ramsay land. When would you prefer to leave?"

Jennie fought to keep her tears at bay. "On the morrow? Would we be able to leave by then? I would like to be by her side soon."

"Aye, I'll see to it. But I don't want to leave you right now. I'll send the messenger to the kitchens for nourishment, and he'll send Neil to me later."

"I'm fine. Do what you must, Aedan. I would rather you settle things so we are prepared to leave on the morrow. Please? Lina and I will comfort each other."

Aedan kissed her brow and asked, "Are you sure? If so, I'll leave you now and make arrangements. I need to choose the guards and..."

"Aye, go, Aedan. Lina and I will go pack our things."

"I love you. If you need me, please just send someone for me." Aedan took his leave and led the messenger to the kitchens for some food.

Jennie got up, straightened their needlework for the bairn, and then took Lina's and led her up the stairs. Lina tried to think of something to say, but naught came out. The only thought that came to her mind, she kept to herself.

But once they were inside Jennie's chamber, she could keep quiet about it no longer.

"'Tis all my fault." Tears welled in her eyes, so she closed them in the hopes to squeeze them away.

Jennie looked at her, aghast. "What is this nonsense? How could it possibly be your fault?"

"Because of the sapphire sword. I am running out of time to find a husband, so the tragedy that is to befall my family has already begun."

For a long moment, the two stood in the middle of the chamber staring at each other. Then Jennie shook her head. "Nay, Lina. You're wrong."

"How can you be so sure?"

"Because the faerie told you that you have two moons. It has not been two moons yet, so this could not have happened because of you."

"But I am no closer to being married." The tears she had forced back finally slid down her cheeks. "This could be the first of many tragedies to befall my family. Oh, saints above, what am I to do?"

"Lina, I refuse to believe such nonsense. Women lose bairns frequently. It happened to my own mother a couple of times. Aren't there some at the Ramsay castle who have lost bairns?"

"Aye, but..."

"But what? 'Tis not an uncommon loss."

"But the fae...sometimes one hears tales of the fae and bairns. I've heard about babes being taken and replaced with changelings."

"My mother never believed in those stories, nor did Brenna. We've heard talk from the old wizened ones about the fae, but nothing of the like has ever happened at our keep. Do you not recall that Erena asked you to place your trust in her? This does not sound like something Erena or the fae would do. Nay, I refuse to hear you blame yourself, and I do not want to hear another word about it, Avelina Ramsay. You have naught to do with my sister losing her bairn."

"I hope you're right, Jennie. But you have no proof."

"Neither do you."

Lina had to admit that Jennie was right about that. She had no proof, and Erena had urged her to believe in herself and the fae.

But what if the curse really was starting to unfold? Lina had an important decision to make, and she had to do so quickly. She would not allow the legend to do any further harm to her family.

She would do what was necessary to protect them.

Drew paced as Aedan and Neil made arrangements for the trip to Ramsay land. Though he had tried to leave earlier, Aedan had stopped him, insisting he needed to speak to him.

As soon as Neil left, Aedan led Drew down a path to a private area to speak. Drew didn't know what it was about, but he respected his friend, and he wasn't going back home for a while, so he needed to establish himself here for a short time until he decided his next step. He had brought Boyd with him, and needed to find a place for him, as well. Not that either of them minded sleeping under the stars at this time of year, but winter would descend before too long.

After looking around, mayhap to ensure they were, indeed, alone, Aedan spun around and punched him in the jaw with such a force that he fell to the ground.

"God's teeth, Cameron. What'd I do?"

"I saw you leave Lina's room last night. Now, I'd be calling a priest right now, but I have to take my wife to see her sister. I thought I'd advise you to be ready to marry Lina when I return. Fortunately for you, now is not the best time for a wedding, else I would force you today."

"Aedan, 'tis not what you think."

"Are you denying that it was you leaving her chamber last

night? If you hadn't been leaving, I would have beaten your arse then and there, but I do not like to disturb my wife's sleep. She has enough trouble sleeping."

Drew stood up, rubbing his jaw, and leaned against a nearby tree. "Aye, 'twas me leaving. Not for what you believe. Well, could have been, but I did naught. Well…"

"Hellfire, Menzie, why must you be so honest down to the most minute detail? Stop mumbling and tell me true. Did you take her maidenhead? Is there to be a wedding?"

"Nay, I did not." He held his hands up to his friend, then let his breath out through pursed lips. "I almost did, but I stopped. I still am not certain if I wish to marry, so I knew it was wrong."

"Saints be praised for that wee bit of enlightenment. I thought at first I heard screaming, so imagine my surprise when I saw you leaving."

"Lina was screaming. 'Twas why I came to her chamber. I was sleeping on a pallet in the hall, and I could hear her over the balcony. She screamed and screamed and did not stop until I awakened her. We talked for a time, but then one thing led to another, and…aye, I stopped in time." He ran his hand down his face in frustration.

"Why was she screaming?"

"Because she had another dream about the lad tied to the bed."

"Did she find out who it was? Did you help her locate the laddie?"

"Nay."

"Why not?"

Drew stared at the leaves on the tree overhead and paced in a circle. Word would probably get around after what he'd done at his keep. And he did need Cameron's support, depending on what he'd decide to do with his life, but 'twould be embarrassing. Awfully embarrassing. He ripped a piece of bark off the tree, then turned to face his friend. "The laddie in the bed was me."

"What? You? Saints above, how could it be you? You're not a laddie."

"Nay, but it happened when I was a laddie. 'Twas me, trust me. She recognized me."

Aedan crossed his arms in front of him. "Your sire tied you to a bed?" He scratched his head as he considered it. "But why?"

Drew refused to look his friend in the eye because he was simply too embarrassed. "Because my mother was afraid she'd lose me, too. The loss of my three brothers drove her daft. She asked Da to tie me to the bed to keep me from doing anything dangerous."

"God's teeth, Menzie. How could you deal with it? 'Twould drive a person to madness."

"I felt mad, many, many times." He breathed in deep and let the air out slowly through pursed lips.

"It happened more than once?"

Drew was surprised to see the shock on his friend's face, but somehow, it made him feel a wee bit better. "Aye, it started when I was about five summers. I was too busy, and they counted on James to watch me, but once he was gone, they could not find anyone else to keep up with me. After I got into trouble a few times, my father had a special bed made." He turned his gaze away from his friend.

"Special bed?"

"Aye, to tie my hands out away from my body. They were so afraid I'd find a way to get out."

"And Lina saw all this in her dream?"

"Aye, enough to know 'twas me. Not at first, but she recognized me last night."

"How in hell do you ever go home, Menzie?"

"I'll not go home again for a while. I need some time away. I intended to speak with you about that."

"All right. I'm listening."

"I would like to stay here if we could come to an arrangement. I left after I chopped up the bed and the lock on the door. I told my parents I would not return for a while, but I have nowhere to go, and was hoping you'd allow Boyd and me to stay on as part of your guard."

Aedan rubbed his chin. "Menzie, I do not know what to say. Of course, you can stay. Boyd can be in my guard, but not you. Mayhap as an advisor with Neil. Mayhap you can help train my guard. You know it has been my goal to make my men stronger. They like you, and you have great ideas."

"I'd appreciate it, Aedan."

Silence settled between the two, both staring off into the

distance.

"Menzie, why not marry Lina? I truly believe you would suit."

Drew ran his hand through his hair. "Because I do not think I could."

"Why not?"

Drew grabbed another piece of bark from the tree and tore it apart, tossing the pieces aside. "What if I am like my sire? I could not bear it…"

"Drew, you are naught like him. I think because of what happened to you, you would probably be wonderful with your bairns. You'll want your bairns to have a better life than you did."

Drew nodded. "I have thought of that, actually. And I must say that Lina is the first lass to make me *want* to marry. I've been set against it for so long. 'Tis hard to see it."

"Lina is a calm and patient lass. I think you would do well together. She's a beauty, too."

Drew rolled his eyes. "Aye, 'struth. She almost pushed me over the edge last night. But I could not do it. My honor would require I marry her, and I'm just not sure yet."

Aedan grasped his shoulder. "Think on it. You could live here with Lina and train my guard. Would make my wife more than happy to have Lina close by. Give it consideration while we're gone?"

"Aye, I will. My thanks, Cameron. I'll start working with your men on the morrow."

"Good. Keep them busy while Neil and I are gone. As I said, we're leaving for the Ramsays with at least a score guards, though I know not how long we'll be. Keep things under control here. Neil rides with me until we're on Ramsay land, then he'll be returning to protect our land."

Drew glanced up as a golden butterfly flew past him and then turned and landed on his arm. If he had not known any better, he would have sworn the butterfly was smiling at him.

Surely, he must be going daft.

CHAPTER TWENTY

Lachlan backhanded the fool standing in front of him.

"But I seen her, Burnes. 'Tis the beauty of all the Scots and she's here in the Highlands. I want her. I can steal her at night and have my taste of her without anyone being the wiser." The fool grabbed his crotch with emphasis. "If'n you want her, I'll bring her back to ye."

"Horse's arse. She's mine, and if any of you touch her, I'll cut off your bollocks."

Lachlan wanted to spit at the thought of any of these louse-laden dolts touching his Avelina Ramsay. He wanted her with a fury now. They'd been talking about her for days, betting what she would look like unclothed. He hocked up a pile of spit and flung it off to the side. He'd learned quite a bit from his new men, taking on many of their characteristics. Men would respect and fear him someday. He was practicing the new Lachlan, one with no mother and in charge of himself.

He'd gone to the Lowlands and found both Scotsmen and Englishmen willing to follow him for coin. His promise to have them all back home within a fortnight had helped, but they were lazy and needed to be pushed.

After much deliberation, he had decided the Ramsay lass was likely the one who had taken the sapphire sword. She was the one who'd had access. Of course, he knew Menzie might have stolen it after beating him, but his plan allowed for either possibility.

Lachlan pulled his pet mouse out of his sporran, fed it a piece of cheese and set him on his lap. He'd named his pet Willy.

"Wee Willy, what think you? Do you think the lass has the sword or Menzie? If you sit on the one side of my lap, 'twill mean the lass. If you sit on the other, 'twill mean Menzie." He gave the rodent a little shove from behind and it ran in a circle before finally settling on one side of his lap, leaning on its hind legs and wiggling his nose up at Lachlan. "Och, mayhap you have the right of it. Menzie must have stolen it. That whoreson never liked me."

If Menzie had the sword, it would be easy to get it from him— he wanted Avelina as much as Lachlan did. All he would need to do was hold a knife to her throat to get what he wanted from Menzie. He had to get the sword back, he just had to.

That was why he kept his good luck charm, Willy. Wee Willy could answer questions for him that no one else could. He fed him another piece of cheese, and the mouse squeaked at him. "I know, Willy. My sire does love me, 'twas all my mother. He proved himself to me at the end." A wide grin crossed his face, and he broke into laughter. "She won't be bothering me anymore, will she?" He snorted and then quieted, listening to his men talk in undertones.

"Do you think he killed his own mother?"

"Don't know if he did or did not, but he is daft. He talks to his pet mouse."

"Mayhap we should leave."

"Nay, he's got a lot of coin. I've seen it, and I want my share. We'll get ours within a fortnight. What else have we got to do?"

"Aye. I agree. Just hope he's not daft enough to get us all killed."

"He swings a mighty sword, and the fool is tough besides. Look at all the scars on him. Appears he's been beaten enough times. I'd wager he can take whatever he gets handed, unless 'tis a sword in his belly."

"That means naught."

"What about the fact that he has another fifty guards waiting for us on the other side of Cameron land? His plan is to squeeze them from both sides."

"That does make me feel a wee bit better. That's close to a hundred guards."

Lachlan smiled as he tucked his pet back into his sporran. "Willy, I'm taking your advice and going after Drew Menzie to set things right. I'll have the sword and my queen, all in less than a moon," he muttered. "Then naught will be able to touch me. Ever."

Lina glanced up at the moon just as an owl hooted nearby, startling her. She pulled the plaid tighter around her shoulders. They were on the way back to Ramsay land, but they had only been on the road less than a day. Not long ago, Aedan had sent Neil off into the forest with a few guards, though she knew not why. They'd settled near a waterfall for the night. Neil and the others had returned to the group after they finished their dinner of roasted rabbit. Now Neil and Aedan were huddled off to the side of the clearing, talking with their heads together. She'd heard Neil use Lachlan's name, and she needed to know what they were saying.

Jennie sat across from her on a nearby log.

"Jennie, I'm going to tend to my needs. Do you need aught?"

Jennie shook her head, absorbed in her own thoughts or so it appeared. Lina thought this was a good time to sneak through the forest closer to Aedan and Neil without raising suspicion.

She hadn't told anyone—nor did she plan to—but her intention was to find Lachlan Burnes, wherever he was hidden, and return the sapphire sword to him. Fear drove her forward, and she was convinced it was her only option to protect her family. She would go ahead with her plan whether Erena approved or not.

Her family would not suffer any more harm if there was aught she could do about it.

Aye, she loved Drew Menzie, and she almost believed he loved her, but he had made it clear to her that he was still not certain he could marry. There was no time to wait. She had to act before it was too late.

She did not need the sapphire sword any more than she needed to be a chosen one. She would just go back to being plain, dull Avelina Ramsay. She slowed her steps to listen to the men and their conversation.

"What did you discover?" Aedan asked Neil.

"He's got guards with him, mayhap around thirty. I overheard his guards discussing two things."

"Aye?" Aedan leaned in toward his second in command.

"One is he's after the sapphire sword."

"No surprise there. We suspected he would come after it sooner rather than later. And the other?"

"They think he's daft. Word is he's killed his own mother and he talks to a mouse."

Aedan paced in a slow circle, chewing on mint leaves. "That bothers me. I knew Lachlan was different, but I hadn't realized his mind had deteriorated that much. We need to be verra aware of what he's doing. How far away are they?"

"Less than an hour away, and they are headed in the opposite direction."

Aedan's eyes went wide. "Toward my land?"

"Aye. He thinks Menzie has the sword."

Lina's heartbeat sped up. This was all her fault. She had stolen the sword, and Drew would pay for something she had done. She chewed on her lower lip and turned away from them, trying to plan the best course of action.

After much deliberation, she decided that perhaps Erena was watching out for her—and approved of her plan—because Neil's information provided her with a perfect opportunity. She would wait until everyone bedded down and then follow the path back toward Cameron land. After she left the sword in Lachlan's camp, she would return without Aedan or Neil realizing she had even left.

She moved back to speak to Jennie. "Where are you and Aedan settling?"

Jennie pointed to a spot a short distance away at the top of a small hill. "Aedan wants to watch the stars together before we sleep."

"I'm jealous," Lina admitted. "Do you think I'll ever share the same with someone?"

"Aye, similar, but most lads do not love the stars like Aedan does. Mayhap your husband will have another interest. Alex and Maddie like to swim together, and Caralyn and Robbie both like to fish. Who knows what your love will share with you?"

Lina sat down and fussed over the pebbles on the ground. "I think I must forget Drew."

"Mayhap. At least you are more comfortable talking to lads now."

"Aye, some. I still get upset sometimes, but I have improved. I can actually speak to Boyd now."

Jennie chuckled and reached over to tuck a loose tendril of Lina's behind her ear. "Lina, your time will come. But I do not think 'tis time to forget Drew. You do not need the other lads, only

Drew Menzie."

Aedan came over and held his hand out to Jennie. "Are you ready to star-gaze with me, love?"

Jennie took her husband's hand and stood up beside him. After she brushed her gown off, she turned back to Lina. "You'll be all right?"

"Aye," Lina smiled. "I'm verra tired. Do not worry about me."

Aedan said, "If you need aught, just holler. I will not be far, and Neil and the rest of the guards will be right there."

Lina took her time to verify where all the men were. She was quite sure she could do this without anyone discovering what she was about. She smiled and waved at Jennie. "Go on. Enjoy your husband and the stars."

Wrapping up tight in her plaid, she feigned sleep for a couple of hours. When all was quiet, she crept to the other side of the clearing and slipped into the woods as if seeing to her needs. After checking her pockets to make sure she had the sword, Lina headed out in search of Lachlan.

A few hours and several blisters later, Lina came upon a group of horses and listened intently. All was quiet except for loud snores from a few of the men. Padding softly around the camp, she did her best to find Lachlan, and as soon as she did, she sneaked over to him and dropped the sword as close to him as she could. With a sigh of relief, she turned around and headed back out of the camp. The stale aromas of whisky, urine, and ale made her nostrils flare, but she hoped the libations were imbibed enough to keep the men fast asleep.

Leaving camp, she thought about taking a horse, but decided it would be stealing, so decided against it. She trudged along through the forest, ignoring her blisters the best she could when she came upon a lone horse munching grass by itself.

She searched the area for the owner, but found no one. Finding a nearby log to mount, she took a slow canter until she dared to move to a gallop, thanking the saints above for offering this gift to help her return quickly.

Just when she thought she was safe, she heard a wild shout behind her. Slowing enough to glance over her shoulder, she groaned and kneed her horse at the same time.

Lachlan Burnes was not far behind her.

Drew woke up to shouts outside the gates. He was wide awake in a matter of seconds since he and Boyd had chosen to sleep under a tree inside the bailey. Puzzled by the shouts, he rushed toward the portcullis just as Neil flew into the bailey.

"What is it? Has something happened?"

"Aye. Lina's missing."

His gut clenched and he closed his eyes and said a quick prayer. "How long?"

"We think since the middle of the night. Jennie thinks she was trying to find Lachlan Burnes so she could return the sapphire sword."

"And where the hell would she find him?"

"Aedan and I discovered they were headed here looking for the sword. He thinks you have it. Lina must have overheard their conversation and gone after him. He sent me back to see if I saw aught along the way, or if I could catch Lachlan. He's not been here?"

"Nay." Drew headed toward the stables for his horse. He'd have to move fast if she was half a night ahead of him. He stopped for a moment and barked back at Neil. "Where's Aedan?"

"Aedan continued on toward Ramsay land with Jennie. He plans to return with Logan and any other guards Quade can spare. He also sent word to the Grant. Lachlan had twenty or thirty warriors with him."

"Then I'll go after her." He mounted his horse and turned toward the gate. Boyd, who'd hurriedly prepared his own horse, was right beside him.

"Menzie," Neil shouted after him. "Take some guards. Burnes has gone daft apparently. There's no telling what he might do."

"You will remain here?"

"Aye, I have instructions to protect the Cameron keep."

"God's teeth, this is not good. Lachlan was only a halfwit to start, and he has no morals. The thought of Lina in his hands scares the hell out of me."

"And there's one more problem."

"Aye?"

"My men tell me Burnes has another fifty guards waiting for his instructions not far from here."

"Hellfire. I hope the Grant sends men. We'll need them."

Laird Alex Grant led his guards across the valley. When they made it to the other side, he held his hands up to signal for those in the front to wait for the rest to gather. They all knew this was the toughest area to traverse in all of the Highlands. Trekking down this next mountain was slow going. Rocks and pebbles and steep drops that could catch the horses' hooves threatened to slow their progress. But at least it wasn't winter.

This was a rare journey for them, one they had never made before as a family, which was why Alex was taking such care. He had two hundred guards with him, but he needed them all. His dear wife, Maddie, rode in a cart behind them with Celestina and the Grant bairns.

After receiving the message about his sister Brenna's loss, he'd made the decision they would go as a family to offer their support to the Ramsays. Most of his clan had traveled out of the Highlands at some time or another except for Maddie, and she had asked him if he would take her to see dear Brenna.

The entire world knew he was unable to turn his wife down. He still adored her as much as the day they'd married, nay, even more. He glanced over his shoulder at the cart. There she sat with their youngest, Eliza, in her lap, next to Celestina, who was cuddling her newest daughter, Catriona, on her lap. Maddie had been telling the little ones stories, but she had stopped short.

Alex didn't like this one bit. He had never seen such a sight. His mother had always sworn that the land was controlled by the fae, who would come out every so often to shake up the land. He hadn't seen it happen yet. But this vision in front of him had him wondering whether this was exactly what his mother had warned them about. The fae came when there was trouble, she had said, and they would help a worthy human, a chosen one, lead the land in the direction they desired, in the direction of good.

He recalled Brenna's question to their mother at the time. "What do you mean, direction of good? Where else would we go?"

They'd waited patiently for their mother to answer. "Sometimes there are evil souls who try to wrest power for themselves," she had said, smoothing back Brenna's hair. "But remember that the fae are always watching us. You will know when they step in to provide us with their protection."

"How?" Alex had asked.

"There will be a strange cast over the land. At first, you'll just think the day is different, yet you'll know not why. You will continue, and you'll feel as though something is there over your shoulder watching you, but there'll be naught there. Even the clouds and the rain will be different—darker and heavier. You'll know it when you feel it. Trust me."

His mother was right. He could feel it.

His gaze narrowed as he searched for any clues, but there were none. They were more than halfway to the Ramsays. His gut told him not to turn back. His sister and her bairns were near the Lowlands.

His decision finally made, he gave crisp instructions. "Once we get to the bottom of the next mountain, Brodie, you'll take the cart, all the bairns, and one hundred guards. You are to head to Ramsay land using the peripheral route that curves away from Cameron land. Robbie, you'll come with me and we'll take the rest of the guards to Cameron land to see if Jennie is safe."

He didn't like it. There had been many skirmishes in the Cameron's land not long ago, right before Jennie and Aedan married. Lochluin Abbey, full of riches, sat near the keep. Apparently, the skirmishes were not over.

Loki, Brodie's eldest son, rode up behind Alex. "My laird, I'd like to request to travel with you to fight. I think my skills would benefit you."

Alex turned slowly to address him. Aye, Loki was a clever, cheeky lad, but he lacked good judgment as of yet. And Alex did not like being questioned.

Brodie barked, "Loki, apologize to your laird."

Alex's hand came up to stop him. He turned his attention to his nephew. "Loki, are you telling me that the job of protecting my bairns and my wife is not important enough for you?"

Loki paled and stuttered, "N-nay, my laird. Forgive me."

"You'll follow the cart and the horses, watching the rear for any threats. I have five bairns that need protecting, and many nieces and nephews."

Jake and Jamie, his twin lads, growing up so fast it frightened him, spoke up. "Da, we can protect…"

"Silence!" His stare raked across the group. "I know not what we are up against, and you are all to do what I say without question. And when I am not with you, you will do as Robbie or Brodie instruct you. Understood?"

A sea of heads nodded, but Alex's youngest, golden-haired Eliza, just a wean, began to cry. "Papa, up?" she asked, outstretching her arms to him from the cart.

Alex turned and gave directions to Robbie and Brodie before they all continued on down the mountain. He couldn't look at his daughter right now. The thought of anything happening to her made him not furious, but ill, quite ill.

He didn't like this one bit. The tales his mother and father had told him of the fae had conveyed one lesson.

Visits from the good fae came when evil threatened to overtake part of the land.

And what he saw in front of him looked purely evil.

CHAPTER TWENTY-ONE

Lina hung onto her horse's mane and flew across the landscape, praying to get away from Lachlan. The lad had already attacked her twice. What would he do to her now, especially now that he knew she was the one who had stolen the sapphire sword? She didn't think she had much farther to go. *Aedan, where are you?*

Lachlan's twisted laughter echoed out across the night. The eerie sound sent chills shooting down her spine, but she did not let herself despair. Somehow, she would prevail.

He drew closer and closer. She spurred the horse on, but not fast enough. Soon, he was almost next to her—a sight which sent panic racing through her veins. Lachlan let out a low growl and leapt straight at her. She tried to duck, but he caught her, and together they toppled onto the ground and rolled down a small grassy knoll.

She did the only thing she thought might help her, even though she risked slicing her tender skin open. The sapphire sword sat sheathed at his waist, right there for her to grab. He wouldn't let go of her arms so she rolled down the small incline with him, and as soon as her hand met the hilt of the sword, she yanked it out, gripping it tight until they stopped moving.

Jumping up, she moved away from him, the sword in her hand.

"You wee bitch, you're quite a good thief, I'll give you that. But I'll not let you keep it. You just returned it, or have you forgotten?"

She brandished the weapon at him as he came toward her, blood dripping down her arm from where she had cut herself. Her heart raced in fear, but she gulped air to keep herself alert. He lunged for her, so she flung the sword over her head and pointed it at the heavens above.

The minute the sword was pointed upward, a furious wind whipped up out of nowhere and lightning shot out of the sky, followed by deafening thunder.

"You evil witch, what are you doing? Give the sword over now. You have no idea the power you're holding, do you?"

She kept the weapon raised over her head even as drenching rains started and the lightning ripped down from the sky, tipping her face up to the heavens, praying the Lord, the angels in Heaven, and the fae were all watching. One strike of lightning hit the tree behind them, bouncing them both into the air. Lina landed with a thud. She had actually felt the power in the sword. A new understanding dawned within her—the power was meant to be hers, not Lachlan's, and it was time she came to accept that.

He seemed to have come to that same conclusion, for he backed away from her, staring up at the light show around them in mingled fear and wonder. His hand guarded his face as he beheld the impressive force of nature she had stirred.

"Do you not see, Lachlan? This sword was meant for me, not you. I am a chosen one. You must leave me alone or the faeries will come for you." Though she was not certain it was true, she decided her best chance of escaping this situation was to convince him that she held all the power. And somehow all the lights and thunder around her made her feel empowered enough to take a chance and grab onto her destiny. She was a chosen one, so she would fight for her right to hold the sapphire sword. It was the only way she could keep him at a distance.

After a short time, she lowered the sword. As soon as she did, the rain and the lightning stopped, but an eerie glow rose up around Lina.

"Hellfire, you *are* a chosen one." He panted as he wiped all the rain from his face. "My sire told me all about it long ago, but I'd forgotten. You'll be my wife. 'Tis the only the way the power will spread to me. I know the story. If you do not marry me, tragedy will befall your family within two moons. My mother told me of this, and you've had the sword for a couple of fortnights. Your time is running out. 'Tis why the lightning is here."

"Nay, I'll never agree to marry you." Lina held her breath as she watched him, so fearful he would find a way to force the marriage.

"Aye, you will. I'll hold you for a sennight until you see all the tragedy start to befall your family. Then you'll agree to be my wife. The marriage must take place. You know it as well as I do."

He pulled his pet mouse out of his sporran and whispered to him, but Lina couldn't understand a word he said. After a few minutes, he climbed onto his horse. Three other horses emerged out of the brush behind them. Lachlan's men. One grinned from ear to ear as soon as he saw her.

"Och, you've got her. Well done, Lachlan. Can I have her after you do?"

Lina backed up, not wanting any of them to touch her.

"Nay, you'll not touch her. Did you not see those storms around us just now? She's been chosen by the fae. Touch her and you'll die. She's to be my wife as soon as we find a priest."

Lina closed her eyes in frustration. She'd messed up everything. Now she held the sword again, so her family would be in danger if she did not marry. What if Lachlan told the truth about holding her until someone was harmed in her family? Then she would have no choice. If she had to make this sacrifice in order to save them, then she would.

Drew? Aedan? Erena? Anyone? Please help me.

Aedan had almost reached the Ramsay land when the dark clouds overtook them. An eerie silence settled, and he glanced at Jennie to see if she sensed anything. He thought her healing abilities gave her a certain intuition others did not possess.

Jennie's eyes widened, but she said naught. The sound of horses' hooves pummeling the ground greeted them. They turned to see five horses approaching, the riders swathed in the Ramsay plaid.

Aedan relaxed when he realized one of the figures was Logan Ramsay. "Jennie, do you need the woods?" he asked. "I do not want to stop unless 'tis absolutely necessary. I have a bad feeling. But if you do, now would be a good time."

She shook her head in denial, her gaze telling him how frightened she was by all that had transpired.

Logan stopped his horse abreast of him. "We have heard of your troubles. Fill me in on everything you know so we can go after her." Gwyneth, Logan's wife, was already sidling her horse up next to her husband's.

Aedan, Jennie, Logan, and Gwyneth all dismounted and moved away from the guards to speak in privacy. The men spread out around the periphery of the area to keep watch.

Aedan began. "Lina and Jennie both wished to come to your land to support Brenna. We were on our way when Lina disappeared in the middle of the night from the clearing where we were resting. There was no sign of a scuffle, my guards swear there were no other horses in the area."

Jennie teared up. "We think she left to find Lachlan."

"Daft lass. Why?" Logan growled.

"Because she thinks 'tis all her fault that Brenna lost the baby. She believes 'tis because she has not yet found someone to marry. The two moons she was given have nearly passed, so the family tragedies are starting." Jennie's tears garbled her words and Aedan wrapped his arm around her shoulder in comfort.

Aedan continued. "Neil discovered Lachlan with an odd group of men last eve, similar to the groups Dermid and Irvine hired to attack me and some of the other Highlanders, and overheard them saying they were coming for the sapphire sword. They believed Drew held it and were seeking him at the Cameron keep."

Gwyneth's puzzled expression changed in an instant to a look of understanding. "Lina thinks if she returns the sword to Lachlan, it will put the curse of the legend back onto him."

"Aye." Jennie sobbed into her husband's shoulder.

"Near dawn, I sent Neil and a few guards back to my keep in the hopes they would find her and warn Drew. I've heard naught about anything."

The wind whipped up out of nowhere, so Aedan pointed to a cave not far away. "Inside, Jennie. I do not like the feel of this."

They barely managed to make it under cover in the cave, which was also large enough to offer protection for some of the horses, before the heavens opened up and drenched the earth all around them. Torrents of rain, streaks of lightning, and loud cracks of thunder echoed from the direction they had come.

Gwyneth glanced up. "The fae are angry."

"What?" Logan stared at his wife, obviously surprised by her declaration.

"Ask my brother Rab. He has always talked about the faeries

and storms. When they get angry, they will use whatever weapon is available to them to stop evil from achieving its goals. Many times, 'tis nature."

All were silent as they watched the light display outside.

"Look for a focal point," Gwyneth said. "Could be where Lina is."

"I've seen the fae," Jennie whispered.

Logan replied, "You have? With Lina?"

"Aye, she was beautiful. She said Lina was a chosen one, but she would have to find her own way."

Logan turned to Aedan, "Lina told us everything about the fae and the queen. We believe her, though I admit it was difficult. But I could not argue what I could see with my own eyes. Gregor healed right in front of us."

Aedan whispered, "You do not need to convince me. I believe the lasses."

A streak of lightning wrested their attention back to the storm.

Jennie pointed off to one spot, "Look. 'Tis centering in that one spot."

As they watched, more and more lightning strikes targeted the same area, but then they immediately ceased. The land took on an eerie glow, almost golden, in the area where the lightning had been the strongest.

"Mount up, wife," Logan said. "We're heading toward the glow. I believe 'tis my sister." The rain and wind had stopped as quickly as it had begun. "Cameron, get your wife to our land. Do not stop for aught."

CHAPTER TWENTY-TWO

Drew felt like he was losing his wits. He'd searched in five different directions, through lightning, a torrential downpour, and heavy winds—all for naught. There was no sign of Lina anywhere.

Aye, he had tracked a group of horses for a distance, but the rain had wiped out every hint of a track.

He forced himself to continue, because if he didn't, he'd surely be ill. If he stopped this very moment, he would jump off his horse and heave into the nearest bushes, but he knew he couldn't. He could not stop until he found Avelina Ramsay. The thought of her in the hands of Lachlan Burnes was sheer torture.

Sweet memories of his time with Avelina kept rebounding in his brain. Visions of her creamy flesh and sumptuous lips, of how she was with her nephews, and of the night she listened to his tales with such compassion continued to haunt him. Hellfire, but he was in love with Lina, and he was glad to admit it.

Why hadn't he agreed to marry her? If he had, this would not be happening. He'd allowed memories of being locked in that chamber to sour him. He'd made the same mistake as his parents by allowing the past to cloud the present and future.

Then his mind shifted. Thoughts of Lachlan Burnes on top of Lina in the grass, of her beautiful face bruised, lit a fire under him, forcing him onward.

Three guards rode with him, and he had sent others off in various directions. He saw a group of horses headed toward his group, so he slowed until he could identify them. When he saw that the riders wore the Ramsay plaid, he finally released the breath he'd been holding. He almost cheered when he recognized Logan and Gwyneth.

Now he had true assistance.

"Have you discovered aught?" Logan asked.

"Nay, I've sent guards in five directions at this point, but there is no sign of them. And you?" He knew that Logan Ramsay would overturn every stone in the entire land to find Lina.

Just as he would do.

"Nay, but we've only just arrived. We followed the golden aura after the storm. I believe 'tis where Lachlan caught up with Lina. She must be with him. I hope she has kept the sword in her possession. 'Tis her only bargaining chip. We did find two of his guards turning tail back to England. My Gwynie," he paused to give her a wink, "convinced them to talk. They had deserted the group. Said they thought Lachlan was daft. The only other information they gave us was that he had a lass with him he planned to marry. That's all they knew."

"Has he hurt her?" Drew asked through a clenched jaw.

"Nay. They said he's afraid of her."

"Lina's smart. She'll keep the sword. The question is, where would he find a priest?"

Gwynie replied, "According to my brother, there are not many in the area, but if Burnes is truly daft, he'll find anyone to marry them."

"You know this land well, Menzie?" Logan asked.

"Aye, 'tis not far from my own."

"Where would he take her? He'd have to keep her well hidden."

Drew thought for a moment before replying. "There are two main areas with large caves, but in two completely different directions. I'll send you in one direction, and I'll head in the other."

"He's got more than four score guards in total. You'll need more than what you have."

"I'll meet up with the others and then we'll have at least a score. I'll not wait any longer. Time is of the essence."

Logan nodded, taking his measure. "She's more to you that just Jennie's friend, is she not, Menzie?"

Drew took a deep breath before answering him. "Aye. I hope you will consider my request for her hand in marriage if this is ever settled."

"If you find a priest, and Lina agrees, marry her. Do not wait for us."

Drew nodded, explained where the two caves were, and headed off to gather his men. There was no time to waste.

~✥~

Lachlan instructed Lina to wait by the entrance to the cave and then headed out to survey the surrounding area on his horse. He knew Lina wouldn't stray. There wasn't far for her to go on foot. The cave was small and dark, and his men had the perimeter surrounded.

He spoke to Duncan, an Englishman he had placed in charge of the others. "Where's the priest?"

"My men are out searching for one. The one on your land was not in the chapel or your keep, so I've sent some to search for him. We'll have one here by dusk."

"Can you hold off all of Cameron's men?"

"Aye, no problem. Only about twenty of them. But we've lost a few men…"

"How many are left?"

Duncan thought. "I've called all our men together, even the ones on the other side of Cameron land. With all my men in the field, including the ones looking for the priest, I'd say we have around eighty."

"Good. 'Twill be enough to contain the others until the lass and I are married. The Ramsays will be here soon. Have you seen any other clans?"

"Nay. How would I know it was Clan Ramsay?"

"When our men start dropping from arrows, 'twill be the Ramsays. They have the finest archers in the land, including Logan Ramsay's wife."

Duncan chuckled. "A lass? As an archer? 'Twould love to see that. I'll keep watch for her. Bet she's a feisty one."

"Take my word on it. You do not want to go near her or she'll tie your bollocks up in knots and then stomp on them. She did almost that to my sire, just missing his bollocks by a hair." Lachlan couldn't help but twitch when he remembered how she had almost shot his sire between the legs. He'd thought it impossible until he'd seen it with his own eyes.

Duncan instinctively covered his privates with his hand. "Shite. A lass would do that?"

"Aye, and more. Run if you see her coming. She'll put an arrow between your eyes before you get near her."

"Well, I have seen a few scouts, but not enough to cause us any trouble."

"Keep it that way. And if we're attacked by more than fifty guards, I'll double everyone's coin to keep fighting until the lass and I are married. Once the priest is here and the deed is done, naught else will matter."

"Aye, Chief."

"Move along and keep me abreast of all."

Once Duncan had departed, Lachlan returned to his lovely bride-to-be, who was presently sitting and leaning against the side of the cave with her eyes closed. Her hand was near the hilt of the sword. If he could just get close enough to grab it, he could have some fun with her before they were married. His mouth watered just looking at her fine shape. Once he got that sword in his hand, the first thing he would do was slice the ribbons off her bodice so he could see those tits for real. He'd have to be careful not to cut her skin though. She already had a wound on her arm.

Though she was still beautiful, of course, she didn't look too good. Her color was pale, and her hands shook as if palsied. He had almost reached her when her eyes flew open and her hand grabbed the hilt of the sword.

"Stay back. I said I would marry you when the priest arrives, but you'll not touch me before." That same haunting glow that had surrounded her after she created the storm welled around her now.

"Suit yourself," he spat out. "I'll be ripping through your maidenhead and planting my seed in you before the night's out. I can wait." He found a nearby rock and sat on it to await the priest's arrival. It couldn't be much longer.

A few moments later, the rumbling of hooves met his ears. He jumped on his horse and rode out to ask his guards who approached.

As soon as he reached them, he cursed. Now there'd be trouble. "You tell all your friends I'll triple their coin if they stay until we're married. We just need to delay battle. All I want is to marry her, then I'll surrender."

Alex Grant and some hundred and fifty guards were lined up opposite his hired men. He recognized the Grant and his brother at the forefront of the group, but they were with another man in a plaid he did not recognize.

"Are all our men here yet?" Lachlan spit out.

"Aye, all but the five gone for the priest. I have four score here."

"Whose plaid is that?" Lachlan snarled, tilting his head toward the newcomers.

"That's Micheil Ramsay in the Drummond plaid," one of his cronies replied.

Hellfire, the Grants *and* the Ramsays were here.

It was near dusk, and Drew was feeling defeated. His men had searched everywhere, to no avail. There was no sign of Lina or Lachlan. They had only run into one small group of Lachlan's marauders. It had been easy enough to take them out, but he'd caught one sword edge on his leg.

"Menzie," Boyd said with a whistle, "you should get that wound sewn up. You're losing too much blood."

"Aye, you may be correct, but I'll not take the time to stop. The bleeding has slowed. I'll survive until I can get to a healer or to Cameron's abbey. A monk there'll sew it up for me."

"Suit yourself. Which direction now?"

"I think we go back to the area where we sent the Ramsays. There's a good chance 'tis where he's keeping Lina."

A golden butterfly flitted in front of him and landed directly on his forearm. He scowled at it and tried to send it away, but it returned to his arm. Then the butterfly took off in one distinct direction before returning to him and fluttering right in front of his face.

"What in hellfire?"

He used his hand to push it away, but it returned.

"Boyd, what the hell do you make of this butterfly?"

Boyd laughed and said, "It must be a lass who thinks you handsome."

Drew sent it off again, but again it returned. Then a memory intruded. The butterfly that had landed on Lina and Gregor was this same color, was it not?

Boyd frowned, "Didn't Lina say something about a yellow butterfly? Or mayhap 'twas you."

Drew thought for a moment and said, "Aye, there is something special about this creature." He stared at the butterfly, which almost seemed to be beckoning to him. He held his hand up and the butterfly took flight in the same direction it had indicated before. It was also, he noticed, where he had sent the Ramsays and their guards.

"I think we should follow it," Boyd said, quirking his brow at him. "Mayhap 'twill lead the way to Lina."

"Mayhap you are right." Though he still had his doubts, Lina was special, and since he believed in that, in *her*, he needed to start believing in her power. "Lead the way, butterfly."

CHAPTER TWENTY-THREE

Lina's strength was waning. She had slept little the night before and hiked until her feet were covered in blisters, all without eating, but she would not go down without a fight.

She prayed Lachlan would not find a priest before someone came to her aid. She didn't argue about marrying him because she had to believe she would be rescued first. The only thing that concerned her was when her time would truly run out. She'd tried to decide exactly what day, what hour, but she could not. If he held her until tragedy started affecting her family, she would give in. She could see no other recourse. But she would fight for as long as she could. Her eyes closed and she drifted off, dreams of butterflies and a certain dark-haired warrior rescuing her filling her mind.

Moments later, something startled her and her eyes flew open. Lachlan was gone, but she heard a rumble not far away. She scrambled to her feet, her gaze following the sound, and in the distance she could see Lachlan, his second, Duncan, and a couple of others watching the landscape. There was still a group of guards around the periphery of the cave.

A smile crept across her face as she realized the cause of the rumble. Someone had come for her. Immediately, she recognized the Drummond plaid in the forefront of the group. Micheil. Thanking God for sending someone, she closed her eyes, only to snap them open a moment later.

The loudest rumbling came not from Micheil's guards, but from a sea of horses headed in their direction from a greater distance. A towering figure rode into view—Alex Grant, the most imposing warrior she had ever seen besides her brother Logan. Flanked by his brother and five other guards, he rode toward Lachlan. There were scores of warriors behind him, she realized with relief. Her heart soared at the possibility of freedom.

Off to the right, she saw more movement. Another smaller group of warriors, Quade's warriors, flanked the Grant guards on the right, while the Drummond clan sat to the left. Logan rode his horse up next to Alex. Lachlan flicked his reins and headed out to meet them.

Finally, this foolishness would come to an end. Lachlan had to see the futility of trying to make a stand against the combined power of the Grants, the Drummonds, and the Ramsays.

"Where's my sister, Burnes?" Logan's bellow could be heard over all else.

"Your sister will be mine soon. We have the power of the sapphire sword behind us. You'll not stop us. She'll be my wife and we'll control all."

Lina could not believe what she was hearing. He was willing to risk his life against all these warriors? She hurried forward, waving toward Logan, because she had to be certain they knew she was present. As soon as she moved into her brother's line of sight, three guards raced to her side and pulled her back, so she screamed to make sure she'd been seen.

As they dragged her back toward the cave, Logan yelled, "Fight, Lina, and be aware!"

Once the guards had pulled her back to the caves, she took a moment to assess the situation. She knew what Logan had been telling her. Sure enough, off in the trees she could make out Gwyneth and two other archers.

Give up, Lachlan, please. Her belly churned as she listened to the negotiations taking place in front of her, but suddenly she became unsettled over one fact—*she* still held the sword.

Aye, if she had been correct in her assumption that tragedy was about to befall her clan because she was still unmarried and still in possession of the weapon, perhaps an even bigger tragedy was about to unfold. This time, when her gaze roamed the sea of warriors in front of her, images of dead men lying in the dirt flashed before her eyes. She could only pray that it would not come to pass.

Both of her brothers sat open to attack at the front of the group.

From behind, she noticed Lachlan send a signal to Duncan, and Duncan in turn motioned to his guards. She screamed, hoping to warn her brothers, and the men surrounding her dropped their hold and took off toward Lachlan.

Thus, the battle began.

War whoops came from all three corners—the Grant call, the Ramsay call, and the Drummond call—and the previously unmoving sea of men turned into chaos.

She thought she heard someone yell, "Lina, get back into the cave!" She backed up, but kept her hand on the hilt of the sword, watching in horror as men fell screaming from their horses. The clash of steel was so loud that she covered her ears and closed her eyes, not wanting to hear the reminder of the fight in front of her. Men were about to die because of her,

Aye, if the dead were all Lachlan's men, she could deal with that. They were unscrupulous men for hire. But what of the Ramsay guards, the Drummonds, the Grant warriors? How many would die because of her? This was all her fault, all because she had taken the sapphire sword.

From a distance, Drew could tell the fighting had already begun. Flashbacks to the skirmishes on Cameron land fueled him forward. This time, he fought for the lass he loved.

He led his men into the chaos and was pleased to see not only Logan and his men, but also the Grant warriors, Quade's men, and Micheil Ramsay and the Drummond guards. Surely, they would win. They must outnumber Burnes and his men by three or four score. The good would triumph on this day.

He swung his sword arm overhead, lunging toward one warrior after another, clashing his weapon against the mercenaries, taking many of them down as he moved through the melee. But as soon as he dispatched one, another took his place. One came so close to his side that he yanked out his dagger and sliced the man across his neck, sending blood spurting over his shoulder.

He yelled and spurred his horse forward, dodging some of the Grant men as they finished off Lachlan's fighters. He fought his way toward the cave, delivering one jarring blow after another, doing all he could to get to Lina, whom he supposed to be inside. Steel against steel rent the air as he clamored his way closer to his goal. He came so close that at one point he thought he could hear her sobbing, but he forced himself to ignore it to focus on the battle in front of him.

Drew watched as Alex Grant's warhorse reared up on its back legs to allow Alex to rearrange his sword to do more damage. The two were incredible to watch. The man fought with a deadly patience, his smooth strokes taking out warrior after warrior in his path. How Drew wished he had the Grant's stamina.

Lachlan's numbers dwindled as they moved closer to the cave. Logan's wife had to be hidden among the trees, for Drew noticed men dropping with arrows lodged in their neck or hearts. The lass had a dead-eye with her bow.

He nearly pitched off his horse when his sword caught the last warrior in his belly, so he decided to battle from the ground. Just as he landed, a sharp pain hit him in the thigh. Drew spun around, catching his attacker across the chest and felling him to the ground, but unfortunately, he was a wee bit late. Blood spread across his breeches, indicating the lout's sword had indeed connected with his thigh, the same one previously injured.

Drew would not allow a couple of wee cuts to deter him. This was for Lina. Gathering all his strength, he moved on and cut down a man who was about to attack a Drummond warrior.

Drew's gaze searched the area, hoping they were near to the end of the mercenaries. Many of his motley group had fallen off their horses, but they continued to fight on foot. They seemed to appear out of the bushes and attack at aught they could.

A sharp scream caught his attention because it sounded like Lina's voice. He turned to his left and noticed Alex Grant was raising his sword to command silence from his men. Was it over? An eerie silence spread through the group.

The men who still lived turned their gazes toward the cave. Finally, Drew understood.

Lina.

Lina stood in front of the chaos sobbing. "No more, please, stop the killing."

Lachlan had a dagger pressed to her throat and her arm wrenched behind her back so she couldn't grab her sapphire sword. She screamed again to stop the killing, tears flooding her cheeks.

Logan moved toward his sister.

"Do not take another step or I'll kill her. If she's dead, I'll have the sword," Lachlan ground out.

Logan laughed, mirth in his eyes. "Burnes, even you know better. My sister is a chosen one. You'll be haunted until the day you die if you kill her."

"Nay, if I let her life's blood decorate the ground, then I'll have the power. She'll be naught but ashes in the wind."

Micheil yelled out, "You are as addled as they say if you believe that. Have you not heard my sister can command butterflies to do her will?"

Lachlan guffawed. "And what could butterflies do to hurt me?"

Logan stared at his sister, "Lina, lean your head to the side so my wife can take care of him."

Lina finally spoke. "Nay, Logan, please. I'll do what he wants if it puts a stop to the bloodshed. I'll marry him. I can't bear to watch any more die. I must marry soon, 'tis the legend."

Out of the corner of his eye, Drew noticed a priest on horseback was pushing his way through the Grant guards.

Lachlan must have seen him at about the same time. He laughed and said, "Father, come marry us. It must be done now."

The priest's horse was being led by one of Lachlan's men. He made it to their side and dismounted. "Lad, I cannot marry you to someone who cannot willingly take her vows."

Drew watched Logan Ramsay and Alex Grant. They were planning something, but daft Lachlan kept moving and his dagger had already pierced Lina's soft skin once.

"You will marry us, Father, or I'll cut the lass's throat right in front of your eyes, and you'll be the cause of it. Do you want such on your conscience?"

Lachlan's few remaining guards built a circle around him, helping to keep Gwyneth from hitting her target easily. Now the priest was also in her way. Aye, Drew had seen two other archers in the trees, but they were not close enough to do any damage.

"Nay. Please, lad. Do not do this." The priest kneaded his hands in front of him after mopping his forehead with a section of linen.

"Start, Father, or I'll do it." He dug the tip of his knife into Lina's skin, and fresh blood trailed a path down her neck.

The priest held his hand up in concession. "All right, lad. No reason to hurt the lass. I'll do it."

"Lina, do not agree to this marriage," Logan shouted.

Drew could tell Lina tried to see exactly who surrounded the cave, but she could not see the periphery at all. He guessed she surely knew her brothers' voices. With a knife at her throat, what choice did she have? If her brothers could have done anything to stop this, they would have by now. They never hesitated to take action. Sweat dripped down Drew's back as he watched the spectacle in front of him. There wasn't a doubt in his mind that Lachlan would cut her throat and take the sword back. Time had run out.

Lina said, "Go ahead, Father. I wish to end this bloodshed. Do it quickly."

Lachlan grinned. "See, Father, my wife-to-be is quite agreeable."

Micheil yelled, "Nay, Lina. Do not do it."

A look of desperation and despair flooded Lina's eyes, but she only shook her head slightly, not enough to jar the dagger.

"Go ahead, Father." Lachlan pushed Lina toward the priest.

Drew wiped his forehead, his vision dimming as he stared at Lina. What the hell was she thinking? "No more," she whispered. "'Tis all my fault."

"Do you…what's your name, lass?"

"Avelina, Father, now get on with it."

The priest cleared his throat and said, "Do you, Avelina, take this man, Lachlan, to be your husband?"

Lina nodded her head.

"Nay!" Drew shouted, just as his knee gave way and he fell to the ground.

CHAPTER TWENTY-FOUR

Lina had seen enough death and injury in a day and could handle no more. All she had to do was say aye and the threat to her family would be lifted.

Father said, "Lass, you must speak up. I cannot accept a nod."

Lachlan pinched her neck. "Do it." Did she have a choice?

Her vision blurred and her legs buckled. How she wished it were Drew standing here, but he had sworn he would never marry. Lachlan yanked her back up.

"Say aye, Avelina," he bellowed.

Someone nearly collapsed in her peripheral vision. She could see the blood running down one side of his plaid, covering his legs. Who was it? Was he hurt? She tried to see, but she was weakening. Her legs threatened to drop her out from under her at any moment. She was holding her knees locked tight to keep from being skewered on Lachlan's knife, but she could not hold out much longer. Closing her eyes, she gave in to the needs of her body, no longer caring what happened. She prayed her life would end quickly. At least this would free her from the terrible choice she was being forced to make.

"Lina!"

Her eyes flew open. Drew? Could it be? She searched the area again, finally recognizing him as the wounded man she'd noticed moments before. He was not far away and covered in blood.

"Drew, nay…" she whispered, hoping he wouldn't come for her. She could not bear to watch him slaughtered. Her heart beat faster in her chest. If she were to live and he died, he would take a part of her with him. Oh, how she loved him.

"Lina, I love you. Marry me!" Drew shouted. He forced himself back into a standing position.

What had he just said? She felt the knife at her throat again. Hell, but it hurt. Her mind was slowing, and she didn't like it. It was getting harder and harder to breathe, to think, to swallow…

She heard her name again.

"Lina," Drew bellowed. "Will you marry me?"

"Lass?" the priest whispered. "Who is it you wish to marry?"

As she stared at Drew, it felt as if her throat were closing, in fact, she didn't know if she'd even be able to speak because the pressure on her neck was so strong. Swallowing and mustering up as much strength as she could, she croaked, "Drew. I wish to marry Drew." Lachlan still had the weapon pressed to her neck, so she knew they might well be her last words. If so, they were worth it.

A horde of butterflies flew out of the trees, straight into Lachlan's face. The hand with the dagger shifted just enough for Drew to leap forward and grasp it. He knocked the dagger out of Lachlan's hand and punched him in the face. Lina fell to the ground, rolling onto her side, but still clutching the sword. Logan hauled Drew away, and while Lina did not understand why at first, as soon as her brother tossed her love aside, an arrow sliced through the air and caught Lachlan between the eyes. He collapsed to the ground, and Lina crawled away on her hands and knees, gasping for air and coughing. A set of hands wrapped around her waist and lifted her onto a nearby horse.

Drew's hand stayed with her as he climbed up behind her. He was about to turn the horse around, but he stopped mid-action. "Father!"

The priest stared at him, obviously still shocked at what he'd witnessed.

"Finish it. We wish to marry. I want her to be my wife."

Sheer chaos reigned around them as Lachlan's remaining men continued to battle or did their best to run off, but Lina didn't care. She only had ears for Drew. Lina turned around to look at him. "Are you certain of this?"

Drew cupped her cheek with one hand and kissed her. "Aye, more certain than I've ever been. I love you, Lina. Will you be my wife?"

Lina wrapped her arm around him. "Aye, I love you." She turned to the priest. "Father, marry us, please?" She clung to her love as if he were about to disappear at any moment.

Logan came over to join them. "Father, I'll serve as your witness, but you must do this quick if it's to happen. You can see the unrest around us. Sorry, Drew, but I'd like my sister away from here and safe."

Drew nodded, "Aye, proceed, please."

The priest took a piece of Drew's plaid and wrapped it around their entwined wrists, then spoke in Gaelic for the short ceremony.

As soon as he finished the blessing and nodded his head, Logan tugged Lina down to kiss her cheek and said, "Congratulations, sister. You've chosen well, and I promise to tell the others. Now on with you." He positioned her back in front of Drew, slapped the flank of the horse and said, "Get her out of here, Menzie. Have her on Ramsay land in two days."

Drew galloped off with his arms wrapped tight around her waist.

As soon as they cleared the sea of warriors, she held up her hand, and Drew slowed the horse.

She turned to gaze into his eyes. "Is it true?"

The gleam in his eyes told her he would tease her. "Is what true?"

"Are we married?"

He wrapped his arms around her and kissed her soundly. "Aye, we are. Does this please you as much as it does me?"

She nodded and sighed, then settled back against him and fell fast asleep.

When she awakened, Drew helped her off the horse. "You all right, my sweet?"

"Aye."

He took her by the hand, grabbed the satchel someone had thrown at him as they were leaving, and led her down a path toward a stone outcropping. As soon as they rounded a corner, Lina gasped. "Oh, Drew. 'Tis the most beautiful spot I've ever seen."

A small pool sat in the center of two walls of stone, its edges covered with moss and lovely flowers, and there was a beautiful waterfall at the far end. He set the satchel on a large rock, threw his plaid and tunic off to the side, and held his other hand out to her. "Come. We need to clean you up."

Lina took one look at his broad chest with the dark hairs scattered across it and her mouth went completely dry. Her gaze trailed all the way down to his toes before her eyes jerked back up to his face. A calm settled in her soul because, at that moment, she was happier than she'd ever been in her life. After tugging on the ribbons of her bodice, she stripped out of her bloodied gown and shift and stood in front of her husband with naught on, just as he was.

His gaze traveled the length of her and back up again. "Lina, you are so beautiful. But please do not distract me from my plan."

She quirked her brow at him. "Plan? What plan?"

He leaned down to kiss the slices on her neck where Lachlan had held the tip of the knife. "I need to wash you first. There must be no reminders of what you've just been through to interfere with this night."

She touched the side of his leg. "Seems you need some washing as well. It looks as if you have two wounds on the same leg. Is that possible?"

"Aye, but they will heal. Do not worry about them." He took her hand and waded into the pool. Once they were in the water, he set the slice of soap he had taken out of the satchel and placed it on a nearby ledge, then let go of her to get in up to his shoulders and duck his head under the water.

"Is it cold?" she asked as soon as his head came above the water.

"Nay. 'Tis summer and still warm. Come."

She tiptoed in up to her knees, squealed, but then followed him the rest of the way.

He tugged her over to the ledge and started washing the dried blood off her neck, kissing each spot that had been cut. Her eyes welled up from both the sting of the soap and the tender way he washed her skin.

As soon as he finished, a swarm of butterflies fluttered around them. "Oh, Drew, you're going to meet her, I hope." Lina glanced up to see Erena standing near the waterfall. She was dressed in a beautiful pink gown decorated with blue feathers. The sun reflected off the tiny pearls decorating the full skirt, and the lace sleeves fell to her wee wrists.

For some reason, she looked more regal today. In fact, Lina

thought she could almost see a pair of wings behind her back, transparent in the fading sun. Her hair was pulled back at the nape, which allowed the multitude of colorful butterflies to rest on her shoulders and all down her arms. She held them out for a moment before sending the winged creatures off into the sky.

"Are you happy, my dear?" the Queen of the Fae asked, her face beaming.

"Aye, I am verra happy." Lina leaned toward Drew, letting herself sink a little deeper into the water as he wrapped his arm around her.

"You needed to have more faith in me," Erena said. She wagged her finger at Lina, but her lively expression assured Lina that she was not very angry.

"My apologies, Erena, but 'twas a bit close with the dagger at my throat."

"Aye, 'twas a bit closer than we would have liked, but so much of what happens in this land is in human hands. Still, all has ended as we wished, and I am verra proud of you. We chose well."

Drew whispered in Lina's ear. "Will she allow me to speak?"

"Of course, Laird Menzie. You are not laird yet, but you will be."

Lina grinned and spun around to catch his reaction to Erena's announcement. Drew hadn't moved a muscle, but his jaw had dropped open in shock.

The Queen of Harmony continued, "Besides, Lina has been chosen by the fae, but you have been chosen by Lina. That makes you quite special on your own merit. What is it you wish to ask me? I'll answer if I can."

"This is true? There is naught more we need to do?" Drew could hardly take his eyes away from the queen, he was so entranced.

"Nay. You have the sapphire sword with you, do you not?"

"Aye." Lina nodded. "I managed to keep it without slicing my own skin open."

"Then take it with you, and when you have decided where you are to live, find a safe hiding place for it, where it will be concealed from prying eyes. Let it be known that you no longer have it in your possession, lest others seek to steal it from you. You will still be protected by it. The sapphire sword is an ancient legend, and most of the Scots know of its value. Be wise in your care of it."

Lina glanced at Drew and nodded, accepting this part of their fate.

"She will not need it at all?" Drew asked.

"Nay, not in the near future. Once your family is older, mayhap a score of years from now, much unrest will come to pass, and it may be needed again. If so, we will come to you. But please do not release it to anyone without my approval. I promise to come to you when it's necessary."

"Erena, the dreams I've had. Sometimes, I know what will happen. Will they continue?"

"Aye, my dear. You have the sight. 'Tis the gift you've been given. The fae have always had a few seers in the Highlands, and you are to be one of them. I trust you will use your sight wisely."

Lina and Drew stared up at the Queen of Harmony, awaiting any further instruction.

She waved her hand. "I am off. I wish you two a most wondrous life together. In time, Drew, you shall forgive your parents, and you will learn to trust them again. They do love you, and will be wonderful grandparents to your bairns."

"Bairns?" Lina asked, raising her brows.

Drew hugged her close. "Aye, bairns. Our bairns." He paused for a moment. "Erena, are you sure our bairns will be safe with my parents?"

"Of course, I shall be watching. Your first-born will be verra special. We shall need another chosen one to replace you someday, Avelina. If you do not mind, please name her Elyse. I love that name. Then she'll feel a wee bit like my verra own daughter." Erena leaned over to wink at them.

Erena held her arms out to beckon the butterflies, then sent them off to the heavens with a smile. "For now, 'tis time for you to soar, as I told you would happen someday. Enjoy."

Lina watched Drew as he stared at the butterflies overhead. "She's something to see, is she not?" He shook his head, still having trouble absorbing all that had transpired.

Once they were no longer in sight, he turned to Lina. "How could you handle all of that on your shoulders? I never thought about it until I saw her. I've not seen anything like her before.

Lina, you are a verra brave lass. I admire you for all you have done. 'Tis amazing that you've accomplished all that you have." He wrapped his arms around her and pulled her in close. "And to think you are all mine. My wife." He growled and ravished her lips.

When he ended the kiss, she whispered, "I do love you, Drew." She bit her lower lip as he soaped her in one last spot, then pronounced her clean.

Once he was finished, he set the soap aside, and settled her back into the water to gently rinse her neck. "Lina, I love you more than I truly comprehend," Drew said, gently pulling her to him, "and I'm so sorry I made you wait. This could have all been avoided."

She set her fingertips against his lip. "Let us *not* talk about how we could have done things differently. It will serve no purpose, and I prefer to enjoy what we have now. I love you, and you love me. What more do we need?"

He nodded and melded his lips to hers. She parted for him, and he invaded her mouth, teasing her with his tongue.

She pulled back and held up her hand to indicate she wanted him to stop. "Please allow me."

He gave her a puzzled look, but he did as she asked, breathing hard. Her hands reached up to the peak at his forehead, and she followed the lines of his face with her fingertips, moving down each side until she traced the angled edge of his jaw. "Do you know how long I have wanted to touch you, but could not?"

He quirked a brow at her, but said naught, a slow grin creeping across his features. She replaced her fingers with her lips, starting with his forehead and moving down to trace each cheek and then his lips. When she was finished, she said, "For a verra long time. Even when I saw you in Lothian, I wondered how your lips would taste."

Her hands traveled down across his chin and his neck before coming to rest on his chest. She teased the coarse hairs, then moved her fingertips to his nipples, flicking her nails over the edge of each peak. "When you came into Cameron's keep, all I wanted to do was run my hands down your chest and feel every bulge, every ridge of the muscles in your arms." She leaned over to whisper in his ear. "But I could not."

She lifted her hands up to the sky and smiled. "But now I am free, am I not? Free to love you and touch you as I wish. Free to be loved as I wish. Finally, we shall be together." She arched her back and stood on the tips of her toes, enough for her breasts to come out of the water as she tossed her head back and swung her hair loose around her. She'd never felt this wondrous before or this bold. Drew and Erena had helped her to come into her own, and she was grateful.

Drew growled and lifted her into his arms. After ravaging her with kisses, he leaned her back in the water so that she floated, allowing him access to her taut nipples and the full mounds of her breasts. Lina moaned at the sensation of his hands moving over her body as the warm water lapped between her thighs, filling her sex with such heat she thought she would explode in his hands.

His tongue replaced his hands and he used it to trace the outside of the twin globes. "Lina, Lina, you are more beautiful than I could have imagined." His tongue fell into the valley between her breasts before licking a trail up to her nipple. Taking the luscious tip into his mouth, he suckled her until she cried out.

"Drew, please." She gripped his shoulders as he played with her, but then trailed her hand down the outside of his arm to his waist, moving inward until she took him in her hand. Groaning, he lifted her out of the water and carried her to a soft mossy mound nearby. Once he settled down beside her, he leaned onto his elbows and gazed into her eyes, trailing his fingers down her belly and into her folds, smiling when she spread her legs for him and he thrust a finger into her easily.

"Do not wait, Drew. I hear 'tis worse if you go slowly."

∞

Hellfire, but she was the most beautiful creature he had ever seen. Lying in the middle of the moss, the leaves, and the soft earth, she looked as if she were fae. He would bring her pleasure first if he had to die doing it.

His mouth descended on hers again as he gripped her hips and slid into the edge of her, waiting just a moment before thrusting forward and burying himself deep inside her. He thought he'd died and gone to heaven. It felt so good to be inside her that he was desperate to pull back and do the same again and again, but he forced himself to wait until she adjusted to him.

She made barely a sound, so he said, "Lina? Talk to me. Are

you all right? I will not move until you tell me."

She took a few short breaths, her forehead pressed against his, her eyes closed, but then said, "I'm fine. Try again."

He could tell she was holding her breath, so he slid out and back in again as slowly as he could. His response was a deep moan from her—her head tipped back, her lips parted. She grasped his biceps and arched her breasts toward him, seeking his touch. When he met her eyes, the passion he saw in her gaze almost undid him in an instant. Her desire for him so unbridled, so innocent and open, he couldn't even think.

Grasping her hips in his hands, he thrust into her again and again until she matched his pace, moving with him in a steady rhythm that threatened to throw him over the edge. She pulsed against him with a small moan, her hands gripping his shoulders, so he reached between them and found her nub, caressing it lightly until he could feel her contract around him. Finally, she shattered, going over the edge as she shouted his name. Without realizing it, she brought him with her. His own orgasm erupted in waves of pleasure as he buried his seed deep inside her.

Attempting to control his breathing, he gazed into her eyes and saw the wonder there, the surprise of what they had shared. If only he could find the words to express how he felt. He'd been with so many, and yet naught could compare with this woman or this eve they had spent together. Loving Lina had surpassed all his expectations.

Aedan had been right all along. Finding the right woman was everything he had said it would be.

"Drew," she panted. "Oh my, that was, that…"

"Shhh, love. There's no rush." He rolled onto his back and took her with him, encasing her in the crook of his arm. Once they could breathe again, he lifted her gaze to his. "You enjoyed it?"

She grinned, "Aye, 'twas wonderful." She ran her hand across his abdomen, pulling herself so she was almost on top of him, her breasts resting against him, her head resting against his chest on her splayed hand. "I had no idea lovemaking could be so wonderful."

He gave her a wicked grin.

"Drew, we should have done this long ago."

When they finally reached the Ramsay land, Lina wished to run up the hill just to tell everyone how happy she was with her marriage.

"Drew, you will not be expected to learn everyone's name the first day." She grinned at him as he helped her dismount near the stable.

He gave her a confused look. "There are that many?"

"Aye, the Grants will likely still be there."

"And how are you kin with them?"

"My brother, Quade, married Alex's oldest sister, Brenna. Of course, you know Jennie. There are many bairns here, you'll see. You've met some of them at Cameron's."

Moments later, a string of bairns rushed toward them through the courtyard. Leading the way were Gavin and Gregor, though she suspected everyone had held back to allow them to greet her first.

"Dabin, look! Aunt Wina is hewe."

Gregor threw himself into her arms, Gavin right behind him.

She picked each one up separately and gave them each a big kiss. "You two do not look sick at all. You are better?"

"Aye, we are not sick," Gavin answered. "Why would we be sick?"

"Short memories," she whispered to Drew.

"Abby," Gregor yelled, "come say hi to Aunt Wina."

The puppy came bounding out to greet Avelina. She picked Abby up and kissed her nose. "Have you been a good girl for Gavin and Gregor?"

By the time she set the dog down, Jennie, Aedan, Micheil, Diana, Logan, and Gwyneth had all circled around to greet the new couple. Behind them stood Brenna and Quade.

Lina stood back, tears welling in her eyes. "Brenna, I'm so sorry." All she could think of was the pain Quade and Brenna had faced. She gave each of them a hug.

Brenna said, "My thanks, but we'll see our bairn again someday." She squeezed Quade's hand and looked into his eyes. "It had naught to do with you."

"Now I understand the truth of that statement, but I did not before. I was hoping you did not believe that I had aught to do with it." Lina stared at the ground.

Brenna lifted Lina's chin. "We are certain of it, and you also saved our son. I told your brother about what you did for Gregor."

Quade leaned over to kiss her cheek. "I'm glad I was not there. I do not believe I would have handled it well. My thanks to you for listening to your dreams."

Drew's hands squeezed her shoulders from behind.

Brenna brushed Lina's loose hairs back from her face. "I'm just pleased to see you married and happy. You are happy, are you not?"

"Aye, I am. I did not think I could ever be this happy." She gave Drew a hug and introduced him to her family. Then they all made their way up to the hall to greet the rest of the group.

At the base of the steps to the keep, Avelina stopped to glance up. Her mother stood at the top, tears running down her cheeks. "Oh, Lina. You look so beautiful. Married life suits you." She gave her daughter a warm hug. "You have always been my chosen lass. I am proud of you. You'll have to tell me all about it when you get settled." Arlene Ramsay turned to Drew and took his hands in hers. "Finally, my clan is complete. Welcome to the Ramsays, Drew Menzie. Many thanks for taking care of my daughter."

Erena was right, Lina realized with a full heart. She had nowhere to go but up.

CHAPTER TWENTY-FIVE

A few days later, Alex clasped Quade's shoulder as they headed out of Quade's solar. Both came to a sudden stop in the middle of the Ramsay great hall.

"Where is everyone?" Alex asked, his gaze searching the empty space.

Quade's mother came down the stairs with several plaids slung over her arm. "They are hoping to tire the weans out by spending the afternoon at the loch. Brenna is excited to show off the improvements Quade has made to try to compete with the famous Grant loch. I've heard much about it, though I have yet to see it. Come, walk with me. I am bringing out more plaids for the bairns for when they get out of the water. 'Tis a lovely day."

Alex followed Quade and his mother out the door and down the hill toward the loch. "Did it take much work to adjust your loch for the bairns to use?"

Quade took the plaids from his mother before he rolled his eyes. "Nay, not to make it as you have arranged your loch, but it took a bit more to please my wife. Aye, creating a gentle slope for the weans on one end and removing the grass was not difficult, and we were pleased to find a soft sand mixed in with the stones. But Brenna came up with a few more things she wanted. And my brothers had their own ideas." Quade clasped his shoulder. "You'll see what I mean. Your sister is like you in many ways. And I'm sure after you leave, she'll have even more ideas for me."

Alex smiled. He and the Ramsay laird had always been a wee bit competitive. He couldn't wait to see how the Ramsay loch compared to the Grant loch. It had not been difficult at all to create a comfortable area at the opposite end of the loch from where

Robbie and Caralyn lived, and the swimming spot had in fact become a clan favorite. Many a clan member spent the warmest days of summer out by the loch.

Quade continued as they drew near. "As you can see, my men had to build stone benches for seats, and we also put a dock out in the middle of the loch as you did. I admit the dock island is a favorite with the older bairns. But Brenna did not stop there."

Alex noticed the edge where all the weans were splashing. "Why do you have rope across the loch?"

"Och, you're catching on to your sister's thinking, are you not? The rope is the limit for the wee bairns. They cannot go beyond it until they learn to swim. 'Tis Brenna's idea. And Molly is gifted at teaching the youngest ones how to swim."

Alex nodded. "I suspect Maddie will be having me create the same as soon as we are home."

A giant old oak leaned gracefully over the water in the middle of the loch. Alex stopped in his tracks and turned his head to the side. "What the devil is that?"

Quade chuckled. "I see you've discovered Logan's contribution to the loch. After watching him try to toss my son and daughter from the lower branches of the big oak tree, I agreed to allow him this instead. But 'tis all Logan's creation. As you can see, the older ones enjoy it."

As Alex watched, Loki grabbed the knotted rope that hung from the highest branch of the oak, pulled it back as far as it would go, then ran down the grassy slope leading to the loch, jumping up and lifting his feet to the knot at the last minute. As soon as he sailed over the water, Loki threw himself into the air and did a flip before landing in the water with a huge splash.

Alex applauded Loki's achievement and watched as all the lassies giggled and collected around the lad as he climbed out of the water, his chest puffed out with pride.

"Do a double flip, Loki," Torrian yelled.

Lily shouted, "Nay, do a backward flip."

But before he could do any of those things, Logan came charging toward the tree, grabbed the rope, and ran back as far as he could, stopping at the top of the slope with a huge grin on his face. "Are you all ready? I'll give you a challenge. This will be the biggest splash ever. Then we shall see if all you wee bairns—" he pointed at Loki, Torrian, Lily, Ashlyn, Molly, Jake, and Jamie, who were all standing around watching, "—can beat me."

Logan flew down the slope and launched himself into the air, letting go of the rope at the last minute to fly out over the water. Landing at an odd angle, Logan created a huge splash that spouted like a fountain, saturating those who were standing nearest to the edge of the loch. The spectators shrieked at getting wet, but all laughed and applauded when Logan climbed out.

While Alex stood to the side, Brodie came running past him from the end of the loch with a grin on his face. "I take up the challenge," he said, grabbing the rope. "We'll see who can make the biggest arsewhacker of all."

Brodie did his best to beat Logan, but he did not quite make it. Micheil followed with a hoot.

Maddie ran up to Alex, who was still watching the display, and flung her arms around his waist. "Alex, is it not wonderful out here? Have you seen the swing? And look at how Quade chopped a tree down and cut off pieces to be used as seats around the loch. And we have to add a rope to our shallow section for the bairns, just as Brenna did."

Quade chuckled just as Alex gave him a pointed look over Maddie's head. "Ramsay, the next thing she'll have me doing is planting an oak tree next to our loch."

"But that would take too long, Alex," Maddie pleaded. "I'm sure the men would be happy to transplant one from another spot. Just choose your strongest men." She gave him a sweet smile as Quade guffawed.

Alex kissed the top of Maddie's head just as their daughter, Eliza, tottered over, all wet, and lifted her arms. "Papa, up?"

Alex picked her up, kissed her cheek with a resounding smack, and then hoisted her up onto his shoulders.

"By the way," Maddie said, "you know the wee lads have been waiting for you to play the tree game, Alex. I promised them 'twould happen." She gave her husband a hug, and Alex rubbed his thumb across her cheek.

"Did you, now? Hmmm…that could cost you later, sweeting."

Quade said, "Alex, play a tree? I'd like to see that."

Alex passed Eliza off to her blushing mother, then made his way over to the shallow end of the loch where the bairns all splashed in the water. As soon as they spied him, the wee ones all ran over yelling, "Tree, Uncle Alex. Please, be the tree." Celestina held her youngest, Catriona, while Caralyn held her wee lad, Padraig.

Maddie smiled up at her husband. "See how they love you, Alex?"

Alex strode into the water up to his knees, holding both arms out to the side, and shouted in his deepest voice, "Watch out, a storm is a brewing." The bairns giggled and ran toward him, each of them reaching up to grasp his enormous arms.

Gregor was last, chasing the older ones into the water. "Dabin, wait for me!"

Once they were all hanging from his arms, he started to swing them back and forth, "Here comes the wind."

The bairns started to swing and squeal, some of them landing in the water with a splash, others hanging on for dear life.

Maddie yelled, "Be careful, Alex. Do not hurt them. There are so many hanging on your arms."

Once all of the bairns had landed in the water, he climbed back out and headed over to greet his sister, Brenna, who was standing off to the side on the hill overlooking the water.

"All is well, Brenna? Is this not too hard for you, watching all the bairns?"

Brenna's eyes teared up. "Nay, 'tis wonderful. You know not how happy you have made me by bringing the family to support me. Alex, look at our clan and all it's become."

As Alex stopped to stare out over the loch, Jennie and Aedan came to join them. "I know," he said. "'Tis hard to believe they are all part of our clan. I wish Mama and Papa could see us now, how we've grown." He wrapped his arm over Jennie's shoulder and kissed her cheek.

"I know, but I believe they are watching." Brenna swiped away a tear as Brodie and Celestina joined them, and Maddie came over to hug her husband. "How could I be sad about losing one child, when we have so many strong bairns?"

"You'll have another," Maddie whispered. "Alex and I lost one before we had Eliza."

Silence settled over the siblings, but the solemn moment was broken when Logan came running at them from the tree, followed by Robbie. Before he reached them, Logan first chased over to Gwyneth, who was sunning herself on her plaid, and proceeded to drip water all over her.

"Logan, you'll pay!" She jumped up and chased him back to the tree.

All the older bairns chased after the two to see what they would do next.

Logan flung himself into the water from the swing, yelling, "Come catch me, Gwynie." He landed with a big splash almost as loud as his first. Gwyneth used the swing next—after flipping in the air, she kicked her legs straight up and landed in the water head first, with her arms leading overhead, not far away from Logan. Dressed in her leggings and a sleeveless tunic, she hardly made a ripple in the water.

"How did she do that?" Robbie whispered, Caralyn right behind him with their babe on her hip.

"Are those two always so playful?" Celestina asked.

Micheil and Diana came over, holding their two lads, David and Daniel, both a bit overwhelmed by everyone. "Aye, Logan loves to tease Gwyneth," Micheil replied.

"But Gwyneth enjoys every moment of his teasing," Diana added.

Celestina said, "I love to see the strong friendships among the cousins. Look at Bethia and Kyla, and Gracie and Sorcha. Roddy and Braden are inseparable until they come here, and then they love spending as much time as they are able with Gavin and Gregor. Those four lads are all within a year of each other, are they not? And look at Molly and Ashlyn, they're so dear together!"

Moments later, Logan and Gwyneth climbed out of the water laughing, arms wrapped around each other.

Brenna glanced around as Quade wrapped his arm over her shoulders. "Who are we missing?"

Lina and Drew emerged from the forest, heading straight for them.

"Well, well, 'tis nice to see you two for a change," Aedan drawled. "You cannot seem to get enough time alone, can you?"

Lina's cheeks blushed a pretty shade of pink, but Quade drew everyone's attention away from this sight of her embarrassment. "And what did you mean by that, Cameron? 'Tis my sister you speak of. Logan, does this meet your approval?" Smirking, he turned to Logan, whose smile had shifted into a fierce expression.

Aedan jumped back, both hands held flat in front of him, as the rest of the group laughed.

"My apologies. 'Twas not meant to be vicious. I meant to tease my friend, not his wife."

As laird of the Grants, Alex had learned when to keep the peace. He stepped in to change the subject. "Good timing, Lina. I need to ask you a question."

"Aye, I'll answer if I'm able."

"Did you not say that the fae consider you a seer?"

"Aye, I have been given the gift of sight."

Gwyneth asked, "What does that mean exactly, Lina? Will you have visions every night? I hope not. If so, you'll never be able to sleep."

"True, but we could have used that gift many times over these last few years," Quade added.

Logan agreed, "Aye, when we were searching for Lily, and Brenna, and…"

Brodie cut in, "And Celestina, and Caralyn, and…"

Alex waved his hands. "Aye, it could have been beneficial before. But I'm grateful that there is someone special in the family who has been given this gift. 'Tis invaluable, do you not all agree?"

Drew hugged her from behind. "And the gift could not have been entrusted to anyone better."

"Most true," Quade said. "I have complete faith in my sister."

Lina added, "And I have not had dreams every night. They are rare."

Alex crossed his arms in thought. "Can you tell me what you see for all our bairns in the coming years?" Staring out over the loch, he continued, "Not specific to each one, but in general terms. What will they see in the years ahead?"

His clan joined him in glancing over at the gaggle of bairns playing near the water. Lady Arlene was watching the youngest while they talked, and the older ones were still playing near the rope swing.

Lina answered. "The Queen of the Fae said all will be peaceful for almost twenty years, but then there will be unrest again in the

Highlands."

Alex thought for a moment, then said, "Then may we all raise strong descendants. We shall need them."

Lina said, "Do not worry, I see verra strong *sìol* in our future, though they will be tested many times."

Brenna whispered, "God bless us all, look at all the descendants, our *sìol*, in the loch. We have so many. I cannot wait to see them grow up, every one of them. I love them all."

Loki came out of the water beaming, squeezing water out of his long bronzed locks as the lasses applauded him. "What did you think of that one, Torrian?"

Torrian ignored him as he gazed over at his clan standing together on the opposite bank, a serious expression on his face.

"What are you looking at?"

"Our elders." Torrian tipped his head in their direction, all clustered in a group. "What do you suppose they're talking about?"

Loki stood shoulder to shoulder next to Torrian. "I have no guess. But I hope someday to be like your Uncle Logan."

Torrian grinned, "Truly? Uncle Logan?"

Loki squinted at his cousin. "Aye, I wish to be a spy like him. To travel the Highlands. Who do you wish to be like?"

"My da. Aye, my da and Uncle Alex. He's a legend."

Loki shrugged. "Aye, you'll be a laird, like your da. I have no chance at that, so mayhap a spy would be a better fit for me."

Torrian grasped Loki's shoulder. "You do not have to be a laird to be legendary."

Loki waggled his eyebrows at Torrian and grinned.

EPILOGUE

The following autumn

Once they dismounted their horse outside the stables, Lina helped Drew unhook the warm pouch he had attached to his chest. As soon as he held the material back, the two wee legs sticking out of the bottom wiggled away.

"What is it, wee Elyse? Were you missing your mama?" Drew asked, kissing his daughter's chubby cheek as soon as he had her unwound.

Lina grabbed the babe out of Drew's hands. "Nay, you are not fooling me at all, wee one. I know who your favored one is. You are your papa's lassie, and I know it." It was a cold autumn, so Lina made sure a hood covered the wee one's head. The lassie was soon to be half a summer, and she had grown like a weed.

"Are you ready, love?" Lina glanced up at her husband, squeezing his hand as she settled their daughter on her hip.

Drew nodded. "Aye, I am." He leaned over to kiss his wife's cheek just as the stable lad came bounding toward them.

"My lord, 'tis so good to have you home, 'tis. We've all been awaiting your return. Your sire's been ill, but he's been asking for you."

Drew patted the lad's shoulder and said, "My thanks."

As they headed toward the great hall in the Menzie keep, Drew's clan members lined the path to greet them.

"Drew, glad you've returned to us."

"Your wife and daughter sure are bonny lassies."

"Drew, are you here to stay? Please say you're home to stay. Your clan needs you."

Gus, the smithy, strode up to him and clasped his shoulder.

"Lad, we've all missed you, for sure. But none more than your sire. 'Tis time for you to come home. They miss you something fierce, and they've seen the error of their ways. 'Tis time to forgive. Your sire is not well."

Drew nodded and hugged Gus. "Gus, this is my wife, Avelina, and our daughter, wee Elyse. My thanks, Gus. I've missed your sage advice."

They continued onward, moving past all the well-wishers to enter the great hall. His parents did not await them outside, but he had expected as much, for his sire was very ill.

Once inside, he turned toward the hearth. His sire's chair was very close to the warmth of the fire, and the big man was wrapped in a thick plaid and a fur. Drew's mother sat in a chair next to him, quietly sobbing, her hands clenched in her lap.

"Mama?" He escorted Lina over to his mother. He leaned down and kissed his mother's cheek, then tugged her to her feet and wrapped his arms around her as she cried. No words came from her, but he could tell how difficult this was. Now that he had a bairn of his own, he had come to understand his parents a bit more.

"Mama," he stood back from her and turned her toward Lina. "I'd like you to meet my wife, Avelina. We call her Lina. And this is our daughter, Elyse."

"Oh, Drew. You have a daughter?" She clutched Lina's hand and said, "I wish to welcome you to our home. My, but you are a pretty one." Her eyes settled on Elyse and she gasped. "I have a granddaughter. Arthur, look." Her eyes met her husband's. "We have a granddaughter. Isn't she beautiful?" Elyse giggled and shoved her fist into her mouth.

Drew moved over to his sire. "Papa. How do you fare?"

"Not as well as I once did, but I'm an old man. I still get around, but my one side drags a bit." Drew noticed his father's face drooped on one side, and his speech was more deliberate than it had been before, but his sharp gaze was as keen as ever. "Introduce me to your family."

Drew finished his introductions, then all of them sat down. The kitchen maids stood nearby, awaiting instructions. "Some cheese and bread, please? Mayhap a goblet of ale for me and some wine for my wife?"

Once the maids had left, his father said. "I know I shouldn't ask this right away, but I must. Have you come home to take over the lairdship as you should? 'Tis your right and your land. You're my son. I wish to leave all to you."

His mother peered up at him. "Everyone is hoping you'll stay home."

His father cleared his throat. Drew wondered which of his many mistakes the older man was about to dredge up.

"Son. You were a better leader years ago at twenty summers than I ever was. I never wished to admit it, but 'struth. All of my guards have been hoping for your return. And I am ready to pass everything on to you. In fact, I see your wee wife is carrying again. It would please me to watch my grandchildren grow and only offer you help when you have need of it."

Drew's shock took him aback. Had his own father just complimented him? And he wished to get to know his grandchildren? Would that not be too painful for him?

His mother smiled at him. "Drew, 'tis different when they are your grandbairns. Think on it, will you? Would you allow me to hold wee Elyse on my lap?"

"Of course," Lina answered. "Let me help you get her settled."

With Lina's help, Elyse soon sat sideways on her grandmother's lap. At first, she gave her a serious look, but then she broke into a big smile, two teeth sticking out of her lower gums.

"Papa, if that's what you want, Lina and I are ready to move here. I miss my clan and I'd like our daughter to get to know her clan members." His voice cracked with emotion at how far he and Lina had come in such a short time. "We may still travel a few times a year as Lina has a large clan, but we would like to make our home here."

"The clan has been waiting for you, son. I've told them how smart you are, and how you remember everything I've taught you..."

As his father talked on, Drew glanced over his mother's head to catch his wife's gaze. He shrugged his shoulders, and she nodded, indicating she agreed with him. They had discussed this possibility before they'd arrived, but Drew wanted to be sure he had Lina's support. He had to admit it felt good to be home, though he would have to get used to hearing his father talk about his good qualities instead of only his bad ones.

Drew only had one more question he needed to ask. He'd struggled with how to go about this exactly, but he had to ask. As he paced the floor, trying to decide how to phrase his question, his mother said, "Drew, your father and I would like you to know something."

He spun around and waited for her to continue. His mother glanced at his father, who nodded for her to continue. She continued. "We're verra sorry for the wrong we did you. We're verra proud of you, and we have deep regrets for the choices we made. 'Twas wrong of us to waste so many years thinking only of the past. We hope, in time, you can forgive us."

His father hung his head and added, "I feel the same, son. You have our deepest apologies."

Drew finally decided how he needed to phrase his question.

"Well, who do you think she looks like? Me, Tomas, or James?" He glanced from his mother to his sire, holding his breath. How he prayed his parents would not think Elyse looked like either of his brothers.

His mother scowled, then peered at his father before staring at the bairn on her lap. "Och, Drew. Nay."

Drew just stared at her, his heart full of hope and fear, and waited for her to continue.

"She looks like Elyse."

The End

NOVELS BY KEIRA MONTCLAIR

DEAR READER,

Thank you so much for reading HIGHLAND HARMONY. I hope you enjoyed Avelina and Drew's story. Alas, this book finishes the series—for now. I can't promise I'll never come back to it, as I think someday I will. But for now, I will be moving on to my new series, and I'll start with Loki's story.

If you like my novels and would like to support me as a self-published author, here's how you can help:

1. **Write a review:** Please consider leaving a review. They can really help an author, particularly one who is self-published as I am.

Go to my Facebook page and 'like' me: You will get updates on any new novels, book signings, and giveaways. **https://www.facebook.com/KeiraMontclair**

2. **Visit my website: www.keiramontclair.com:** Don't forget to sign up for my **newsletter** while you're there.

3. **Stop by my Pinterest page: http://www.pinterest.com/KeiraMontclair/** You'll see how I envision Avelina, Drew, along with Gregor and Gavin.

After Loki's story, I'll probably return to write the third in my Summerhill Series. After that, who knows where I'll go! I must admit I have a wee series about Avelina's gift churning in my brain, too.

Once again, thank you for all your support.

Happy reading!
Keira Montclair

ABOUT THE AUTHOR

Keira Montclair is the pen name of an author who lives in Florida with her husband. She loves to write fast-paced, emotional romance, especially with children as secondary characters in her stories.

She has worked as a registered nurse in pediatrics and recovery room nursing. Teaching is another of her loves, as she has taught both high school mathematics and practical nursing.

Now she loves to spend her time writing, but there isn't enough time to write everything she wants! Her Highlander Clan Grant Series is a reader favorite and is a series of eight stand-alone novels. The Summerhill Series is a contemporary romance series set in the beautiful Finger Lakes Region in Western New York. Her third series will be set twenty years after the Clan Grant Series and will focus on the Grant/Ramsay descendants.

You may contact her through her website at www.keiramontclair.com. She also has a Facebook account and a twitter account through Keira Montclair. If you send her an email through her website, she promises to respond.

Printed in Great Britain
by Amazon